DINOSAUR TIME

It came from the gloom with a roar and a crashing of young trees. It was Death in lizard form, stalking on two enormous legs like great, heavy pistons. The great beast's skin rippled like beaded leather over vast muscles; the smaller, clawed forelegs clenched, ripping branches from its path. The long mouth opened, spiked with daggered teeth; and the monster roared with the wail of centuries long gone, its breath a wind from the grave, all rotting meat and bones and corruption.

Death incarnate. A beast from fevered nightmares.

Allosaurus.

They all screamed back at it—Aaron, Peter, and Jennifer—an animal fear rising in them that compelled them to answer the call of the predator. It seemed to scent them first. Then smallish, copper-gold eyes fastened on them...

D1414792

Avon Books are available at special quantity discounts for bulk purchases for sales promotions, premiums, fund raising or educational use. Special books, or book excerpts, can also be created to fit specific needs.

For details write or telephone the office of the Director of Special Markets, Avon Books, Dept. FP, 1350 Avenue of the Americas, New York, New York 10019, 1-800-238-0658.

RAY BRADBURY
PRESENTS
DINOSAUR WORLD

A NOVEL BY
STEPHEN LEIGH

Illustrated by Wayne Barlowe

A Byron Preiss Book

AVON BOOKS • NEW YORK

If you purchased this book without a cover, you should be aware that this book is stolen property. It was reported as ''unsold and destroyed'' to the publisher, and neither the author nor the publisher has received any payment for this ''stripped book.''

RAY BRADBURY PRESENTS DINOSAUR WORLD is an original publication of Avon Books. This work has never before appeared in book form. This work is a novel. Any similarity to actual persons or events is purely coincidental.

AVON BOOKS
A division of
The Hearst Corporation
1350 Avenue of the Americas
New York, New York 10019

Copyright © 1992 by Byron Preiss Visual Publications, Inc.
Illustrations by Wayne Barlowe
Published by arrangement with Byron Preiss Visual Publications, Inc.
Library of Congress Catalog Card Number: 91-92450
ISBN: 0-380-76277-3

All rights reserved, which includes the right to reproduce this book or portions thereof in any form whatsoever except as provided by the U.S. Copyright Law. For information address Byron Preiss Visual Publications, Inc., 24 West 25th Street, 12th floor, New York, New York 10010.

First AvoNova Printing: June 1992

AVONOVA TRADEMARK REG. U.S. PAT. OFF. AND IN OTHER COUNTRIES, MARCA REGISTRADA, HECHO EN U.S.A.

Printed in the U.S.A.

RA   10   9   8   7   6   5   4   3   2   1

This is for Megen
who dreams of dinosaurs and misty forests
lost in time

CONTENTS

THE EGG-LAYING BEAR

Green Town sweltered.

The August sun was a blast furnace suspended in the sky, pouring molten light down on the landscape. Paint cracked like dried mud on cedar shingles; heat demons waltzed madly through the dusty streets. The air shimmered and swayed over dark-shingled roofs. You could almost imagine aluminum siding sagging like old candle wax and collapsing into silvery metallic puddles on the sidewalks.

It was one of those bright, lazy, humid midwestern summer days when you knew that storm clouds would soon bloom like dark flowers in the evening. First you'd see massive, vaulted thunderheads swelling with black, wide castle towers on the horizon. As the clouds spread and turned from black to a sickly dull green, the failing sun would duck behind them in fear. The fortresses of cloud would throw quick, bright lightnings at each others' ramparts and then burst open with torrents of rain.

Afterward, the water would vanish from the gutters as if someone had toweled the streets instantly dry; the heat would return, heavy with the rain's humidity. Yet...

During those few moments of the storm,

summer's grip would briefly loosen. In those fleeting instants, you might feel a hint of autumn's touch in the cool barrage of rain and wind. The outriders of autumn rode the storms of late August, staring down with greedy eyes at the ripening fields below.

Aaron Cofield wasn't quite sure that he liked the thought of autumn, even though the sweat kept dripping into his eyes and the sunburn on his forearms was tender.

"Hey, you should put some sunblock on that. I've seen boiled lobsters that were less red."

Jennifer Mason reached over with a forefinger and pressed Aaron's skin to prove her point. Her touch left behind a glaring white circle on his arm that slowly returned to blotchy, angry scarlet. "Ouch," Jennifer said in sympathy. "Aaron, that's *got* to hurt."

"Nah. Not really," Aaron lied. Actually, the sunburn *was* beginning to feel prickly. He could feel dry skin pulling whenever he moved, and he could already tell that he was going to be peeling like a molting snake in a few days, but . . . If he admitted that he should get out of the sun, then the two of them would have to go back to the house, and Aaron was comfortable where they were. He didn't want to move. It felt too good to be sitting there next to her. Alone.

The two of them were sitting in the tall grass behind Aaron's house, on a steep, rocky slope that plunged into a ravine of tangled woods. From deep within the emerald shade under the thick canopy of oaks and maples, a cool breeze would sometimes rise, fragrant with the scent of moist earth and hidden things. The woods—indeed, the whole area around the Cofield house—had always been a locus of magic for Aaron. Like all of his friends, he'd spent most of his youth in among those trees, half-believing that he might find Merlin hidden behind a moss-furred ancient oak or a hidden pirate treasure under a fallen log. The woods had always been a special place. Even now, at eighteen, he still found himself often wandering along the old trails.

The magic had never faded. It was sometimes a little harder to find now and there were moments when he found himself scoffing at his own feelings, but the spell was still there.

The Cofield house itself—an old rambling Victorian structure some ten miles from Green Town itself, a turn-of-the-century dwelling that Aaron's parents called a "money-eating monstrosity"—was hidden from where the two teenagers sat. Aaron and Jennifer could imagine themselves all alone in a primeval world, with only the sounds of birds and the hushing of waving grass to bother them.

This was a special place, *their* place.

"What are you thinking about?" Jennifer asked Aaron. "I'd swear that you've said a total of about four words today. I'm beginning to wonder if you want me here at all." She grinned at him to soften the words. "So you'd better answer that one carefully, huh?"

"That's not it. Not at all, Jen. Not even slightly." Aaron wiped at the sweat and swatted at a persistent gnat that buzzed around his head. He rubbed fingers through dark, longish hair and yawned, then had to smile at her mock-offended expression. "Okay, okay. . . . I'm sorry. It's just . . . well, I guess I'm starting to realize how close I am to going away, leaving this spot and the old house and Green Town. You know how it is—I mean . . ."

Aaron exhaled loudly and shook his head, then started again. "The summer starts and you think you've been gifted with an *eternity* before school rolls around again. Jen, I had a whole incredible summer lifetime to look forward to, working at the museum during the day, going out with you and the gang at night. And then— *boom, crash*—June's gone marching by and July's followed it and now August's almost done. The summer's flickered by like heat lightning and there's only a few weeks left. The world is pressing in again. . . . I keep thinking about what's coming."

Aaron plucked a piece of grass and rolled it between his fingers, looking at the trees down the hills from them. "I'm going to miss this place. I've never been away from Green Town for more than a few weeks before. This house is the only home I've ever known. I've spent a lot of years roaming through those woods: chasing tadpoles and minnows in the creek, collecting frogs and turtles and snakes, hunting for fossils. . . ."

"Anything else you're going to miss?"

Aaron turned to glance at Jenny from underneath deep eyebrows. There was a half smile on her full lips, one hand holding back a fall of corn-yellow hair, a few ringlets sweat damp on her forehead.

"Yeah," he answered huskily. "There is." He cupped her cheek with a hand and held her gaze with his own intense eyes. "Grandpa Carl's peanut butter sandwiches," he told her. "I'm *really* going to miss those."

An instant later, Jenny playfully bit at his hand. Aaron snatched it away. "Oww! Take it easy! That was a *joke*. . . ."

"Peanut butter sandwiches . . ." Jenny said with outraged, exaggerated tones.

The laughter faded quickly. The air seemed to absorb the humor. "Jen, you know it's you I'm going to miss most of all." Aaron pulled Jenny into his arms. He stroked her hair, lying back in the grass. "Jenny, I'll be back for breaks between quarters. Dad said he'll drive up and get me if I want to come home on weekends—at least once a month or so, or maybe I can get my own car if I keep working and all the tuition's paid. Then after school's out I'll be back here for all next summer. You can come to State after you graduate next year; their premed school's pretty good. . . ."

"That's a year away, Aaron. A year apart. An awfully long time."

"I know . . . I know. . . ."

They'd been avoiding the subject all summer, talking around it though they both knew that the topic lurked in the background of their thoughts. In the last year, Aaron and Jenny had become inseparable. They'd known each other since fourth grade, when Jennifer's parents had moved to Green Town from Cincinnati. As kids, they'd spent the requisite number of years alternately liking and hating each other—best friends and best enemies. Through most of high school, they'd been in the same group, dating the other's friends but never each other. It seemed that whenever Aaron had broken up with whoever he was seeing, Jennifer was involved with someone else, and vice versa.

Until last summer. Last summer when Aaron and Susan Monroe had their final argument, when Jenny had told Peter Finnigan that they'd be better off as "just friends." As usual, Aaron and Jenny had sought out each other to talk about their common problems.

Aaron was never quite sure just when the landscape of their relationship had shifted. Somewhere in those conversations, a boundary had been passed, a barrier destroyed. Neither Aaron nor Jenny was quite sure when that line had been crossed or what had triggered the revelation. Now, Aaron wondered how he could ever have been so blind not to see that his best friend was also something more.

He was very glad that the blindfold had been lifted.

"Jen, our relationship can survive a few

months' separation. I know it can. And if it can't . . ."

"Then it wouldn't have lasted anyway," Jennifer finished for him. "I know—I've said the same thing to myself a few hundred times in the last few months. In fact, I think I've had everyone from my parents to Great-aunt Ethel give me the same advice. I still don't like the idea. I'm . . . well, I'm a little scared. College changes people, Aaron. Being away changes people."

"I'm not going to change."

"Uh-huh. Courageous but stupid, that's how I like my men." Jennifer smiled down at Aaron and kissed him lightly. "Yes, you *will* change, love. You won't have a choice. I know that and you know it, too."

"It won't change the way I feel about you. It really won't. That's a promise."

"Good. Just keep thinking that, but it's a promise I won't hold you to." For a moment, Aaron thought she was going to say more, but Jennifer sat up again, hugging her legs to her chest, her chin on her knees as she stared into the woods. "It's too bad," she said.

"What's too bad?" Aaron moved so that he could rub Jennifer's back with one hand and stared up at the drifting islands of clouds.

"That Green Town is such a *small* town. If we had a good university near here instead of just the dinky junior college . . ."

"I didn't have much choice for paleontology, Jen. State has one of the best curriculums, Dr.

Morris is a top person in her field, and I could get the Roberts Scholarship grant."

"I know." Jennifer sighed. "I know. It would have been the same decision for me if I'd been the one going to college this year. The school I go to has to have a strong premed. I *understand*, Aaron. I just don't like—"

Her voice cut off, and Aaron felt the muscles in her back tense. "What is it?" he asked, sitting up quickly. Jennifer was shading her eyes with a hand, staring into the woods.

"Listen," she whispered. "You hear that?"

Aaron had. From behind the screening mulberry and bramble, well back among the trees, they could hear a crashing like a drunken army thrashing in the underbrush. The clamor seemed to be coming toward them, stopping just short of where the line of trees ended and the field began.

For an instant, Aaron and Jennifer could glimpse *something* moving at the edge of the woods, a hulking shadow patterned with leafy darkness and hidden behind the willowy bars of young trees. In the vagrant breeze, there was a smell—alien and unfamiliar—a sharp tang that made their nostrils wrinkle. The creature paused, snuffled throatily, and then moved deeper into the underbrush, only the waving fronds betraying its passage. In a few moments, they could no longer even hear it.

Aaron blinked away sweat. "What was *that*?" he exclaimed.

"I don't know," Jennifer answered. "It was big, I know that. . . ."

"A bear," Aaron said decisively. "It had to be a bear. Grandpa Carl says there used to be some browns back up in the hills. Maybe . . ."

Jen shook her head in puzzled disagreement. Aaron echoed the gesture, knowing that his explanation hadn't even convinced himself.

"It was too large for a bear," Jennifer said. "Besides, I don't think there really are any more bears around here, no matter what your grandpa says, and I don't think a bear would smell like that. That thing looked like it was the size of an elephant. It had to be something else."

It was Aaron's turn to shake his head. "What else makes any sense, Jen? Look, the more likely an assumption is, the more likely it is to be true, right? It's too crazy to think that it's anything but a bear. If there was a circus around, or if we had a zoo, I might—*might*, mind you—believe that an elephant had escaped. But what do you think's more plausible, an elephant roaming the Illinois woods or a brown bear with a pituitary problem who also smells bad. . . ."

He let his voice trail off, realizing how pedantic he was sounding. Jennifer was openly grinning at him. "Okay," he said. "So what's *your* explanation, Dr. Mason?"

"I don't have one," Jennifer answered. "But I do know how to find out"—another grin—"besides talking it to death," she added.

She stood, holding out her hand to Aaron. He ignored the gesture, getting to his feet with a grunt. "This is stupid," he said. "Bet you dinner at Arnold's that we find bear fur snagged in the brambles."

"You're on, Sherlock." Jennifer glanced again at the woods. "Whatever it was, it's gone now, anyway."

"C'mon."

Aaron took Jenny's hand. Together they made their way down the rocky slope to where the high grass gave way to blackberry bushes and vine-tangled undergrowth. There was a well-worn path leading under the trees—the legacy of Aaron's frequent visits. The two teen-agers followed the winding, packed dirt trail until they stood near where they thought the bear (as Aaron insisted on calling it) had been.

"It blundered in from that way," he said, pointing. "See how it knocked down all the brush?"

"Awfully clumsy for a bear," Jennifer told him. She moved away from the path and bent down to take a closer look at the foliage. "No fur, either."

Aaron had moved to the other side of the path. The grass and weeds were just beginning to lift up again. He found a place where the animal had gone through a patch of thorns; he examined the area carefully. Several of the thick needles had broken off, but the "bear" hadn't left any evidence of bearhood behind. The ground was hard from several days of sunshine and well-cushioned with growth. Aaron couldn't find any clear footprints.

He began following their quarry's trail, hoping to come across a muddy spot where he could find footprints or maybe some spoor the animal had left behind. He made his way through the tangle of bushes and around the larger tree trunks, cursing the heat and the flies that seemed to have materialized from nowhere to plague him. Aaron was fairly certain that he was going to be buying Jennifer's dinner tonight.

Maybe there *was* a circus or something in the area that he hadn't known about, or maybe one had been passing nearby, possibly along the Penn tracks down by the river. . . .

Aaron stopped. He found himself holding his breath, looking at what he'd almost just stepped on.

"No . . ." he breathed. "Now *that* isn't possible."

The object was lying there on top of the crushed grass, an elongated spheroid a foot and a half long, like a ball of clay some giant had taken and rolled between his hands a few times. Its smooth, matte surface was a mottled white flecked with dark brown. The worst thing about it was that Aaron had seen one before—more precisely, he'd seen some casts and artist's renderings.

"Jenny!" he called.

She rushed over to him, coming to a stunned halt next to him. "That's an *egg*," she said, then—a moment later and with less certainty: "Umm, it is, isn't it?"

"Yeah. It looks just like a *dinosaur* egg," Aaron replied slowly.

"Uh-huh."

"No, I mean it, Jen."

"I'm sure you do."

When Aaron heard Jennifer's involuntary giggle at his pronouncement, he continued defensively. "Hey, I've seen them: in textbooks, in the museum's fossil collection, in photographs." Aaron didn't believe it himself, even as he said it. Sure, it *had* to be something else. "I'm not saying it *is* a dinosaur egg, you understand," he continued, hedging. "It just *looks* like one."

Jennifer's gaze kept sliding from Aaron to the egg. She was trying—mostly unsuccessfully—to keep the amusement from her face.

"Aaron, a few minutes ago you were insisting that the animal had to be a bear because it was nuts to think it was anything else. Great. *Now* you're telling me that this is a dinosaur's egg. That's no fossil, love; it's real. So who's being unreasonable now?"

Aaron crouched next to the egg. No, it certainly wasn't a fossil, though the shell looked thick and durable. A few blades of grass clung to the surface, as if it had been wet when it was laid here. Aaron touched it gingerly; the shell was warm against his fingertips and the surface, like hard rubber, gave slightly under the pressure. This egg, whatever kind of egg it was, was fresh and living.

"Maybe my elephant married an ostrich," Jennifer said, playfully.

"It's not funny, Jen." Aaron stood up again. He stared at the woods around them, listening. There was no sound, no sight, no smell that shouldn't have been there, that he didn't already know. There was only the egg. He shivered despite the heat, and tried to cover his uneasiness with a shrug. "We all know bears don't lay eggs, don't we?"

"So you owe me dinner, right?"

Aaron nodded. "No problem."

There was a long silence. Aaron knew they were both thinking, both speculating. "Elephants don't lay eggs, either," Jennifer said at last.

"What's that mean?"

Jennifer moved closer to Aaron, touching his arm softly.

"So what *did* lay it?"

Aaron let all the air out of his lungs in a long *whuff*. The woods—*his* woods—were no longer so comfortable and familiar to him. The shadows under the canopy of branches were darker; the green depths further in were somehow endless, ancient and enchanted and it didn't seem so strange to be thinking that the egg was exactly what he thought it was.

But he didn't say any of that to Jennifer.

"Nothing that normally lives around here, that's for sure. Ostriches lay big eggs, but I've seen pictures of those and they don't look anything like that. Snakes and lizards lay eggs, but I can't think of any reptile that lays eggs this large."

"How about an alligator?" she answered. "Maybe someone brought a baby up from Florida and it's been living down at the creek or in the sewers."

"I poke around these woods all the time. So do you and Peter, Ken, Bruce, Sandi. . . . Heck, half of Green Town from age six to twenty is down at the creek at one time or another during the year. Somebody would've seen it before now, Jen. Besides, do you really think an alligator did all that thrashing around? Do you think an alligator could lay this egg? Look—" He pulled at a young tree nearby. A branch was hanging broken from the trunk about five feet up from the ground. "You ever see an alligator climbing trees?"

"Are you telling me that we're back to dinosaurs? Let's call the *National Enquirer*!" Jennifer laughed again. "I can see the headline now: **Elvis Spotted Riding Dinosaur in Illinois**."

Aaron spread his hands wide. He made a noise halfway between a chuckle and exasperation. "Neither one of us really knows what it is. That's all I'm saying."

"So let's pick the egg up and take it back to the house," Jennifer suggested.

Jennifer moved as if to grab the egg, her long hair swirling as she started to bend down, but

Aaron held her back. "Wait, Jen. We shouldn't do anything yet. Leave it where it is; if it *is* something strange."

"Like a dinosaur," Jennifer interrupted, teasingly.

Aaron ignored the jibe. "Then we should document all of this first. Take some pictures, some measurements. . . ." He stopped, frowned. "Except that my folks have our camera with them in Chicago."

"Peter has a good camera," Jennifer suggested. "C'mon, we'll go call him."

Aaron didn't like the suggestion at all for reasons of his own, but there didn't seem much else to do. "We're probably going to find that there's a reasonable explanation for all this," he said as they made their way from the woods. "I just wish I knew what it was."

He heard an insect at his ear and swatted it away. Buzzing angrily, a fly as big as a matchbook skittered off.

"Big sucker," said Jen.

"Biggest I've ever seen," replied Aaron, as he watched it vanish into the woods.

DEATH IN THE WOODS

Peter Finnigan had been Aaron's best friend for as long as Aaron could remember. It was Peter who had been the first mate to Aaron's pirate captain, who had been Arthur to Aaron's Merlin, who had explored all the hidden places deep within the trees with him. Peter had half carried a broken-legged Aaron out of the ravine the time they'd been swinging on vines and Aaron's had snapped; he'd been the quarterback who tossed halfback Aaron touchdown passes during grade school football games.

It was only in the past few years that deep fissures had begun to appear in their friendship, and the hammer that had caused the most damage had been Jennifer. Still, the cracks had begun to develop long before. . . .

Somewhere in the summer between eighth grade and high school, Peter had magically transformed from a gawky, awkward youth into a handsome, red-haired athlete. It was in those first years at Green Town High that Pete and Aaron began to grow apart.

They had both decided that they wanted to study a martial art and started taking aikido classes together; Peter quickly found aikido too difficult and slow to master. He switched to karate; Aaron didn't. They both went out for the freshman football team. Pete became the first-string quarterback, while Aaron was relegated to a replacement tight end, mostly blocking for running plays. Peter joined the varsity squad the next year while Aaron didn't even try out. Aaron was always at the top of his class scholastically, while Peter was content to lie back, giving only the minimum effort needed to pass.

They still called each other friend; they always ran with the same crowd. They pretended that nothing had changed since their childhood days, though they both knew it had.

Watching Pete flirt with Jen, having them begin to date and seeing them embracing one another had always caused a flare of unbidden jealousy in Aaron, even as he smiled and laughed and pretended to be happy for both of them. When the two had broken up after several months and Aaron began dating Jennifer himself, it seemed that the friendship between the two young men had shattered completely. Pete and Aaron didn't talk about the problem; for most of their senior year they avoided each other's company. Even at the graduation party at Trapp's Farm, Pete always seemed to be just leaving whenever Aaron drifted into a room.

It was only over this last summer that Pete and Aaron had made the first efforts to see if the damage could be repaired. There remained a certain amount of tension, and Aaron was never quite sure that he liked the way Pete looked at Jen sometimes or the fact that she and Pete could laugh over some shared remembrance. At times like that, Aaron felt left out and resentful.

"Aaron says it looks like a dinosaur egg," Jennifer told Peter. Aaron and Jennifer had coaxed Peter away from his air-conditioned living room and the Bruce Lee movie he'd been watching on television. Aaron was certain that it was more Jennifer's presence than his own that had finally convinced Peter to leave the comfort of his house and follow them into the woods. Now they stood around the nest, staring down at the odd-shaped shell.

"Dinosaur egg," Peter repeated carefully. He raised one orange-red eyebrow. He was looking at Jennifer, not Aaron. "Oh, yeah. Sure."

"I only said that's what it *looked* like," Aaron told him. "And it does, no matter what anyone says. But I didn't say it *was* one."

"Right, buddy. I hear you." With a grin, Pete lifted his camera, checking the exposure. "Well, *something* went through here, I'll grant you that. Good thing I have some fast film in the Pentax; it's dark under the trees. Put your pen down in front of it, Aaron—that'll give some idea of the scale." Crouching, Peter snapped a few pictures of the egg, moving around to get different angles. Aaron watched intently, directing Pete and making certain that he also took a close-up of the granular surface.

"When you're done, we'll take it back to the

house, show it to Grandpa Carl, and maybe call the museum, see if someone can tell us what it is—"

"Aaron! Pete!" Jennifer had moved a few yards away. She was standing in knee-high weeds, waving urgently to them. They came on the run: Peter, then Aaron. They stared down at what she'd found.

In what was obviously a hastily-made nest of dirt and weeds, three more of the strange eggs had been laid, half buried with the larger end of the rounded cone at the bottom. Aaron stared at the nest dumbfounded. He's seen *that* before, too—in artist's reproductions. This was the way certain hadrosaurs—the duckbill dinosaurs—arranged their nests, judging by the fossilized remains that had been found. He didn't say anything to Jennifer or Pete, but he *knew*. He was certain now.

Something impossible had happened here. Something miraculous.

And something was wrong, too. Aaron couldn't put it into words, but a vague uneasiness prickled his spine and made him raise his head. Jennifer and Pete were talking excitedly and snapping pictures. Their commotion suddenly made him realize what was missing. "Hey, guys," he said softly, then louder. "Listen!"

Peter glanced up, puzzled. Under the shock of unruly red hair, his forehead wrinkled. "I don't hear anything."

"I know," Aaron said. "That's just it. I don't hear *anything*."

They could all feel it now. The forest seemed to be holding its breath. The background chatter of birds and insects was gone, the rippling of water in the creek bed had been stilled. Nothing moved. Even the leaves hung like dead things from their branches. Nothing moved. It was as if the trees themselves were waiting.

"I don't like—" Aaron began.

He got no further. At that moment, an apparition burst from the trees with a yell: a man, dressed in strange clothing and holding what was obviously a rifle of some sort. He was running at full speed, looking back over his shoulder at something unseen. He plowed into the trio, knocking down Aaron and Jennifer as Peter spun out of the way. The stranger—hard faced, scowling, bleeding from cuts on his arms and face—pointed his weapon at them for just an instant, then whipped around to face the way he'd come. Aaron and Jennifer struggled back to their feet. Aaron looked at Peter, who shrugged wide-eyed.

They had no time to react.

It came from the gloom with a roar and a crashing of young trees. It was Death in lizard form, stalking on two enormous legs like great, heavy pistons. The great beast's skin rippled like beaded leather over vast muscles; the smaller, clawed forelegs clenched, ripping branches from its path. The long mouth opened, spiked with daggered teeth; and the monster roared with the wail of centuries long gone, its breath a wind from the grave, all rotting meat and bones and corruption.

Death incarnate. A beast from fevered nightmares.

Allosaurus.

They all screamed back at it—Aaron, Peter, and Jennifer—an animal fear rising in them that compelled them to answer the call of the predator. It seemed to scent them first, snuffling with wide, cavernous nostrils. Then smallish, copper-gold eyes fastened on them from the heights. The thing snarled, saliva frothing in the charnel house of its mouth, its tail lashing.

There was a moment when Aaron noticed that the scaly flesh was a vivid, patterned azure and gold, that in the creature's chest were several seeping wounds, holes that looked insignificant and unimportant compared to the immense bulk of the thing.

Then the beast roared once more in challenge and rage, and Aaron knew that they were going to die, right there and then. He knew that the immense head would bend to rend and tear, that to struggle would be as futile as an insect resisting the shoe about to crush it.

The stranger fired his rifle as the carnivore drew back to strike. There was a stuttering of gunfire and a line of blood-red dots appeared on the beast's chest, angling up toward the terrible head. The allosaurus screamed, its voice shaking the very ground, and it beat at the air with its diminutive forearms as if swatting at flies. Then it bent down once more, opening its jaws and engulfing the four people before it in its fetid breath. Again the stranger opened fire; again the brute reared back. Blood was streaming down its chest now, and it wavered.

And struck.

Lightning fast, the jaws opened and closed, clashing and opening again as it snapped at the group. The stranger continued to hold down the trigger, the endless report of his weapon echoing among the trees. Aaron clutched Jennifer to him, as if together they could ward off this monstrosity.

The creature's attack veered aside at the last instant, the jaws closing on earth instead as the huge body toppled to its side. The tail raked the ground in a violent dust storm, then went still. The forelegs twitched.

The creature seemed to give a vexed grunt.

The stranger collapsed.

A MYSTERIOUS STRANGER

"Well, this sure isn't what I expected when you guys called me."

Peter's attempt at irony didn't quite come off—the quaver of residual fright in his voice ruined the effect. He stood well back from the sprawled body of the allosaurus, staring at the trees the beast had shattered in its fall and at the gouged pit where its jaws had closed on dirt and brush instead of its intended human prey. Jennifer had already run to the unconscious stranger; Aaron walked carefully over to the dinosaur, touching—wonderingly—the flesh of a fevered dream. Under Aaron's fingertips, the skin was cool and leathery, the bright scales as smooth as wave-polished pebbles. The skin was warm, and he could feel immense striated muscles just underneath. The body hissed and burbled internally like a steam engine cooling down. Even as Aaron examined it, its right arm twitched reflexively.

Aaron jumped back. Behind him, he could hear the metallic snap of Peter's camera shutter.

"Hey, I could use some help here."

Aaron and Peter, with a last glance back at

the dinosaur, went to where Jennifer was ripping the man's already tattered shirt into makeshift bandages. The stranger was sweating, his
head rolling as if some vision tormented him
even though his eyes were closed. He looked
in his late thirties, maybe early forties, dark
haired and skinned, with a shadow of stubble
on his cheeks. Several deep scratches furrowed
his arms; a jagged gash wandered from his left
eyebrow nearly to his hairline, and bruises pur-
pled his chest. He moaned, his lips parting.

"How is he, Jen?" Aaron asked.

Jennifer knotted one of the strips of cloth
around the worst of the cuts, glancing up at
Aaron with concern in her eyes. "He's lost a
lot of blood—that's probably why he's so weak.
He's also broken a few ribs, and he's lucky he
doesn't have a punctured lung to go with them.
Something gave him a good wallop on the chest;
my bet's on that thing's tail." Jennifer glared
at the toppled dinosaur with a strange mixture
of revulsion and fascination. "Umm, it *is* dead,
isn't it?"

"I think—I *hope*—so. I don't know for sure,"
Aaron answered.

"A better question might be, 'What is it and
where did it come from?'" Peter interjected.
"For that matter, who's this guy? I've never
seen him around here before." Peter stooped
down and picked up the weapon the man had
used. He very carefully kept the ugly, black-
ened snout pointed away from them. He hefted
the device, sighted down the thick, ringed bar-

rel at a nearby tree. "This isn't any type of automatic rifle I've ever seen before, either. He gonna live, Jen?"

"Yes," Jennifer answered, almost angrily it seemed to Aaron. "He's just beat up and exhausted, that's all. But we need to get him to a hospital."

"Want me to run and call the life squad?" Peter asked.

Aaron's gaze skittered around the grove, taking in the allosaurus, the injured man, the weapon in Peter's hands, the nest of eggs nearby. He found that he didn't want anyone else to see this. Not yet. Jennifer's steady regard caught Aaron then, and they exchanged a long, understanding look.

"No, Peter. We can move him," she said. "I've got the worst of the bleeding stopped, and we can be careful with the ribs. Nothing else is broken, and I don't see any obvious signs of internal injuries. If we get him back to your house, I can clean up the rest. For now, anyway."

"Then let's do it," Aaron agreed, somehow relieved that, for the moment, this would remain their secret. "Peter, give me a hand, huh?"

In a way, Aaron was glad that his parents happened to be away for the week. His mother would have been phoning the police as soon as she saw Aaron, Jennifer, and Peter carrying the man from the woods. His father would have notified the authorities if she hadn't, without pausing to hear explanations.

Grandpa Carl was different. Carl Cofield had always been independent and eccentric, sometimes to Aaron's father's embarrassment.

His grandfather didn't say much as he helped the trio lay the man on his own bed, or as the three excitedly told him what had happened. He glanced blandly from Aaron to the stranger to the odd weapon that Peter had propped against the wall, and nodded. He murmured footnotes to the conversation, nudging them into explanation. "Allosaurus, you say . . . Dinosaur eggs, eh? . . ."

"You don't believe us," Aaron said after they finished. "I'm not surprised. I wouldn't believe it either. A crazy story like that—" He almost laughed.

His grandfather gave him a slow smile and sidled to the foot of the bed. It hurt Aaron to watch Grandpa Carl walk. In the last several years, arthritis had taken its toll. Aaron's grandfather was no longer the slight, wiry figure Aaron remembered working endlessly in the fields or repairing the cars out in the barn. Carl moved slowly now, carefully, and the pain would sometimes—when he thought no one was watching—deepen the wrinkles around his eyes and mouth.

"Didn't say I don't believe you, boy," he said, his voice as slow and cautious and wary as his movements. "Seems to me that you brought back pretty good evidence that something out of the ordinary happened, no matter what I might like to think." He nodded toward the man on the bed, still unconscious as Jennifer cleaned his wounds. "Jenny girl, you're the doctor. What do you think about your patient here?"

Jennifer straightened and brushed her hair back from her eyes. "We need to get him to the hospital. He needs to have those ribs x-rayed, that cut on the head should be stitched, and someone should check to make sure there's nothing else wrong."

"No." The voice had come from the bed. They all turned. The stranger's eyes had opened—nut brown pupils rimmed with bloodshot whites. "No hospital and no authorities. Please. I have to find him."

His voice was deep and weary, and though the words were English, he gave the sentences a strong, guttural accent that none of them could place. They had to strain to understand him.

"Who do you have to find?" Carl asked. "What's your name?"

The man shook his head. He tried to sit up as Jennifer made a motion to restrain him, but he sank back before she touched him. "So tired . . ." His eyes suddenly widened in a memory of terror. "The dinosaur—"

"It's dead," Aaron told him. "It went down, anyway."

The stranger's eyes closed. "Where am I?"

"Green Town," Jennifer told him. When

there was no response but a slight shaking of the man's head, she added. "Illinois."

Nothing. Aaron thought the man had drifted into unconsciousness once more when the man gave a hoarse, bass whisper. "Everything's changed," he said. "All of it."

They waited for him to say more, but he didn't. The lines of his face slowly relaxed and his eyes remained closed. His chest rose and fell slowly. "I think he's asleep," Jennifer said.

Carl nodded thoughtfully, rubbing his chin as he regarded the man. "He looks pretty ragged. Jenny, we need to get him to the hospital fast, you say?"

Jennifer shrugged. "I don't think so, Mr. Cofield. He's breathing okay, and the bleeding's not a problem. . . ." She wrung out the washcloth she'd used to clean his face and wiped her hands dry on her jeans. "But I'm not a doctor, either. I . . . I really don't know. If he has a concussion, the sleeping could be a sign of something serious. . . ."

Carl smiled at her. "I understand. Listen, you kids stay here and watch him for a few minutes. I need to go check something, and then maybe we'll go ahead and call Sheriff Tate."

He left the room. A few moments later, Aaron heard the back screen door thump against the jamb. Aaron smiled—watching through the window, he saw his grandfather striding carefully across the lawn toward the ravine and woods. When Aaron turned back, he found the

stranger staring at them. "What's your name?"
Aaron asked again.

The man hesitated, as if choosing between
answers. He licked dry lips. "Travis," he said
at last.

"Travis? Just Travis? That's it?"

A grim-faced nod. "Close enough, I guess."

"Sit back and rest," Jennifer told Travis.
"You're tired and hurt. We're going to take you
to the hospital soon. They'll take care of you."

"*No!*" Travis shouted the word, pushing
against Jennifer's restraining hands. The muscles stood out on his neck, throbbing with the
effort. Peter and Aaron rushed to help Jenny.
Travis struggled against them for a few seconds,
then gave it up, collapsing back against the
pillow with a sigh. "No," he insisted again. His
hands clenched into fists, then opened again
like umber flowers. His eyes were bright with
an interior passion. "You can't do that. Please
. . . I *am* begging you. You don't know how important this is. If I don't find him soon—"

Then a suspicion clouded the fire in his gaze.
He closed his mouth angrily, as if he felt he'd
already said too much.

"Find *who*?" Aaron insisted. "What's going
on here? Where are you from, where was that
thing from?"

"You wouldn't believe me. I'm not sure you
can believe me."

"Try us, because otherwise you don't leave
us much choice," Peter told him. "You can't

expect us to just ignore what happened, mister."

"That's just what I am asking you. Ignore it, forget it. Help me get up and out of here. You don't know how much is at risk."

"That's an awfully big pile of meat we left back in the woods," Aaron said. "Kids go back there all the time. We need an explanation."

"I don't know what to tell you."

"Try the truth," Jennifer answered softly.

He gave her a long, lingering gaze. "The truth," he said at last. "That's a very difficult thing to find." He closed his eyes once more.

When he opened them again, he nodded.

"All right," he said. "The truth."

TRAVIS'S TALE

The truth . . .

I'm not sure exactly where to start (Travis began). Or 'when,' which might even be the harder choice. No, don't start interrupting now; you people wanted the whole story, so you're going to have to let me go about it my own way.

What year is this? I'd make a guess that you're somewhere near the end of the twentieth century, but maybe Eckels changed everything so much that nothing's recognizable.

Ninety-two, is it? You look so puzzled that I'd even ask . . .

No, stop asking all the questions and listen. I'll explain it all, I promise. Let me start by telling you about me. You'll have to believe me or not, but just keep remembering what you saw out there when your disbelief gets too large to carry. Remember the dinosaur, the terrible lizard. . . .

I'm a hunter. More precisely, a safari guide. Only I don't take people on expeditions through some uncharted wilderness on a far continent. Where—or *when*—I come from, there aren't any such places, and nothing's there to hunt, in any case. I hunt in time. I stalk the creatures of myth and stone, the chimeras that fought and bred and died so long ago that they aren't even dim racial memories to us newcomer mammals.

You see? You'd forgotten already, but that sarcastic laughter died quickly, didn't it? After all, you *saw* that walking terror, that allosaurus. You felt its anger shake your bones and you smelled the raw blood on its breath. You *know*, even though you don't want to believe me. Your whole sense of reality rebels against the very idea. This is the kind of tall tale you make jokes about, but there's that dinosaur for evidence. . . .

Well, they're my prey. I hunt them as they hunt me—it's an even enough game. In two years of operation, the company has lost four guides and their parties. Two years. Sometimes we win; sometimes we disappear into history ourselves. Someone always has to go back to make sure that it isn't just an equipment problem. Someone has to witness what happened just to be certain. . . . That's a hard task, because we aren't allowed to change any of it, just watch. That's regulations.

We have—had? It gets so confusing, even for me—lots of regulations: pyramids of restrictions, skyscrapers of rules, entire forests of paper dictating how and when and where and what.

None of it did any good. None of it.

I'm getting ahead of myself again. . . .

For those two years, everything meshed. We

were making money; we were growing. Guides like me, we enjoyed the kick, the thrill of hunting the biggest, deadliest, fiercest creatures that nature's frenzied imagination had ever dreamed up. We told ourselves that, hey, we were furthering humankind's knowledge, too, since the safaris allowed us to fund research we otherwise couldn't have afforded.

I don't know if it's the same way here. Frankly, we've lost a lot of records from the late twentieth, early twenty-first centuries, and it was never my period, anyway. War destroys written history quite effectively. It does a *lot* of nasty things. Yet it also moves technology forward, sometimes in a deadly sort of way. That's where our research into the temporal drive started, with defense research. Weapons' research . . . From what I understand, they'd almost had a working model completed when the active fighting stopped. When the defense funds dried up after the Cairo Armistice, when it looked like all the work was going to go to waste, the corporation decided to work on a commercial application. Like with so many things, economics was the engine that drove us.

We were careful, so careful. . . .

You're right. I'm drifting. Let me tell you how it worked. The regulations of the corporation restricted us to prehistoric times, pre-*human* times. Everyone was cautious: there was to be no mucking about with known history. We were all aware of the possible paradoxes, of the damage that we might be able to do. Some of our theorists argued that it wasn't even possible to change history in any significant manner, but the corporation, if it erred, was going to err on the side of caution. We wanted to study history; none of us was crazy enough to want to *change* it.

How did we set up the safaris? Even at the exorbitant fees we charged, we still needed three or four 'hunters' to finance a trip. Once we had our customers—or rather, when we had their very substantial and nonrefundable down payments in our hands—a guide—me, if it was my turn in the rotation—would take one of the machines back. Going DownTime, we called it.

We prowled the Mesozoic for the most part. It was a slow process, one of the many reasons we were so expensive. Hunting in time was for the very wealthy, period. After arriving in the proper era, I'd begin prowling the local territory. What I was looking for was simple: a corpse, preferably that of one of the big carnivores: allosaurus, tyrannosaurus, something like that—and there are more varieties of them than we ever dreamed of from the fossil record.

My corpse didn't have to be particularly fresh. Once I'd located some remains, I'd move off a few hundred meters and begin taking little shunts DownTime, maybe a day, maybe only a few hours or so depending on the condition of the body I'd found. What I was trying to zero in on was the precise moment of death.

You see, most of the time I wasn't going to see what I wanted to see. I needed an animal that had perished through accident or old age— anything relatively innocuous. Regulations again. If the creature had died through fighting another dinosaur, for instance, and that was quite a common end, then I couldn't make use of it—this era was already far too dangerous for us. I had to make sure that there weren't others of its kind lurking nearby, no protective mates or rivals: that was how the first expedition deaths occurred, after all. We did learn from our mistakes . . . sometimes.

And then Eckels showed up. He disobeyed the rules. He turned into a babbling idiot the moment he spotted T. rex. He left the path. I swore I'd kill him if he had caused any changes.

When we returned to HomeTime, it was clear what Eckels had done. He fell into a cold panic, scrabbling at the muck and filth on his boots, tearing at it. Finally he held up a clod of dirt. There, in his grimy fingers, a dusted iridescence shimmered gold and green. "No," he said. "It can't be. It's just a *butterfly*, for God's sake. . . ."

The fury was a scarlet veil in front of my eyes. I could feel my finger tighten around the barrel of my rifle, the skin white with tension. Half of me was screaming to stop, telling me that it wouldn't do any good to kill Eckels any- way, but I wanted it. I wanted *some* revenge. The man had destroyed my world. He'd turned it into something strange, grotesque, and dark.

I raised my weapon. I pointed the muzzle right at Eckels's chest. He was still babbling and apologizing. I squeezed the trigger.

There was a sound of thunder.

But Lesperance had moved at the same time. She knocked the rifle aside. My shot tore chunks of masonry from the walls and everyone screeched and ducked. Eckels screamed himself, and even as I wrenched my weapon from Lesperance's grasp and brought it up again, he ran. He made for the time machine, dove inside, and slammed shut the door. He pounded at the controls wildly. The device whined and shuddered.

Faded.

Disappeared.

I went after him. Our second machine was powered up and waiting—the cleanup crew would have used it to return to the Mesozoic a few minutes after our departure so they could dismantle the floating path and retrieve any 'foreign' objects. I closed the door on the shouting, confused lab and went DownTime.

I . . . I wasn't expecting what I saw when I arrived. The machine materialized in mayhem. I knew what had happened, knew it immediately. Remember the 'bumps,' remember how careful we were never to have ourselves appear in too close a spatial or temporal proximity? Eckels hadn't reset any of the controls. His machine tried to materialize in the same time and same place as itself. Time really does abhor a paradox: the temporal shock waves ripped apart Eckels's machine. The explosion shredded the path like paper.

The pieces were still smoldering when I arrived. A black crater marked where the center of the path had once been. The mud steamed underneath. Some of the larger fragments of the path had been flung a few meters away, ripping holes in the carpet of small ferns and mosses. Smaller bright scraps littered the ground like confetti, a few landing to decorate the still-warm body of the *Tyrannosaurus rex*. The biggest sections of the path, the ones powered by the antigrav modules, were thrown God knows where, out into the swampy jungle itself. I couldn't even see them.

A mess. The thought kept hammering at me: if Eckels's little tramp through the woods had given such a horrible twist to HomeTime, what would *this* have done?

I brought my craft to rest on one of the remaining intact sections of path and got out. I don't know what I expected to accomplish. I guess I thought I'd see if I could find Eckels's body. It seemed a fitting place for Eckels to have died, right beside the corpse of the dinosaur.

But I couldn't find Eckels. There was plenty of blood, but most of it seemed to have come from our rex. I wondered if Eckels wasn't still out there, maybe dazed. I called for him, shouting.

No one answered. Well, not precisely . . . The explosion of the time machine had caused most of the animals to flee. But not all. One, at least, had come to investigate.

You've met him yourselves—the allosarus.

I know, I know. How did we get *here*? I think I can explain it, but my theory's only that—an educated guess. Let me finish . . . I'm almost done and if I stop, I don't think I'll be able to keep going. I'm so tired. . . .

Allosaurs hunt in packs, did you know that? Like a pride of lions. I saw them come out of the jungle, about six of them. The closest allosaurus was between me and the machine. The pack noticed me almost immediately. I fired in the air, hoping to scare them away but without any real hope. I've met too many of them in the last few years. Allosaurs are built like tanks and they don't seem to *feel* much. They just keep going until the body refuses to stay erect. They're just one huge Hunger trying to feed itself: nothing else matters.

They came at me.

I ran—I didn't have much choice. Now it was *me* trying to flail my way through the muck, trying to stay ahead of those nightmare creatures behind me. I ran across the clearing and into the jungle itself, vines snatching at me like fingers, the ground sucking at my feet, and those monsters roaring and crashing after me. I lost most of them. Ahead, I saw a section of the path, still hovering above the ground. My movement was more reflex than anything else.

I jumped for it.

Ever have an inner ear infection, a bad one where the world refuses to stand up straight and things seem to whirl around no matter how you try to hang on? That's what I felt, along with a cold so intense that it seemed to suck all the heat from my body. Only my motion kept me going; I stumbled off the path again.

The rest you know.

I ended up here. So did one of them.

ANOTHER VISITATION

Travis sighed. His eyes had been closed for the last several minutes, even while he'd been speaking. Now his mouth shut and his hoarse, weary voice trailed off as his head lolled to one side on the pillow. Aaron started to ask him yet another question, but Jennifer shook her head. "No. He's out again. Let him be; he needs the rest."

"What'd you guys make of all that?" Peter asked.

"Like he said, remember the allosaurus," Aaron told him. "If it's a lie, the special effects were really good."

Jennifer and Peter both laughed nervously. Jennifer patted Travis's forehead with a damp washcloth. "I think he's going to be down for a while. What are we going to *do*, guys?"

"I don't know," Aaron admitted. "Let's go to the kitchen—we can talk there."

Aaron's grandfather came back in as Aaron was making a lunch of peanut butter sandwiches. Aaron was concerned by his grandfather's appearance; Carl was breathing heavily and he leaned against the doorway to wipe the sweat from his brow.

"I'm fine, Aaron," he said when Aaron expressed his worry. "I'm just an old man. It seems to take a lot more effort to go down to the creek and back now." They looked at him expectantly, but he shook his head. "Didn't see your dinosaur," he said.

Aaron, Jennifer, and Peter erupted in surprised shouts. "You don't believe us," Aaron said when the tumult had died down slightly.

"Aaron, that ain't the case. I saw that something big had torn up those woods pretty good, and there was a lot more blood on the ground than ever came from our friend. But whatever it was, it ain't there no more." Carl's eyes, snared in deep wrinkles, glistened. "But something else was. . . ."

He went back out to the porch and returned with a large cardboard box. There, placed gently on a layer of dirt, were the dinosaur eggs.

"Too big for a chicken and too strange shaped, ain't they?" Carl said, setting the box down on the kitchen table. They gathered around to look at the eggs once more. Aaron found himself touching them, just to make sure they were real. Carl nodded to Jennifer. "So, how's our visitor, Jenny girl?"

The three of them took turns repeating Travis's tale to the older man. Carl listened patiently, occasionally shaking his head. "I've got to say that I agree with you, Aaron," he said afterward. "If it's a hoax, it's a damn big one and I can't figure out any reason for it. He don't want the authorities nosing about, don't want to go to a hospital. . . ." Carl grimaced.

"Well, that fine, if that's what he wants," Peter said. "It's his business. Why worry about it?"

"Because he could be seriously hurt," Jennifer snapped back. "Internal bleeding, a concussion. I think we need to call someone."

Peter scoffed. "Right, Jen. And what are we gonna say? 'Hi, we just found this guy who'd been chewed on by a dinosaur. Oh, he's from the future, too, and his time machine's double-parked down in the woods. Oh no, we can't prove a word of it; the dinosaur either got up and walked away or someone stole the body, but we can give you one heck of an omelette.' You think Sheriff Tate's gonna buy any of that?"

"We don't have to tell the sheriff everything, Peter," Jennifer answered. Her face was flushed and angry; that made Aaron perversely happy. "And there's no reason for you to be so sarcastic. We found Travis in the woods. That's all we need to say."

"Yeah? And what happens when old Travis starts rattling off his story again?"

"Aaron?" Carl interrupted.

Aaron smiled kindly at his grandfather. Aaron knew that his parents wouldn't have listened at all. They wouldn't have mulled over any of this. For better or worse, if they'd been home Travis would already be in County General and Sheriff Tate and his deputies would be prowling the woods. He and his friends would be in for long hours of questioning, disbelief, and anger. The imagined scenario wasn't pleasant.

At least his grandfather was letting them come to their own decision, even if Aaron had the suspicion that Carl knew from the start that—like it or not—there was really only one path to follow. He was going to let them come to that conclusion by themselves. Carl's trust in their judgment made Aaron grin inside with affection before he replied.

"Travis is hurt," Aaron said slowly. "That's one point. He might die if we don't get him to a doctor soon, and we'd be responsible for that. In fact, we probably should have done that already. If his story's just that—a story—"

"Then I want to know how he got that monster here," Peter burst in.

"Then we'll know that soon enough, and like Jen said, we don't have to tell the sheriff everything."

"And what if the story's true?" Peter insisted.

"You think it is, Pete?" Carl asked.

"I don't *know*," Peter answered, exasperated. "I guess not. Though maybe . . ."

"It doesn't matter," Aaron said. "True or not. It doesn't change anything, does it? The man's hurt."

"Which means we're stuck with getting involved. I wish you two had never needed a cameraman. My folks are going be really—" Peter stopped, looked at Carl "—irritated," he finished.

"The sheriff's number's on the fridge," Carl

told Aaron. "I think you should make the call, boy. And I think you're underestimating everyone, Peter. Something strange happened here, granted, but it ain't any of your fault. I'll be the first to say so."

Aaron looked at his friends. "I'll go check Travis," Jennifer said. Peter shook his head and leaned back against the wall in his chair.

"You got a better idea, Pete?" Aaron asked.

Peter fiddled with his camera, focused on the eggs, and then set the camera back on the table without taking a shot. "Nah," he said. "You're right. I just don't like it, that's all." He looked up at Aaron and gave him a shrug. "Go on, give old Tate a call. We're going away to college in a few weeks—how much grief can our parents put us through anyway? No offense, Mr. Cofield."

"None taken, Peter. I'd've been thinking the same thing when I was your age." He chuckled. "Though I can't say as anything this odd ever happened to me."

Jenny left the kitchen. Aaron went to the wall phone and found the number on the scribbled list held to the refrigerator by a mushroom-shaped magnet. He picked up the receiver and started to dial.

"Aaron!"

Jenny's call came from the bedroom. The boys came running, Carl following more slowly. "He's gone," she said.

The covers were thrown aside; the window was open and the screen lifted up. The weapon which Peter had left leaning against the wall was missing. Travis wasn't visible on the lawn.

"So much for that problem," Peter commented.

Carl watched from the back porch as Peter ran to where the lawn sloped down to the woods. Jennifer and Peter had gone to the front to check the roadway. From the various shouts Carl heard, Travis wasn't in sight anywhere. Carl nodded to himself. It was just as well— the whole situation scared him.

You're an old man, Carl Cofield. Fifty years ago you were the one who would have loved nothing better than finding a dinosaur in the forest. Remember? The air was magic in your imagination and you took in great gulps of the spell, laughing. Now you wheeze and air that vital and cold makes you cough. But you want to believe, don't you? You can still feel it. Still . . .

Still . . .

Carl left the door and went to the table. He stooped over the cardboard box of wonder, looking at the spiderwebbed flesh of his long fingers against the white of the eggs. He picked up one, holding it to the light streaming in from the window. "Are you real?" he asked of the shape. "Are you magic or sham, wonder or mockery?"

"I'll bet Travis was faking it all along," Peter said behind Carl. The older man started, clutching the egg, then gently laid it back down in the nest of grass. Jennifer and Aaron had returned also; they took seats around the table. "The eggs are fakes, too," Peter said with conviction.

Carl saw Aaron regarding him. *Aaron knows. We're a lot alike, that boy and I. He and I both want to believe. We both want a world where there are still unknown creatures to find and new lands to explore.*

"Travis was really hurt," Jennifer insisted. "I know that much. He may have faked how tired he was so we'd leave him, but those cuts and bruises were real."

"I can cut and bruise myself." Peter sniffed. "That don't prove nothing. Right, Aaron?"

Aaron smiled at Carl, as if he knew what his grandfather was thinking and agreed. He turned back to Peter, his mouth opening as he started to speak. Nothing came out. He was staring at the window. Peter raised an eyebrow.

Then, with a whoop and a holler, Aaron was up, his chair clattering to the linoleum floor. "What the—" Peter began, then glanced at the window himself.

Carl saw it too, a wavy image beyond the old glass. Out near the edge of the back lawn, what looked like a small rhinoceros with a frilled head and three horns was grazing, pulling up the long grass. "Triceratops!" Aaron shouted gleefully from the porch. "Come on!"

"Aaron!" Carl called, limping to the screen door as Jennifer and Peter shot out after Aaron.

"It's a plant eater, Grandpa!"

"Don't . . . You can't . . ." The words came out as a reflex, and he hated himself for saying them.

The admonition was too late, anyway. They were already halfway across the yard, running full tilt toward the startled dinosaur, which snorted, tossed its magnificent head, and lumbered downslope toward the woods. "Follow it!" Aaron called to his friends. "Come on, come on!"

"Aaron!" Carl called once more.

"I'll be careful, Grandpa. Don't worry!"

No! That's not what I was going to say. "Wait for me!"—those are the words. "Let me chase it, too." I would have, if I were your age.

But he wasn't their age anymore, and his bones were brittle and stiff and his muscles ached just from watching them run and leap and his joints burned with an eternal smouldering fire. "Be careful, Aaron," he said, but it was only a whisper. "Go on. Go on."

And they were gone, bounding down the slope into the woods. He could hear them shouting at each other, crystalline voices in the afternoon heat. And then even the sound was gone.

Carl shaded his eyes against the sun. He waited, wanting more than anything else to go after them anyway and knowing that the distance between them wasn't measured in yards but in years. And even with Travis's time machine, there was no way to reverse the biological clock.

He went back into the kitchen. For a long, long time, he sat looking at the eggs.

THE BROKEN PATH

When Aaron reached the edge of the lawn, he could look down the slope and see the triceratops, which had returned to grazing on the blackberry bushes at the edge of the woods. As Jennifer and Peter came up, the dinosaur lifted its head. It peered sharply up the slope, its nostrils widening as it sniffed the air. Then, with an odd mewling sound, it bolted like a startled horse, crashing into and through the bushes and under the shelter of small maples.

"Let's go!" Aaron shouted. He half ran, half tumbled down the hill in wild, frantic, laughing pursuit, his two friends following. They plunged into the woods like wild creatures themselves, blackberry vines scratching them through their jeans, snagging their clothes and holding them back. Their quarry had run into a tangled, brush-choked area. The dinosaur's great bulk and strength had enabled it to tear free of the snarl; Aaron and the others were not so strong, thick-skinned, or lucky. It took them several precious seconds to force their way through the stubborn growth and into more open woods. By that time, the triceratops was no longer in sight.

"Another phantom," Peter commented,

breathing hard with his hands on his knees. "Just great."

"Look, Peter, it proves that Travis was telling the truth—or that *something* weird is going on."

"I'll grant you that much, for sure."

"We can still follow—" Jennifer began, then tilted her head. "Listen . . ."

From deeper in the stand, where the maples gave way to oaks and other hardwoods, they could hear several faint voices calling and shouting. "Hey, guys! Aaron! Jen! Peter!"

Peter cupped his hands over his mouth and shouted back. "Who's that? Where are you?"

No answer returned, at least none that they could decipher. The voices still halloed, but they couldn't quite make out the words. "Probably some of the Harper kids," Aaron said worriedly. "They're down this way a lot. They could be in trouble."

"So could we be if we keep going deeper into here," Peter commented.

"Thought you didn't believe Travis, Peter."

"I don't, but I've seen enough in the last few hours to make me just a little cautious. Somebody here needs to be the voice of reason. We don't even have a lousy .22 . . .." Peter stopped and grinned at Aaron's sour expression. "Okay, Great Dinosaur Hunter, I can see that your mind's all made up. Let's go rescue the Harpers. After all, you'd hate to have someone else get the credit for your little discovery, right?"

There was a sarcastic edge to Peter's voice that made Aaron want to respond with something angry and harsh. Instead, he swallowed the irritation. Silent, he turned to dart into the underbrush again—into the emerald-shadowed heart of the forest. In a moment, he had vanished like the dinosaur.

"Aaron, you idiot!" Peter called after him. Still annoyed with Peter, Aaron didn't answer. He kept going. At his back, he heard Peter start to bicker with Jennifer. "How can you *stand* him, Jenny . . ."

The trees were thicker here; it was impossible to move in anything resembling a straight line. Aaron moved as best as he could in the direction of the voices, which had faded entirely away. Aaron was beginning to wonder if they'd ever heard them at all, or whether they had simply been some trick of the wind hushing through the leaves. Here, the hills were steep, shaped by some giant's hands into accordion folds. The incline sloped down sharply in the direction of the river to the south. Aaron labored up one hill and down another, crossed the small creek there, and hauled himself up the next rise.

He was winded by the time he reached the summit; he stopped to catch his breath. Somewhere not far behind him, he could hear Jenny and Peter thrashing their way through the late summer undergrowth. Seated on a fallen, grub-infested log, Aaron surveyed the landscape in front of him. There was *something* just a bit down the hill, a patch of white shining through green. Aaron moved a few steps to his right to get a better view and immediately forgot his fatigue. The sudden adrenaline surge made him laugh out loud.

A quarter of the way down the hill, suspended at an odd angle but *floating* an inch or two above the ground, was a long section of what looked like rigid plastic sheeting, about six feet wide and ten long. The front edge was jagged and splintered, and something black and oily had stained the surface at that point.

"I'll be ... That's Travis's path," Aaron whispered to himself. He laughed again. "It *was* true." Turning to face the way he'd come, he shouted, waving his arms. "Jen! Peter! Over here! Quick! I've found something!" He thought he heard an answering shout. Aaron jumped on top of the log to get a better view, still shouting: "Jen!"

Afterward, he'd wonder how he could have been so incredibly clumsy.

The bark was loose, the wood underneath rotten and insect riddled. His foot slipped, the log shooting forward and pitching him backward. Flailing for balance, Aaron tumbled. His other foot hit loose dirt; he found himself rolling backward down the slope in an avalanche of dust, trying to grab anything to stop his fall and regain his footing.

What he found was the roadway.

* * *

"Peter, you can really be a total idiot sometimes," Jennifer told him.

"Hey, look, all I said was—"

"I know what you said. And you said it just to make Aaron mad."

Jennifer had started to follow Aaron into the woods, but Peter grabbed at her arm. "Jenny, we've lost this dinosaur just like the other one. There's no sense in getting all scratched up and sweaty and bug bit. Let's go back to the house and wait for Aaron. He'll come back soon."

"I'm going with him, Peter. You can wait here if you want. He might need help."

Jennifer tugged away from Peter's insistent grasp. He let her go, shaking his head in exasperation. She started to say more, then shut her mouth—there was no sense in trying to explain anything.

Peter had been the same way when they were dating: anything he didn't understand or agree with was wrong. Everything in Peter's world was black and white. No shades of gray were allowed and certainly there couldn't be two valid positions on any topic. He wasn't much for discussion, either—any time she'd disagreed with him the debate had quickly disintegrated into argument. She still liked Peter (though it was dangerous to admit that to Aaron, who was a little tender on the subject) and she considered him a friend, but she wished he'd grow up.

This was another of those times when she knew it was useless to try to talk with him. "It's up to you if you want to come," she said. "But I'm going."

She stalked off along Aaron's trail; behind her, she heard Peter exhale loudly, mutter something under his breath, and then follow.

The Harper kids' voices—if it had been them, Jennifer reminded herself—were gone. Aaron had moved south and east, and she thought she could hear him crashing through some tangle just over the next hill. Peter was right about one thing: it was indeed hot and sweaty going. The vines, tree falls, and patches of dense undergrowth seemed designed to keep them from moving in any straight direction. Jennifer tugged aside a branch that had entwined its leafy fingers in her shirt and kept going. Just behind her, Peter trailed in her wake, still muttering and complaining.

They heard Aaron call, his voice echoing. "Here we are!" Jennifer shouted back. "Jen!" came the shout again, very close by, and then . . .

Nothing.

"Aaron! Hey, we're over this way!" Jennifer waited, hearing little but the squirrels racing through the branches overhead and the soft whisper of the creek at the bottom of the hillside.

"Aaron?"

No answer. Jennifer was suddenly very frightened. "Aaron," she said again, but this time her voice was hardly more than a whisper. Thinking of him suddenly evoked a horrifying sense of distance and separation. "Peter, something's wrong."

"Nothing's wrong, Jenny," Peter answered querulously. "He's just over the ridge. He can't hear us or he's being too bullheaded to answer."

"No. It's more than that." Jennifer pushed her way through the brush to the top of the ridge. She called for Aaron again, causing birds to flutter from the nearby treetops, but there was still no reply. She looked down into the valley and the creek bed, where she and Aaron and Peter had gone exploring since the time when their parents first allowed them to play alone in the woods. What was there *now* had never been there before. "Peter—"

"What?" he grumbled, coming up behind her and then stopping. "I'll be . . . Is that thing *floating*?"

At the bottom of the valley and nearly bridging the small stream, lay a large piece of white plastic. Jennifer knew what it was; knowing made the fear in her stomach even tighter. She scrambled down to the bottom of the hill, crashing through the carpet of dead leaves and weeds until she stood alongside the odd structure.

"It's Travis's path," she told Peter vehemently, her tone quite effectively saying I told you so. "There's where the explosion tore it loose, and it's still floating, just like he said." She reached out to touch the piece, but Peter pulled her hand back.

"Don't."

"Why not?"

"Because you don't know what might happen or where it might lead. Travis said that it transported him here. I wouldn't touch it."

"Thought you didn't believe anything Travis said."

Peter grimaced. "I still don't. But why take chances? Leave the thing alone. This is getting too strange and too big for us. I think old man Cofield's right; we need some help here."

"It's too late for that. Aaron's missing."

"He's *not* missing, Jenny." Peter's voice was exasperated and out of patience. "He's out there ahead of us somewhere."

Jennifer shook her head. "I don't think so, Peter." She looked at the path, only the path. The pristine white surface seemed to sway in the slight wind. "I think he went this way."

Peter was shaking his head. "Jenny, Aaron wouldn't have done that without letting us know. C'mon, not even Aaron'd be that stu—"

Jennifer glared at Peter; he raised his hands, palms out. "Hey, sorry. But Jenny, *if* any of Travis's tale is true and *if* this path does lead into our prehistory, then we're not prepared for whatever's on the other side. I don't have any desire to be dinosaur sushi."

"Very funny."

"Besides, didn't Travis say that running around there would change our history here? What if we come back to find everything totally different?"

"Aaron could be hurt," Jennifer persisted.

"We don't need to go exploring, Peter; he could be right on the other side."

"He could be right around *here*, Jenny," Peter retorted. "There's still the triceratops roaming around, and the Harper kids. . . ."

"Aaron's not here," Jennifer repeated emphatically. "I know. I *feel* it."

"'I *feel* it'" Peter mimicked, grimacing. "That's just great. I'm really glad you have true-love radar like that. But let's at least make sure of it before we do something foolish. That's all I'm saying." Peter started to call Aaron's name again, first loudly and then with increasing irritation as Aaron didn't answer. At last, his voice hoarse, he stopped.

The woods were silent and ominous.

"He's not here, Pete. I told you that. I'm going to try the path."

"Jenny—"

"Come or stay, whichever you want, Finnigan. Just make up your mind now, either way."

Jennifer started to step up onto the path itself. "Wait," Peter said. "If we're gonna do this, let's do it together, at least."

He held out his hand. Reluctantly, Jennifer took it.

Together, they stepped onto the pathway.

THE TRUTH OF THE TALE

It was worse than Jennifer had expected.

The cold was instantaneous and bone chilling, like being plucked from the Illinois summer and slammed down in the Arctic Circle. Jennifer's inner ears screamed to her mind that she was being twirled end over end while her eyes gave no indication of motion at all. She could taste the bile rising in her throat; the landscape beyond the fragment of path was blurring like a smeared chalkboard: green, blue, and umber streaks running together like wet paint in strange swirls.

The motion of stepping up onto the path, combined with the dizziness that immediately hit her, made Jennifer tumble from the path in the next second. She found herself facedown on moist earth, a bushy plant of some sort tickling her cheek and moisture dripping on her forehead from somewhere above. A second, later, Peter lay sprawled alongside her, breathless. It took a few moments for the world to settle down again. Peter was already rising to his feet; Jennifer ignored his proffered hand and stood up by herself.

"I don't think we're in Kansas anymore, Toto," Peter said shakily.

"Oh my God, Peter . . ."

The hardwood forest was gone. There was no creek, no rolling southern Illinois hills. The two of them were standing in a damp hollow in a stand of tall conifers whose lowest branches were perhaps twenty feet or more above the ground. A few oaks, birches, and alders were sprinkled here and there, but the firs dominated. There was no grass underfoot, only a threadbare carpet of tiny plants and mosses, punctuated by dense growths of larger flowering plants. The soles of their sneakers were deep in thick, clinging mud, but outside the hollow the ground seemed dry. Vines draped coiling from every branch; in and around them, animal life moved: large dragonflies, butterflies, lizards, even small ratlike creatures. There were calls echoing through the foliage above them: bizarre trills and rumbles, froglike *harrumphs* and booming nasal honks. None of those were sounds that Jennifer or Peter had ever heard before; this was a soundtrack from some alien world. The land smelled of sweet flowers and rotting wood.

Punctuating the scene and denying any possibility that this was simply some strange, lost section of the forest in their own world, a winged, feathered lizard the size of a crow fluttered overhead, peering down at them and banking away on leathery wings.

A shiver of fright, or perhaps a remnant of the intense cold of the transition, made Jennifer clutch herself.

Peter placed his arm around her shoulder; she made no move to shrug it away—at that moment she needed the comfort of his familiarity. Right now she felt very far away from anything normal.

"Aaron!" she called. The sounds of this forest went silent for a moment, then the rustling in the shadows of the tall trees began again. "Aaron?" Aaron didn't answer.

"Jenny, let's go back." Peter spoke in a whisper, as if he were afraid to disturb this place again. Neither one of them had moved. They stood stock still, both remembering Travis's story and staring at the mud staining their clothing. He looked at the path; it appeared to be the twin of the one that had been floating above the creek back in Green Town. "Or try to go back, anyway."

"Aaron came this way," Jennifer said. "We can't go until we find him."

A bright, emerald green lizard the size of a Siamese cat trundled from under a leafy fern a few feet away, licked at the air with a long, flickering tongue, and darted away again. "We aren't going to find him, Jenny. There's just the two of us, and a big, hungry world to search. I don't see Aaron's footprints or any sign of him, and we're a long, long way from home. Home's where Aaron probably is, too."

"No," Jennifer insisted. "He left. I know; I felt it."

"Great. Woman's intuition, right?"

Jennifer glared. "Don't, Peter. I mean it. I

don't need that from you right now."

"Sorry," he said, but he sounded more aggravated than apologetic. "I still think we should go back, Jennifer. While we can."

"We're only a step from home." Jennifer shook her head defiantly, pointing at the floating path. "We haven't gone anywhere, really, not if Travis told us the truth—and if he hasn't, it's too late anyway. All we have to do is make sure we can find our way back to this point."

"*If* Travis told the truth," Peter repeated. "It seems to me that we're missing something important, like a big tree with a tyrannosaurus body underneath it. Travis said the place was a jungle, too. This is weird, but it isn't exactly what I'd call a jungle; it's too open. None of it matches what Travis was talking about."

"Travis said that the explosion threw pieces of the path all around. The dinosaur body could be anywhere nearby and we'd never see it in the undergrowth."

Peter took his arm away, running his hand though short, thick hair. "Jenny, I'm sorry but this is really *stupid*. We aren't prepared for this. Let's at least go back and get some stuff: a compass, a medical kit, Aaron's dad's shotgun. For that matter, let's do what old man Cofield said and call in the cops. Let *them* go prowling through here."

"Aaron might need us now, Peter. He's your friend; he's my . . ." Jennifer stopped. She looked at Peter's face and decided that she didn't care what he was thinking. "He's a lot more than a friend to me," she finished. "You do what you think you need to do, okay? Go back if you want and get help. Fine. But I'm staying here and at least looking for him."

Peter sighed. She could almost read his thoughts: *No use arguing with her when she gets that way.* "All right. Wonderful," he said. "So pick a direction, any direction."

She ignored the sarcasm. She pointed into the forest, away from the hidden sun. "This way. It's as good as any."

They circled the hollow. The going was difficult. A thousand species of insects hummed and darted through the warm air; smaller animals, mostly lizards, darted underfoot. After a short time, both Jennifer and Peter were tired and irritable. They'd made nearly a complete circuit of the area when they came to an open glade in the midst of the trees. There, clear and well-defined in the shadowed, bare earth, they saw the prints of shoes.

Jennifer gave a glad cry, but Peter's eyes narrowed as he bent down to examine the prints more closely. "This isn't Aaron," he said. "These shoes are too small, and Aaron was wearing his Nikes. These are bootprints or something like that. They're new prints, though. . . ." He straightened, peering around anxiously. "There's someone else around, Jenny. Gotta be."

"Travis," Jennifer suggested.

"Maybe." Peter scratched at the insect bites on his arms. "My advice's still to go back to the path and get help. Now more than ever."

"I want to follow the prints. Travis didn't seem dangerous to me. Maybe he knows where Aaron is."

"You're awfully damn stubborn."

"You're awfully damn right I am," she retorted. Angry, Jennifer ignored Peter entirely. Moving as carefully as she could to avoid stepping on anything alive, she followed the direction of the footprints away from the glade and the path.

"Jennifer—"

She kept going.

Peter stood with his hands on his hips, watching her. When she didn't even look back and he began to lose sight of her among the trees, he followed.

The prints, sometimes lost and then found once more, led them in a winding loop away from the path. They climbed a hill where bare outcroppings of limestone punctuated the greenery. The footprints led to a cleft between two large boulders. There, down a short and steep incline, the jagged mouth of a cave nestled. The prints ended at the edge of that blackness.

"That's it," Peter said. He sounded relieved. "We don't have flashlights or anything for this kind of thing."

Jennifer had gone down closer to the cave mouth, peering into the inky depths beyond. "There's light a little further in," she said. "I can see it—something like a torch or a camp fire."

She took a step down into the cave itself. A damp coolness welling up from below hit her. The smell of earth and rock mingled with the scent of smoke. Jennifer let her eyes adjust to the dimness and found that between the sunlight spilling in and the fire's illumination another hundred yards further in, she could see fairly well. A distinct, hard trail had been trampled in the dirt near the entrance; beyond, it seemed to wind down among the rockfalls.

Peter came up behind her suddenly, startling her. "Jenny, look . . . I—I hate caves," he said. "You remember?"

She did. They'd gone to Mammoth Cave in Kentucky one weekend with Aaron and a group of friends. Peter had been extremely uncomfortable in the dark, enclosed caverns; he'd gone on one short excursion, then stayed outside the rest of the day while the others went on one of the long walking tours.

"I know," she said, more gently. "Look, you can stay here. I'm going in as far as the fire, just to see."

"Jenny, we can't go spelunking here. We can't afford to get lost in this place or hurt—nobody's going to come rescue us."

"I know that. I just want to check this out. If Travis isn't here, we'll go back, I promise."

She could feel his muscles tensing alongside her. "All right. I'll go with you," he said at last. "We should stay together. Be careful and go slow, huh? There's no park rangers to turn the lights on."

She smiled at that. *One minute he's insisting we go back and the next he's Mr. Bravery. I wish he'd make up his mind. . . .* "Thanks," she told him.

"Just remember that we're going right back after this, okay?"

"It's a deal."

The footing was treacherous and the passageway so narrow that they were forced to go in single file. Loose slabs of rock fallen from the ceiling tilted underfoot and raised booming, dull echoes when they fell back into place. "Great alarm system," Peter muttered. "No sneaking up on anyone here." Jennifer had to agree, but no one called out to them as they continued forward.

The corridor opened out shortly into a small room. Jennifer could tell immediately that this was someone's dwelling. A fire burned in the center of the cavern, the smoke coiling upward to a crevice in the ceiling. The ruddy, wavering light revealed crudely made furniture: a chair made of rope-lashed branches; a table that was a sawed-off, sanded stump; a few unglazed pottery cups set on a cave ledge; a mattress on the ground that looked made from denim stuffed with straw. The place had evidently been inhabited for some time—everything had a used look: old rings of moisture on the table, scratches on the ledges, the floor hard packed from use.

"This can't be Travis's place," Peter said. "He left Green Town at the most an hour ago."

"Eckels's?" Jennifer ventured, then shook

her head at her own guess. "That can't be. If Travis was telling the truth, then Eckels has only been in the past for a day himself, at the most."

"*If* Travis was telling the truth, indeed."

The voice came from behind them. Peter and Jennifer whirled, startled and frightened. A shape came from an alcove they hadn't seen. Firelit shadows traced the figure: a thin, roughly bearded man with dark shadows under his eyes, his clothing half in tatters. He limped forward into the firelight, holding his right leg stiffly.

He also cradled a rifle in his arms, the ugly snout pointing directly at them. "A fresh body or two to send back to that SOB might just give him the message to leave me alone, don't you think?" the man said.

With those words, Peter screamed and launched himself at Eckels in desperation. Eckels's reflexes were far quicker than either one of them expected from his bedraggled appearance. He easily parried Peter's flying kick with the rifle's muzzle, then smashed the stock into the young man's chin. Jennifer heard Peter's mouth slam shut as his head whipped backward from the blow.

Peter crumpled to the ground, his limbs sprawling.

Eckels grinned down at Peter's unconscious body. "A budding martial artist. What a pity he didn't learn his lessons as well as I did, eh?" Still grinning, he looked back at Jenny. His crooked leering smile was like a mask of horror, and his deep-set eyes held no compassion at all.

"Well now," Eckels said. "It's just you and me, isn't it?"

ESCAPE AND RECAPTURE

The man talked. Long and confusingly. Words flowed out of him endlessly, as constant as a groundwater spring and just as chilling.

"Now," Eckels told Jennifer, still grinning lopsidedly at her. "There's some rope under the table. Made it myself from vines, did you know that? Tough stuff, those vines; they'll fray your hands if you don't soak 'em in water first so they're soft. Try braiding them as they are and you'll end up with your palms raw and bloody like you scraped 'em with sandpaper. I've had to learn lots of stuff. Gotta know how to take care of things, you see. The dinosaurs aren't any help, most of them; they don't like me and they're quite willing to tell me so. I don't think you can reason with them at all—they'd as soon eat you as talk to you. So get the rope and tie up our Mr. Hero—we wouldn't want him to do something really stupid and get shot, would we? And Peter'll certainly do something stupid, won't he, Jenny?"

Jennifer's intake of breath sounded loud in the darkness of the cavern. "You know our names. . . ."

Eckels looked confused for a moment, then the grin returned. So did the nonstop monologue. "Of course I do. Sure I know your names. Yeah. I watched you coming here when I was out spying on the big lizards, didn't I? They're always looking for me. Always. They're searching for me all over the valley, but I'm too smart for 'em. You two talk too much and way too loudly, did you know that? These corridors are great amplifiers. I heard you coming long before you got here. Learned your names then, I did."

A look—almost of pain—seemed to pass across his thin, haggard face. Jennifer wondered at Eckels's appearance. For a man who Travis had described as rich and pampered, he looked starved.

"Let us go, Eckels," Jennifer said. "Please. We don't mean you any harm. Just let us go and we'll leave. We won't tell Travis you're here."

Eckels barked laughter and waved his weapon at Jennifer. "Right. I'm gonna make *sure* you never tell Travis. I got my own surprises for old Travis, I can tell you now; things he never thought of, things he never dreamed about. He doesn't think I can fix things but I can. He thinks I'm useless and stupid. Hey— you just do what I said, huh?"

"What are you going to do with us?"

Eckels's finger prowled the scraggly beard on his cheek with one hand, and the rifle barrel dropped. Jennifer almost made a move toward

the weapon, but Eckels anticipated the movement. His hand went back to the gun stock.
"Haven't quite figured out yet what I'm going
to do. But I will. Maybe I'll talk with the Big
Greenies, see if I can sell you two to 'em.
They'd do that, y'know. We could work out
some kind of fair trade, something equitable.
They'd find you tasty. Eat you for lunch, they
would. Yum, yum."

Eckels made exaggerated chewing motions
and then cackled. The manic sound sent shiv-
ers down Jennifer's back. She'd already decided
that Eckels was mad, mad and raving. Half of
what he said made no sense at all—talking with
dinosaurs?—but the rifle in his hand was com-
pelling. Jennifer took a deep calming breath
and fetched the rope.

Kneeling on the dirt floor, she checked Peter.
He was still out, but his breathing was steady
and strong. He already had a puffy bruise along
one side of his face and he'd very likely wake
up with a nasty headache, but the jaw didn't
look broken. Eckels talked continuously as Jennifer tied Peter's hands and feet with the rope.
She didn't listen much to what the man said,
concentrating on making the knots tight enough
to fool Eckels but loose enough that Peter
might be able to slip out of them later.

"Good, good," Eckels told her abruptly.
"Now get away from him." He didn't bother
to check the bindings, just pulled a flint-
knapped blade from his belt and motioned her

away from Peter. Jennifer was suddenly very frightened.

"Ah, am I scaring the poor young lady?" He laughed again, the hideous sound reverberating in the hidden dark passages of the caves. "Let's see, I could just slice his throat, couldn't I, since you did such a good job of trussing him, but that'd be cruel, wouldn't it? Hardly sporting, all things considered. Nope—" The blade flicked and darted as Eckels leaned forward toward Peter. Jennifer nearly screamed until she realized that Eckels was just slicing the remaining coils of rope from Peter's bonds.

"Your turn," he said. "You can sit in the chair there while I give you the same treatment."

There didn't seem to be a choice. Jennifer sat while Eckels bound her to the makeshift chair. He wasn't nearly as gentle as she had been with Peter—his knots were tight and the vines uncomfortable. When he'd finished, he came in front of her and smiled. He touched her cheek and she turned her face away, hardly daring to breathe.

Eckels pulled his hand away—far too slowly for Jennifer—and smiled again.

"You should remember," he said, "that you are the only woman in this world. The only one at all. We'll be seeing a lot of each other; I just know it."

Jennifer refused to look at him, but she could feel his gaze on her. He wasn't saying anything now, just staring at her. Then he moved away with an explosive sigh.

"Lots to do first, though. Lots of big lizards to meet now. Got an appointment with one of 'em, as a matter of fact. Maybe I'll clear up this mess at last, you know. Old Eckels, he was always to blame. But I've put things right, finally."

He was still talking as he walked away down the twisting cavern trail, leaving Jenny and Peter alone in the room. Jennifer listened to his voice for a long time—Eckels was right; the stone passages did transmit sound well. After a time, she couldn't hear him anymore.

Jennifer struggled desperately against her ropes and succeeded only in rubbing her skin raw. Her fingers were beginning to tingle from lack of circulation. "Peter!" she half whispered, half shouted. "Wake up, would you! Peter!"

The youth groaned and stirred. His eyes, still shut, he tried to sit upright and found that he couldn't; he fell back heavily to the earth, moaning. His eyes opened and glanced dully at Jennifer. "Wha—?"

"Are you okay?"

Peter worked his jaw slowly, running his tongue around his mouth. "My jaw hurts like crazy, and I've got two loose front teeth. I also have the great-granddaddy of all headaches. Where's Eckels?"

"Eckels is gone. He had me tie you up, but

I made the knots pretty loose. Can you get out?"

Peter was already tugging at the ropes, his face strained. It took him several minutes, alternately resting and working, to get his hands free. He sat up, rubbing his wrists, which were scratched and bleeding from the rough fiber of the crude rope. "You could have tied them a little looser, Jen."

"I did the best I could," she replied, irritated. "Just get over here and untie me, please."

Peter reached into his pocket and took out his Swiss Army knife. He slashed away the rest of the bonds from his feet and went over to do the same for Jenny. She sighed with relief and tried to rub some feeling back into her limbs. The circulation returned with needles of pain. She forced herself to stand on her unsteady legs. "C'mon," she said. "Let's get out of here."

"Now *that* I can agree with," Peter said heartily.

Cautiously, they made their way back through the cavern to the cave opening. Squinting into the bright sunlight, they peered out. Eckels was nowhere to be seen. They could hear strange animal cries from somewhere nearby, and a pterosaur glided overhead, its long narrow head swiveling to glance down at them. "He's gone," Jennifer said. "Good."

"I'm almost sorry," Peter retorted, grim

faced. "I'd love to pay him back for almost breaking my jaw."

Right. Why not give the madman a second chance at it . . . Jennifer kept the words to herself. *Let Peter have his macho image if it's that important to him. But it's so stupid.* . . . "He was bonkers, Pete," she told him instead. "You didn't hear him, but I did. Ranting and raving, going on about talking dinosaurs and going back to fix things, and—"

"And what?"

Muscles knotted along Jenny's jawline. "Other stuff," she said.

"Did he *do* anything to you? Did he bother you? If he did—"

"What, Peter? What are you going to do? Listen, Peter, I'm not your property, and I don't need your protection. It seems to me that you were out the whole time. If something *had* happened—and it didn't—a heck of a lot of good you were going to do me."

Peter glared at Jennifer; she tossed him a contemptuous glance. "Let's just go," she said. "I want to find that roadway and get home. Maybe Aaron's back by now."

"Aaron—" Peter muttered. There was a mocking petulance in his voice that made Jennifer swing around again.

"Stuff it, Peter." She prodded him in the chest with each word. "You understand me?"

He sniffed. He smiled at her—patronizingly, she thought. "Hey, it's cool, Jen. Whatever you say."

There was a lot more that Jennifer wanted to say, but not here, not so near Eckels's cave. She shook her head again at Peter and stalked off, heading back in the direction they'd come. Peter followed her a few seconds later.

They were well within the cover of the trees when Jennifer stopped. She gestured to Peter for silence. "What'd you hear?" he whispered.

She didn't answer immediately, still listening. "Someone else is out there," she whispered back, pointing to where several large trees twined together into a living wall. "It stopped when we did. Like it was trailing us."

"Eckels." Peter clenched his fists. "I'll get the bastard this time."

"He's got a rifle," Jennifer reminded Peter. At the same moment, she felt a premonition that whoever was shadowing them wasn't Eckels. She was certain of it. She felt that someone was watching and appraising them with hard, hidden eyes. A cold, nameless fear knotted her stomach. *Aaron, I wish you were here. I wouldn't care what happened then. Not as much, anyway.*

The silence continued. Peter seemed to relax, but the twisting uneasiness in Jennifer's stomach refused to go away. "Whoever it is, they're not making a move," Peter said. "If anyone's there at all. Let's get going."

Peter started to rise from his crouch but Jennifer caught his arm. "Not to Travis's roadway," she whispered urgently. "Not yet, anyway."

"I thought you wanted to get home to Aaron."

"I did." She lifted her chin, refusing to let Peter's mocking tone irritate her any further. "I'm just thinking—what if it *is* Eckels? Maybe he's trapped here and doesn't know where the path is. Or maybe someone else is looking for it."

"Like who?"

"I don't *know*." Jennifer sighed. "Just humor me, okay? For a few minutes. If nothing happens, we'll head for home."

Peter rolled his eyes. "You are the most—" He shook his head, not finishing the statement. Instead, he reached down and plucked a thick piece of dead wood from the ground. "Okay, let's go. This way . . ."

They moved off again. Jennifer let Peter take the lead, angling away from the clearing where the roadway sat. Though they tried to move quietly and carefully, she knew that they were making too much noise to avoid notice. Small lizards scuttled out of their way; pterosaurs clucked angrily overhead and drifted off through the trees to new roosts; large flying insects whirred from their wake. Jennifer worried about each step they took—if Travis had been right, then with each footfall, they might be changing history once more. If Eckels's blundering from the path had caused so much damage to the future, then what major alterations had the three of them made?

You can't worry about it. It's already done. You need to find Aaron and get back home, that's all. But she couldn't shake the feeling of dread. She moved closer to Peter, wanting nothing more than to feel his comfortable familiarity in an alien world.

The confrontation, when it came, was totally unexpected.

One moment Jennifer was striding through the trees. The next, she was tumbling to the ground, her ankles snared in a loop of vines. She didn't quite manage to break her fall; a tree root hit her side and all the air went out of her lungs in a quick *whuff*. She looked up, gasping, to see Peter trying to run, then falling himself with a cry.

Jennifer tried to lever herself up from the dirt when something hard and sharp prodded her back down harshly. She could hear someone breathing behind her; turning her head, she saw a pair of clawed, scaled feet. Whoever belonged to those feet made a sound, a highly articulated burst of noise.

"*Aarti*"—snort—"*Keeshi*"—trill.

The pressure on her back lifted and Jennifer rolled to her side so that she could see, her hands up for protection. She gasped.

A spear was pointed at her throat, the head of the weapon fashioned from what looked like polished bone or ivory lashed to a length of black wood. The hands that held the weapon had three long taloned fingers; the skin of those hands, like that of the body behind, was scaled with a rich, marbled emerald that shimmered in the patterned sunlight beneath the trees. A pendant of some dull metal, tied with bright feathers, hung against the reptilian chest.

And the face that peered down at her, the mouth slightly open to reveal the crowns of ridged teeth, was nothing human at all.

ANOTHER PATH TAKEN

It was the strangest experience Aaron had ever had. One second he was doing a back roll down a hill, then there was a sudden, intense cold and a nauseating disorientation, and *then* he was deposited unceremoniously facedown in a mud hole in the middle of a fern-filled steam bath.

Pushing himself up to his hands and knees, Aaron shook his head and lifted it cautiously above the three-foot-high cover of the plants. He blinked away water and mud. He knew where he was even as he gazed at the jungle before him; he'd seen this world a million times in his imagination.

The jungle in front of him was unlike any that existed in his world, but he could recognize many of the plants from their renderings in textbooks. Huge hardwood trees formed the frame of the scene, their multirooted feet planted in shallow ponds and mud banks. They lanced upward toward an unseen sky, branchless until—a hundred feet or more above Aaron's head—they blossomed suddenly into a thick, interlacing roof of green. Between these giants, the tree ferns crowded, nearly as high as the hardwoods themselves, an explosion of emerald shapes and textures like a greenhouse gone mad. Aaron could see a few lycopods among the ferns, like telephone poles with a small brush of stubby branches at their summits, lingering relics of even more ancient swamplands. Among this arboreal wilderness, wildlife skittered and scurried and chattered—not the monkeys, lemurs, or exotic birds Aaron would have expected of an Amazonian jungle, but large, agile lizards, huge millipedes with bulbous eyes, and primitive-looking marsupials.

Lower down were the palmlike cycadeoids and ginkgoes. Horsetails poked their heads from the water, small ferns graced the low mud banks, and everywhere on the ground the flowering plants with leathery, thick petals took hold with bright splashes of fragrant color.

A Mezosoic era jungle, maybe in the early or mid-Cretaceous period, Aaron realized. Which meant one thing: Travis had been telling the truth after all.

The path was floating a few feet away over a patch of marsh. Aaron realized that he must have hit this section in his free fall down the hillside and been transported back into prehistory. He rose to his feet, wiping his clothes in a futile attempt to brush away the worst of the dirt. He forced himself to wait and catch his breath.

No sense in worrying. The path's right here—I should be able to just hop onto it and go back home, right? Take advantage of this, Aaron. You're in every paleontologist's dream. No one else has ever had this opportunity before. This is your chance.

As he looked around, he found himself more and more excited, grinning to himself with each new creature or plant he glimpsed. This *was* a dream come true. The plants, the moist air, the animals: every one of them was a living fossil, no longer just a dead shape embedded in stone but a real, moving and breathing thing. The path hovered enticingly, but Aaron wasn't even slightly tempted to step back onto it.

As if to confirm all his speculations, he noticed booted tracks leading from near the path deeper into the jungle—Travis, he was certain. Despite Aaron's feeling a distinct distrust of the man, Travis at least had some experience here. He also had a weapon, and from what Aaron had seen leaking out from this time into his own, that might be necessary. Aaron's only other choice was to return to Green Town, find Peter and Jennifer, and then go back to the house to get (at the very least) a camera and his dad's twelve gauge.

But returning home would mean having to explain everything to Grandpa Carl. While Aaron loved his grandfather dearly, Aaron wasn't at all sure that he'd approve of any of this. Going back now might mean not being able to return.

You're here, now stay as long as you can. Stay until you have *to leave.*

Aaron could hear the sound of someone thrashing through the foliage to his right—at least, he hoped it was a some*one* and not a some*thing*. Cautiously, he followed the sound; remembering Travis's tale, he watched his footsteps carefully, trying to avoid doing any permanent damage to the plants underfoot. As soon as he'd gone a few yards, he could no longer see the piece of roadway through which he'd come. The jungle closed behind him as if he'd never been here at all. Aaron hesitated, wondering whether he should go back right now, then decided that he'd be able to find the roadway again. He looked around quickly for some kind of a landmark. There: that lycopod with the white gash in its bark leaning tiredly against a tree fern nearby. He set the scene firmly in his mind and continued on.

A few hundred yards further, he broke through into a clearing.

Aaron gasped.

In many ways, he still hadn't believed Travis, despite all that had happened. Yet now it was obvious that at least the basics of Travis's story were true. In front of Aaron was more of the roadway, sitting a few inches above the marshy ground and broken in half by what had evidently been a powerful explosion. The body of the tyrannosaurus huddled like a drunken dragon at the foot of a gigantic vine-covered tree, half covered by the broken limb that had fallen from above. Smaller scavenger dromaeosaurids, quick flesh eaters the size of German shepherds, were already tearing at the carcass. A strange gleaming device like a cross between an overgrown passenger van and a speedboat bobbed above the fronds nearby: the time machine.

Travis was there too. Hobbling and obviously in pain, he raged at the dead T-rex like a madman, shouting at it, cursing, kicking it with his feet. The scavengers screeched at him, moving away briefly and then scurrying back to their feast. Travis moved aside, tearing at the vines and branches snarling the periphery of the clearing, scuffing at the mud and ripping up plants by the roots. Then, abruptly, he reached down and brought up the rifle he'd evidently set aside.

"Eckels! Where are you, you ass?" Travis waved his rifle about and fired blindly into the jungle. "It's useless," he said loudly to himself. "He's destroyed everything. Everything!"

Travis kicked at one of the dromaeosaurids; it squawked at him, snapped once, and retreated. This time, Travis brought his rifle to his shoulder. Before Aaron could move, Travis had aimed and pressed the trigger. The scavenger jumped at the report, then flopped lifelessly to the ground. Before it even stopped moving, a half dozen of its companions were fighting over the body. Travis laughed, a horrible, ugly sound.

"Bang! Another future gone! I'll show you, you ugly little thing. I'll fix it so none of you beasts ever show up at all. You think I can't do it? Just watch me."

Travis turned and limped across the clearing, still cursing. His destination was clear: the time machine. Aaron, with a sickening lurch of his stomach, suddenly knew what Travis intended to do. An image came to him: Travis, rampaging through the past, further and further back into time, every so often stopping and destroying things and with each destruction irrevocably altering the future into something strange and unknown, further and further from any reality that he could imagine.

"No!" Aaron shouted. He ran forward into the clearing between Travis and the time machine.

Travis whirled around. The gun came up. "So you found your way here, huh, kid? How you like it? A dream world, isn't it. A damn nightmare." Travis's face was flushed and feverish. Sweat was rolling from his forehead down the sides of his face. The gun trembled in his hands.

"Travis, please—"

"Get out of my way."

"I can't let you do this."

"Why *not?*" The last word was a bellow, a sob. Travis's whole body shook with the effort. "Don't you understand, kid? You've stepped out of your world now. When you go back, it's not going to be the same. Not now. You might as well be dead, because your HomeTime is. If Eckels's one little butterfly could change the whole shape of the future, think of what *this* mess has done."

Travis waved a hand around to indicate the clearing and the shattered roadway. He staggered and would have fallen had Aaron not moved forward to catch him. Aaron steadied the man. He tried to gently take the rifle, but Travis suddenly pulled away with all his strength, his dark eyes narrowing. The muzzle was pointed at Aaron's chest.

"Get in," Travis told him, nodding at the time machine. Then, when Aaron failed to move: "I mean it, kid. Get in or I'll leave you here for the dromaes to pick over."

Almost, Aaron refused. The man was ill, Aaron had a year of aikido study and had practiced a few techniques for taking away a knife or a staff. Yet this was real, not a practice on the mat with a willing partner. That was a rifle and not a wooden knife. Aaron had a very vivid image of the way the dromaeosaurid had looked when Travis had shot it. Aaron took a deep breath.

He went to the machine.

He fumbled for the door. There didn't seem to be any obvious catches or handles. Finally, Travis snarled with irritation and reached around Aaron to press a small contact he hadn't noticed. The door hissed like one of the lizards and slid into a recess above him. A small step extruded downward at the same time. "Inside," Travis grunted. Aaron obeyed.

The smell was strange—almost medicinal, like air washed and scrubbed and disinfected until it was sterile and dead. The interior was larger than it had seemed from the outside, with enough headroom to walk upright and a narrow corridor between three rows of double seats. Shelves of equipment were snugged against the walls; a rack holding weapons like Travis's was in the rear. A persistent, low-frequency rumble thrummed in Aaron's ears and vibrated the floor under his feet, as if the machine were alive and angry at his intrusion.

Travis waggled the rifle muzzle at the leftmost of the three cushioned seats at the front of the craft. "Sit."

Aaron sat.

Travis lowered himself into the right-hand seat, groaning as he did so. Aaron could see fresh blood dark and wet on the cloth of his shirt. "Travis, you're still bleeding. Listen, Jen said that you've got to be careful—"

"Careful?" Travis barked. He snorted. "Why? You want to see what Eckels did, kid? You want to look at it firsthand? Here, let me show you—"

Travis set the rifle on the floor, close enough for him to reach but too far from Aaron to make lunging for it anything but reckless. "Controls out," he said.

An androgynous voice answered from the air. "Activating..." The windshield in front of Travis lit with an orangish, ghostly display while part of the wall below levered up. Travis's hands did a quick dance over a trackball, and then he typed quickly on the touchscreen set in the slanting shelf in front of him.

The time machine wailed in response and the Mesozoic world outside the window melted like a watercolor left in rain, leaving behind a streaked blackness. The time machine whined and shook; the feeling of intense cold and disorientation that Aaron had experienced when he'd tumbled through the roadway into this world returned. On the windshield, the display was now all he could see. There was a prominent readout where numbers obviously clicked off the passing millennia. They were racing through unseen time, slashing through the ages like fleet ghosts. Aaron watched the numbers, watched the history he knew pass unseen.

Outside in the blind world, the dinosaurs died and left their bones to mud and sand. The mammals began their long climb to ascendancy. A shivering breath, and the crust of continents broke apart and floated slowly across the molten rock supporting them. As Aaron hugged himself, trying to find some relief from the chill and nausea, on some distant continent an ape grasped a bone in its hand and wondered. Mountains rose to be washed away by slow, endless rains. Neanderthals huddled in dark caves and lit fires against the invading night. Blink, and entire civilizations arose and fell again in ashes. Waves of conquering armies fled like ants across ancient landscapes. As the cold began to recede and the numbers in the readout changed from millennia to centuries to years and the voice of the machine went from wail to cry to whimper, Rome came and went, the Byzantine empire flourished and withered, Islam arose.

The craft shook, then steadied itself. The engine settled into a quiet, ever-present hum. Aaron leaned forward, peering into the murk outside the glass, waiting for his first glimpse of the future and the laboratory from which this strange machine had come. The darkness behind the windows dissolved to let in harsh light. Sunlight.

Travis looked at the world beyond the windows and howled like a lost beast. Aaron gasped as well.

BATTLE IN THE PAST

"All right, I'm getting up," Jennifer said to the creature who stood over her with a spear. She raised her hands, her fingers spread wide in an effort to show that she wasn't a threat. The spear tip followed her movements, always just a few inches from her throat. The edges of the thin, shiny point looked very sharp and well used.

"Honest, you don't need to aim that at me," she said to it. "How stupid do I look?"

Stupid enough to be talking to a big lizard like it's going to answer, she told herself. *Just get up and be quiet, Jennifer. Maybe this is just a bad dream.*

Jennifer stared at the apparition confronting her. If the creature stood entirely upright it might have topped eight feet, but it was leaning forward as it guarded her, the thick tail held out almost straight behind it and its chest and long, thick neck canted forward so that the head was about six feet above the ground. The spear was clasped in delicate, three-fingered hands with long, slender fingers tipped with curved claws; around the massive neck was a large metal ornament, decorated with hammered grooves and patterns and tied in place with woven vine much like the rope in Eckels's cave.

The dinosaur spoke again. There was no doubt in Jennifer's mind that it was speaking words in some language of its own—this was not simply the grunting of some mindless beast. If the spear and the pendant were not enough proof, the sounds it made were too articulated and varied, the inflections too wide. It peered at her strangely when it spoke, as if waiting for an answer. When she just shrugged helplessly, it canted its head and the ridges of the eyes deepened, as if it were scowling.

Whatever this was, it was sentient. It made tools; it spoke a language; it wore ornaments.

From the corner of her eyes, she could see Peter getting to his feet. He tried to break away from his captor, but was slowed by the vine still around his ankle. His dinosaur adroitly reversed its spear and took Peter's legs out from under him with sweep. Peter went down hard, face first, getting his hands down just at the last moment. The creature who had upended him snorted once. Jennifer wondered if that was laughter, satisfaction, or disgust.

At the same time, three more of the same species emerged from a nearby grove of ferns. They were all armed with spears. Each of the newcomers had the same forward-leaning bearing of Jennifer's dinosaur—Jennifer decided that this must be the normal stance for them, the rigid tail balancing the rest of the body and keeping them upright. She seemed to remember Aaron talking about "ossified tail structures" or something like that. . . .

And thinking of Aaron brought her abruptly back to grim reality.

The adrenaline rush vanished. She was suddenly very frightened: for herself and Peter, for Aaron.

Jennifer watched her guard carefully. "Peter?" Her voice sounded very small and uncertain.

"I'm all right." Jennifer could hear the anger in his voice even though she didn't look at him, not wanting to take her gaze from the weapon threatening her in case the dinosaur decided to thrust. Maybe, just maybe, she could dodge quickly enough. . . .

"At least I'd be all right if this animal weren't trying to take a blood sample," Peter continued. "I guess this is my day for getting beat on." His humor sounded false and desperate. "How about you?"

"I'm okay. Peter, these aren't animals. Animals don't dress in armor and use spears. Peter . . ." Her throat had gone dry; she licked her lips. "I'm really scared," she admitted.

"We'll be okay, Jenny," Peter said, but there wasn't much confidence in his voice.

"*Asai*"—trill—"*weg*"—warble. Jennifer's dinosaur spoke again. The spear pointed briefly back the way they'd come, toward Eckels's cave, then came back to her again.

Jennifer spread her hands helplessly and shrugged once more. "I don't understand you," she said, uselessly. "I wish I did, but I don't."

It gave her a barrage of words then, sibilant phrases all mixed in with odd honks, bleats, and nasal snorts. It stared at her unblinkingly. She tried to read something, anything, in that inhuman face, but there were no recognizable emotions there, at least none that she trusted. The gold-flecked eyes looked almost angry, but the long mouth had an upturned half smile that jarred against the threatening stance. Jennifer felt adrift. She had nothing familiar to work with, no hints of body language or expression to give her a clue to what the creature wanted or how dangerous it actually was.

She was lost.

Her entire world had been changed in the space of the last four or five hours, since she and Aaron had found the eggs in the woods. She felt cut loose from reality.

Peter's captor had entered the conversation now, along with the other three. Jennifer and Peter moved closer together, encircled as the creatures bleated at each other, gesticulating with their weapons. There were occasional glances in their direction as well.

"Looks like they're not sure exactly what's going on, either," Jennifer whispered. "Eckels said something about talking dinosaurs. I thought he was crazy." He had said other things about them, too, she remembered. *Eat you for lunch* . . . Jennifer shuddered and drove the image that conjured up from her mind.

The band of dinosaurs had evidently come to a conclusion. While the other four stood guard, Jennifer's dinosaur put its spear aside and squatted in front of Jennifer, so that its head was nearly level with hers. It reached out with long, spindly arms; Jennifer held her breath, trying to remain still. She could feel its warm, not unpleasant breath, and see the short, stubby, peglike teeth.

That brought back memories of Aaron too, of standing beside him at the museum and looking at fossil skulls. *"You can tell about their diet by looking at their teeth. Old T-rex couldn't be anything but a meat eater with those fangs. . . ."* These were a plant eater's teeth, a grazer's teeth made for grinding vegetable matter. Aaron had shown her fossilized teeth from maiasaurs, too. No matter what Eckels had said, Jennifer was certain that these creatures wouldn't be eating her for lunch.

With surprisingly gentle fingers, the creature examined the blue denim of her jeans wonderingly, tugging at it and rubbing the cloth between its scaly fingertips. It did the same with her sneakers, lifting her foot to peer at the soles and then daintily touching the laces. The creature made inquisitive grunts and throaty mewlings all the while. Its curiosity satisfied, it then quickly hobbled Jennifer's legs with the length of rope they'd used to trip her.

Satisfied that Jennifer could walk but wouldn't be able to run, the dinosaur went to Peter and did the same. Then they herded the two humans between them and, prodding them with the blunt ends of their spears to move them, the group set off through the trees.

The short length of vine linking her ankles chafed and rubbed even through her jeans. She kept trying to stride too far and the hobble would painfully draw her up short. More than once she stumbled and had to catch her balance, glad that the dinosaurs had at least left her hands free. Peter plodded sullenly alongside her, the side of his face purpling and swelling from Eckels's blow. His jaw was clenched tightly; Jennifer could see the bunched muscles below his ear. She knew that the anger was his way of dealing with the situation; knowing that he must be frightened too made her own fears more bearable.

"Peter, there's nothing you could have done," she whispered to him. "Maybe later we'll get a chance."

He was starting to answer when one of the dinosaurs grunted and thumped Jennifer on the back with its spear handle. When she gasped and nearly fell, it snuffled at her loudly. The implication was clear enough; Jennifer and Peter continued to walk along in silence.

The dinosaurs plodded alongside them. Their gait was strange yet somehow familiar. For some time, Jennifer couldn't place what it reminded her of, then the image came to her: flocks of pigeons moving across Fountain Square in the middle of Green Town. The dinosaurs had the same rhythmic forward-and-back motion of the head, the same strutting pace with tails held out stiffly behind, their bodies inclined forward rather than held upright.

They had been moving sideways up a long slope and were now moving along a ridge. Near the top of the low rise, the tree line ended and they were able to see better the lie of the land. They stood on the rim of a long valley; somewhere down there and behind them lay the path back to Green Town. Jennifer tried to fix the location in her mind, looking over the valley. From the intense gaze on Peter's face, she knew he was trying to do the same. The dinosaurs had paused, a few of them hunkering down as if to rest.

It was nearing midday here—the sun was hot enough but the air was less humid than that of Green Town. Jennifer scanned the valley. If she had managed to keep her sense of direction, the path had to be over there to the right, in that swampy area.

A half mile or so ahead and down in the valley, there was a clearing with clumps of primitive grasses dotting the sandy dirt. There were buildings there, a large grouping of tall cones and domes, looking like they were built of mud and grass and left to dry in the sun. Other dinosaurs were moving among them; Jennifer assumed that this must be their destination.

As if to confirm her thought, one of the dinosaurs stood and half snorted, half bellowed an order. The others stood up; Peter shrugged at Jennifer and followed suit. At a pace that made the two captives pay close attention to their footing lest they fall and tumble down the steep hillside, the group moved to a cleft in the ridge and then down toward the village.

They lost sight of the clearing as soon as they descended into the trees again. They crossed a slow, shallow stream and clambered up the muddy bank. Jennifer and Peter both needed to use their hands to grab branches and roots, though the dinosaurs managed well enough. They had just reached dry ground again, their jeans soaked and heavy below their knees, when the dinosaurs halted once more. One of them gave a querulous honk, staring at the brush in front of them and keeping its spear outthrust in front of it.

Peter moved closer to Jennifer. "What's going—?" he whispered, but the rest of his question was lost in a sudden flurry of movement.

Two figures—humans—burst from the cover of the brush with a shout. In that first instant, Jennifer had time only to see the sun glinting from the polished blades of long, curved swords, to glimpse the Oriental hue of the faces and the bulky, intricate, and beautiful armor and ornate helmets.

Jennifer had taken classes in Eastern history; she'd studied Japanese for the last two years, thinking that the language would be an advantageous one to learn. She'd seen enough of Eastern culture to recognize who these people were in that first glimpse: samurai, dressed in medieval Japanese armor and bearing the two-handed swords called *katana*. Jennifer stared, too confused at that moment to react at all; Peter gave a strangled cry and tried to move frantically toward Jenny. The hobble tripped him, sending him down hard.

The warriors rushed directly at the dinosaurs, a headlong charge precipitated by high, angry, guttural cries—a *kiai* to focus energy and startle the opponent. They ran toward the group like fierce demons, their *katana* upraised. The quicker of the two swung his weapon, the keen-edged blade making a bright, frightening *whhhikk* as it slashed. The blow missed its mark; the dinosaur—far more nimbly than Jennifer would have expected—had taken a quick step backward. As the blade passed harmlessly, the creature stepped in again, thrusting with its spear. Jennifer looked away in horror, too late.

The warrior grunted in surprise as the spear tip slithered between the seams of his armor and into his midriff. The grisly image of the samurai impaled on that spear like a fish would stay with her for a long time. Jennifer heard rather than saw the huge reptile yank the spear back out, letting the body flop to the ground.

The other samurai reached the group at the same time. His fate was just as quick and just as final. As Jennifer forced herself to open her eyes again and Peter pushed himself from the ground, the dinosaurs gathered together and engaged in a quick, fast discussion in their strange mixture of vocalized grunts, snorts, and nasal honks. Once or twice, one of them made a roaring sound that caused Jennifer to start in alarm, though their attention seemed to be more on the landscape around them than on their prisoners.

Jennifer made herself look at the slain men as the dinosaurs conversed. *Just like the emergency room at the hospital. You've seen enough blood there. You've seen people hurt in car accidents. You've watched doctors stitch up knife cuts and gunshot wounds. It can't be much worse than that.*

But it was.

She wanted to go to them, to see if there was something, *anything* she could do. From the stillness of the bodies, the way their limbs were sprawled awkwardly over the ground and the amount of bright blood staining the grass, she was certain they were dead. She began to move toward them when Peter took her arm. He was breathing hard and fast, as if trying to hold back nausea.

"No," he said. "I wouldn't, Jenny."

"They might still be alive. I can't just leave them."

Jennifer shrugged away from Peter and moved to the samurai as quickly as her hobble would let her. Peter made no move to stop her this time; the dinosaurs didn't seem to care. They watched for a moment, then turned back to their conversation. The dinosaur Jennifer thought of as the leader gestured at one of the slain men and spoke a word: a syllable, a bleet, another syllable, and a strange trill. *"Daiiku-bee."* Jennifer had always been good at languages. She tried to fix that sound in her memory as she knelt beside the bodies, whispering it under her breath. It was something to do, something to focus on and take her mind off the gruesome sight before her. The sounds were difficult to reproduce; she wondered if they would be able to understand her at all if she ever attempted to speak their language back to them.

She wondered if she'd ever get the chance.

She turned the bodies over, inhaling through gritted teeth at the sight of the wounds. They were dead, both of them. No pulse, no breath. Jennifer, steeling herself, reached out and closed the open eyelids. She started to pry one of the *katanas* away from clutching fingers when one of the dinosaurs hissed loudly at her. She dropped the sword, swallowed hard, and went back to Peter.

"Dead?" he asked. She just nodded, not wanting to speak.

"Where in the world did *they* come from?"

That seemed like a truly classic Dumb Question. "I haven't any idea, and I didn't get much of a chance to ask them."

Peter glared at her. "Look, I just want to figure out what's going on, okay? I want to get out of here. I want to get on that piece of Travis's path, go back to Green Town, and never, ever talk about dinosaurs again. I *hate* dinosaurs. I never liked listening to Aaron talk about them. I mean, I had a *date* tonight. Man, is Susan gonna be ticked off." He started to laugh, a little wildly and too loud.

That brought back all of Jennifer's fears, both for herself and for Aaron. "You're really an idiot sometimes, you know that, Peter?" she said angrily, then didn't trust herself to say more. She wasn't going to give him the satisfaction of seeing her upset.

Peter looked as if he were about to press the point, but the dinosaurs ended their talk at the same time. Once again, they boxed in the two humans and—with judicious spear prodding—indicated that they wanted them to begin walking again.

"The samurai—" Jennifer began, but the dinosaur she thought of as hers simply snorted at her. "Khiisoo," it said, interspersing the syllables with a bleet and a roar.

"Khiisoo it is," she muttered. "Whatever that means."

They moved on. The dinosaurs paid no more attention to the dead humans. As they left the small clearing, the scavengers were already beginning to make their claims.

A FUTURE DESTROYED

"Don't open the door!"

The words burst from Aaron as Travis rose from his seat. Beyond the windshield of the time traveling vehicle, dark vapors swirled in a burnt orange sky. The land seemed to languish under an oppressive, glaring sun that was doing nothing to heat the earth. Aaron could feel the chill from the world beyond emanating from the glass in front of him; frost was spreading lacy fingers at the corners of the glass. Dotting the sandy soil were towering plants that might have been cacti except for the widespread fleshy canopies girdling their trunks like skirts around a twirling skater. Tendrils of crystalline snow piled at the twisting roots of their feet. Nearby, rocks thrust up like the bones of the earth through the thin, granular soil of the hills, their flanks icy and glittering.

There was life here, too: massive, thick-carapaced snails three and four feet high moved slowly over the snow and sand, their swirled shells bright spots of royal blue. The nearest one seemed to glance over at their machine, and Aaron saw eyes set in the twin stalks of the gelatinous head. The creature blinked, a trans-lucent, shimmering membrane passing over the eyelids, first the right and then the left; afterward, incurious, the thing continued on its slow way.

"You must have set the controls wrong, Travis. This isn't your world. Can't be. This isn't anything recognizable at all, future *or* past."

There were tight knots of muscles around Travis's bitter eyes. He shook his head slightly. "No," he grunted. He snatched up the rifle and got to his feet. "The controls were set correctly."

"Then where's—" Aaron shut his mouth, choking off the words as the implication hit him.

There's no laboratory because the future has changed too much. The destruction of the path, Eckels still back there blundering around, along with Travis and me both. . . . Too much change, rippling all down through the centuries until there's no lab here at all, no town, no humans at all. . . .

Nothing familiar at all.

Suddenly he didn't want to think, because if this had happened here, what of Green Town, only next door in terms of time?

Oh God, Jen!

"That's right, my friend," Travis told him, echoing Aaron's thoughts. The man had his hand on the door control now, and that motion shook Aaron from reverie. "All gone."

Aaron was suddenly panicked. "Travis—hey, it doesn't look good out there. If this much has changed, maybe the air—"

"Who cares, kid?" Travis sniffed. "Not me, that's for sure." He punched hard at the contact. The door yawned wide and the cold rolled in, fogging the windshield. An instant dew beaded every hard surface in the compartment.

Aaron held his breath. He pushed himself off his seat and half dove, half fell toward the door contact. His fingers brushed it, then Travis unexpectedly backhanded him in the ribs with the butt of his rifle.

His intake of breath was reflex. Aaron could taste something acetic and harsh in his lungs, could smell a hint of sulfur that reminded him of experiments in the chem lab. He coughed; that made his throat hurt, but he was still alive.

"It's breathable," Travis said. "Barely. Consider yourself lucky."

Travis stepped out of the craft as Aaron was still trying to catch his breath in the strange air. The older man's boots made a curious crunching sound as he walked, as if he were walking on a friable, thin crust of snow. A frigid wind pressed Aaron's clothes against goose-bumped skin; he shivered involuntarily. He was dressed for Green Town summer, not this. "Travis, it's gotta be below zero out here."

"It's autumn," Travis replied. "I left here in November. We were having one of the warmest falls ever. Everyone was talking about it, when we weren't talking about the election." Travis's back was turned to Aaron; there was a strange catch to his accented voice.

"Travis—"

The man swung around heavily. He was panting, as if the labor of breathing this foul air had already tired him. "The lab was right *here.*" He stamped his foot. "Right here. Had been for years and years, long before the war. Heck, my father worked here too, before they started the temporal research. I knew most of the lab people here. *Here.*" Travis laughed, mocking himself with the word. "They were my friends. They were all I knew. And they're gone."

"Couldn't there have been some mistake, Travis?" Aaron asked desperately.

"Like what? You watched me set the coordinates; hell, the machine's simple enough that you could use it yourself. There's nothing mysterious about it at all. It moves you DownTime; it brings you back again. It moves in time, not space. I've done it dozens of times. Dozens."

Travis laughed again, with a harsh manic edge. Clouds of vapor wreathed around him with the sound. The man stalked around the time machine, kicking at the sand and muttering.

"If this is your time, then what happened?" Aaron insisted. Despite the cold, the caustic air seemed to burn in his windpipe. It was like breathing a mild acid.

"How should I know? A war, a disease. Hey, maybe humankind never got a foothold here at all, kid. Maybe the apes all became saber-tooth meals, maybe they never showed up in the first place. I certainly don't see any evidence of us."

"There's some kind of glitch, then," Aaron

persisted, desperately. All he wanted was for Travis to come back inside the machine and close the door again. He wanted to get away from here; he hated the cold and the alien landscape. "You set the coordinates wrong. Maybe we went backward instead of forward. Maybe your machine's broke."

"Deny it all you want, kid. Go ahead. It doesn't change a thing. Not a thing."

With that proclamation, Travis flung his hands wide. The strange rifle in his right hand brushed the edge of one of the plants. The touch was enough: the skin of the thick ridge ruptured and a cloud of spores erupted from the fissure, the cloud engulfing Travis's head. Travis screamed, dropping the weapon and beating at the air with his hands. Choking and writhing, he collapsed to the sand. One of the snails hissed like a teakettle and swerved toward Travis, moving far quicker than Aaron would have thought possible. Aaron ran from the open doorway onto the sand. The spore cloud had fallen to the ground, leaving behind tiny wriggling things that burrowed underneath the ground in the few seconds it took Aaron to cover the distance.

"Travis!" The man was still breathing, but his eyes were closed. The snail was only a few feet away; a pseudopod lashed out from under the shell, a slimy rope of flesh that coiled around Travis's leg. Aaron kicked the tentacle with his foot and the snail hissed again as if offended, and withdrew its arm. The creature backed off.

Grunting, Aaron half dragged Travis away from the plant back to the machine. He pulled the man into the vehicle, then ran back and retrieved the weapon from the sand.

He hit the contact and the door slid shut. Warm, oxygen-rich, and clean air flooded back into the compartment. Aaron turned Travis over. The man's face was a pasty blue white, his eyes shut.

"No!" Aaron shouted. "You're not allowed to die."

Images from the CPR class he'd taken last fall hammered at him: *if the person isn't breathing, check the airways for blockage.* Aaron tilted Travis's head back, opening his mouth. He gagged reflexively at what he saw there, recoiling backward a step. A white, cottony mass filled Travis's mouth and nostrils. The filaments wriggled. "Gross," Aaron muttered. He took two deep breaths to calm his stomach. He got behind Travis and lifted the man, grimacing as the man's full dead weight leaned against him. He placed a fist on Travis's diaphragm, put his other hand over the fist, and pulled in as hard as he could: the Heimlich manuever. Nothing. The lungs pumped but nothing was expelled.

Aaron was sweating now. He tried the Heimlich again, muttering "C'mon, Travis" to himself, but it did no good. Whatever it was in Travis's throat wasn't going to budge.

Aaron let Travis's body slide down to the floor again. He wished he had gloves or something to cover his fingers, but there was no time to go looking. He tilted Travis's head back once more and opened his mouth. Grimacing, he stuck two fingers into the doughy matter filling the cavity, trying to pry it out. It yielded under his fingers, like scooping up strings of cold vermicelli. The stuff wriggled and flailed in his fingers and Aaron resisted the impulse to just fling it away. He slapped at the door contact again and tossed the stuff outside, then returned to Travis. He repeated the process, getting more of it from well back in Travis's mouth, and this time, Travis choked and took a long, gasping breath. Aaron rolled him to the doorway; Travis's eyes fluttered open, he groaned, and his stomach heaved.

Once the nausea had passed, Aaron handed the man a towel he'd found in one of the craft's compartments. "Here."

"Thanks." Travis wiped his face, grimacing. "I guess I owe you one. Whatever that stuff was, it sprayed right into my mouth. I could feel it growing, swelling, blocking off the air. . . ." Travis stopped. Despite the lingering chill in the cabin, he was sweating and his hands were trembling.

"Yeah, look, we're probably about even, considering that allosaurus back in Green Town would have had us for dinner if you hadn't killed it first. You'd've done the same for me, right?"

The answer came a few seconds too late. "Sure. You're right, kid." Travis didn't look at Aaron; his eyes were closed as, sitting, he leaned back against the wall of the craft. "You should've just left me, you know. Look around out there. There's nothing here for us. It's all over, everything."

Aaron glanced at that cold landscape once more. A trio of snails slithered by; what looked like a rippling wool blanket with eyestalks rode the wind. "The settings are wrong," Aaron insisted again. "They have to be."

Travis groaned and got to his feet. "Uh-uh. C'mere. Look." He went to the control panel and touched a trackball; on the window display, a pointer moved in concert. When the pointer touched the icon of the time machine, Travis said: "Systems check." The icon blinked. A few seconds later, a voice sounded. Her—or maybe his, the voice was a deep alto—voice spoke with warm and soothing tones, though there was a synthesized edge to it, a telltale lack of true inflection.

"Calibration within tolerance. Support systems functioning, backups ready. Power system at sixty-five percent."

"Date check," Travis said.

"Two-thousand two-hundred five, November twenty-seventh, nine hours fifteen minutes forty-three seconds."

Travis looked at Aaron. He didn't say anything; he didn't need to. Travis lowered himself into the pilot's seat. "Sit down, kid. You look worse than me."

"I want to see nineteen-ninety-two," Aaron insisted. "My own time. I have to make sure."

Travis was shaking his head. "Give it up." He pointed at the surreal landscape outside. "That didn't happen in a little more than two centuries. Those plants and animals took eons to evolve."

"You said it before—what about a nuclear war?" Aaron persisted. "Radiation mutation? Some kind of disease?"

"Not a chance. Don't you understand?— Eckels made a botch of everything. The time-stream's gone off in an entirely different direction than the branch that led to our existence. We're not even ancient history here. This might as well be Venus or Mars, because it isn't the earth we know."

"I want to see," Aaron said stubbornly. There was an emptiness in the pit of his stomach. *Grandpa Carl, Jen, my mom and dad, every-one. All of it gone, Green Town vanished like a mirage, the whole United States nothing but a name, not even forgotten because it never existed. Just words in a language no one ever spoke. It can't be.*

"Travis, I have to know. Please."

Aaron thought for a moment that Travis was going to refuse, that he'd have to argue with the wounded, exhausted man or even see if he could muddle through the controls himself. Travis stared at him balefully, his eyes blood-shot and the pouches of skin under his eyes dark and sagging. Then he shrugged and sat forward, reaching for the controls of the machine. This time, Aaron paid close attention. The interface to the computer was simplicity itself, something any of his friends would have been comfortable with quickly. Something about that nagged at Aaron. *His people had almost two centuries to enhance their technology. . . . Would a person from eighteen-hundred have been able to understand what I was doing with my personal computer at home? No, he'd be totally lost. Why didn't things change much between my time and theirs?*

Then the thought was driven away as he leaned forward in his seat to watch Travis.

The icon of a clock sat to one side of the display; Travis moved the pointer toward it and clicked the trackball button. A series of fields appeared on the display with a blinking cursor set in the first. Travis filled in the year, the month, the day, the time. He clicked a button that said Set and Initiate. Another dialog box appeared to verify the information; Travis did so.

Aaron expected the craft's engines to begin to whine and scream once more. Nothing happened. The computer's androgynous alto voice spoke again. "The requested year and location is proscribed due to extensive human habitation. Please choose again."

"That's a safeguard," Travis told Aaron. "We weren't supposed to meddle with anything close to our own time. We wanted to stay away from human history entirely. Didn't want to foul things up." He gave a bark of sarcastic laughter. "Override request. Priority," Travis told the computer.

"Please enter your password and press your

thumb against the touchscreen."

A cursor had appeared on the screen once more. Travis leaned over to the keyboard and tapped in a sequence of seven letters too fast for Aaron to see—a series of X's appeared on the screen as he typed. He placed the pad of his thumb over the touchscreen; a bright scarlet light played under it.

"Override acknowledged," the computer said. "Identity confirmed. Initiating."

Aaron heard the temporal machinery click and begin that long, throbbing jet-takeoff thundering. "Sit back," Travis told Aaron. "This'll be a short one."

INTRODUCTIONS

It was twilight before they reached their destination.

Jenny and Peter saw very little of the dinosaurs' city. They were unceremoniously thrust through a low gate into an open enclosure made of stripped saplings. One of the dinosaurs followed behind them and untied their hobbles. From the gate, a lizard the size and color of a komodo dragon watched intently. The dinosaur finished its task, stared briefly at the two humans, then went to the lizard. It spoke to the creature in a chorus of hisses, warbles, and clicks, stroking its head all the while. The dinosaur scratched the lizard under the chin affectionately, looked at the humans once more, and left the enclosure.

The lizard stayed behind. Peter moved toward the gate. As he did so, the lizard scuttled between him and the gate, hissing and flicking its tongue at him. Its claws suddenly looked very threatening.

"Great," he said. "They've got guard dogs, too." He went back to Jenny, standing beside with his hands on his hips. "I hate this. I really do."

Jenny looked around. The compound was

bare earth surrounded by vine-lashed walls of young tree trunks perhaps fifteen feet high. There were gaps between the trunks, but none was big enough to slip through easily. The gate was crudely hinged with rope, and there didn't seem to be any locks or bars—only the lizard guard prevented them from opening it. Beyond that, there was nothing in the enclosure at all.

"Peter . . ." Jenny started to talk, then found that there was just too much to say. She just shook her head, staring around her with a breath that was suddenly hard to catch and eyes that shimmered.

"I know, Jen. We're in big trouble."

She almost laughed at that. "That's the understatement of the year. We've been gone for *hours*—someone has to be missing us at home by now. There's no shelter here; it's getting dark and I'm hungry and tired and getting cold and we've nothing to wear except what's on our backs—" She stopped herself, taking a deep breath. *All right, what* can *we do? Stop moaning and think.*

As if the self-rebuke had sparked action, the gate opened again and the same dinosaur stepped through. It had shed the armor and spear and was wearing only an intricate pendant around its neck, the jewelry made of broken pieces of shell, mother of pearl, and feathers. It—or she, since by its smaller size and drabber coloring it was evidently a female—was carrying a wooden platter on which were stacked a small pile of assorted fruits. She set it down in the middle of the enclosure, looked at the two humans with her unblinking stare, and then turned away.

"Wait!" Jenny cried. The dinosaur turned at the sound of her voice. Jenny tapped herself on the chest. "Jenny," she said. "My name is Jenny." She went up to the dinosaur—who was standing in its usual inclined attitude—and reached out with an open, palm-up hand. The dinosaur drew back slightly, then allowed Jennifer to touch the colorful azure scales below the necklace. Jenny then touched herself once more, spoke her name, and then tapped the dinosaur. She repeated the process a few times: "Jenny . . ."

The dinosaur snorted, seeming to glare down at her. "Jen, don't push it," Peter said warningly, then the dinosaur's nostrils flared and she harrumphed noisily. "SStragh," she said: a hissing sibilance began the word and a snort punctuated the middle.

Jenny tried to repeat the sound; the best she could manage was *Struth*. "Struth? Is that your name? Struth?"

She harrumphed again.

"Yeah," Peter said. "Struth probably means 'Go away.' "

"Shut up, Peter," Jenny said. The dinosaur was walking away. She seemed tired and lethargic. Jenny wondered if Struth was just tired or if they were always this slow during the night. "Struth!" she called out.

Struth craned her neck to look back. "Jhenini," she said, putting a bleet in the name. Despite the strange pronunciation, it was recognizable.

Jenny looked at Peter in triumph. "We're going to get cold, Struth." Jenny hugged herself, shivering overdramatically. She pantomimed putting something over herself. "Cold. *Brrrr*. We need blankets or something. Shelter." Jenny shivered again. She knew that speaking the request was useless, but she couldn't help it. She hoped that her actions communicated what the words obviously could not.

Struth watched her carefully, occasionally grunting and snuffling, the big nostrils flaring. A fleshy ridge down the back of her head was standing up, as if she had shaken off her lethargy and were suddenly alert. Then the dinosaur spat out a cacophony of her own words and left the shelter. She returned a few moments later with a small pile of stiff and smelly furs. These she dumped alongside the platter of fruit. "Jhenini," she said again.

"Thank you, Struth," Jenny answered. Struth stared at her once more, long and thoughtfully. Jenny wished there were something human in the expression on the dinosaur's face, something she could read, but there wasn't. It seemed expressive enough, small muscles moving around the eyes and mouth and jaws, but none of the expressions translated.

Struth left the enclosure once more and Jenny went to the stack of furs. She picked up half the pile. "Here," she said to Peter. "These are yours."

He took them gingerly. The pelts were coarse and ragged. "Phew!" he said. "We'll get fleas or worse."

"It's either that or freeze, Peter. I'll bet it's no more than forty-five or fifty out here now, and we're both dressed for summer. If you can stand it, great. If not, be glad for what we've got." Jenny pointed to one corner of the enclosure. "That's your space. I'll take the other corner over there. Way back there . . ."

"I know. That'll be the latrine." Peter grinned. "I'll help you rig the rest of these furs for privacy." Then the grin faded. "Jen, we gotta get out of here. Real soon."

"Tell me about it. As quick as we can."

"Then let's do it tonight."

Jenny nodded. "Fine," she said. "Tonight."

Sandwiched between two layers of furs, Jenny was almost comfortable, though the sour smell made her nose twitch irritably and she could feel every stone and lump in the ground beneath her. Through the snarled vines of the enclosure, Jenny could see the moon-drenched dwellings of the dinosaurs—or, she realized now, it was more one large building than separate houses: a series of tall, irregular cones connected by arched passageways, some of them fully enclosed, others only a roofed-over walkway. The larger rooms varied in size from one huge, intricate structure with balconies sprouting from an upper level to sections that looked as if they could barely house one dinosaur. They seemed to be built on bases of stone, with the upper portions made of something like poured concrete—maybe even adobe. The rooms clustered together in a wandering maze with no pattern that Jenny could detect, nor could she figure out if each type of building had a distinct purpose. The dinosaurs simply wandered through the labyrinth purposefully.

Most of the cones had separate entrances. Some of these were simple open arches, others had furs covering the opening. There were no windows, no glass, no doors. The dinosaurs didn't seem to use fire, either—except for the light from the thankfully-full moon and the stars, there were no lights in this village at all.

As soon as darkness had fallen, the dinosaurs had all retired inside. As the light failed, so had their energy. Peter had whispered something about them maybe being active only during the day. That might be true of the ones like Struth, Jenny had to admit, but more of the guard dog lizards like the one in their enclosure wandered the complex. Jenny didn't like the look of them: they were prowling, active, and they seemed to see quite well in the dark.

There were noises in the landscape beyond the village as well—lots of hoots and calls and roars. As they waited, Peter's idea of escaping the enclosure during the night seemed less and less attractive. Whatever was out there sounded hungry, big, and perfectly at home.

Home. Green Town seemed very far away in both distance and time. Somewhere there, people were sleeping or watching the news. Her friends would be out at Arnold's Café or at the movies or at Becca's usual Friday night party. Her parents . . . by now they must be really frightened and concerned. Probably Aaron's Grandpa Carl had gone looking for them. Aaron's mom and dad had been called, so had Peter's. . . . They'd be scouring the woods . . . or maybe they'd have called off the search until morning. . . .

Her mom would be frantic, her dad out thrashing through the underbrush with that big Maglight he kept under the seat of his car. Maybe Aaron was with them, wondering where she and Peter had gone. The sheriff would have been shown the eggs, told the whole impossible tale. . . .

I'm not going to get upset. I'm just going to get out of here and back home as soon as I can.

She hoped that the plan she and Peter had devised would work. She was already tired, thirsty, and very hungry. That plate of fruit was looking more tempting every moment, but she was afraid to try them. She licked dry, chapped lips—it did no good. "Peter?" she whispered.

"Okay, Jen," came the reply from the opposite corner.

Jenny threw back the fur and stood up. The lizard by the gate watched her movements with a sudden alertness, cocking its head. Dark eyes glittered in the moonlight, and it stood up on its bowed front legs.

"Hi," she told it, thinking that it really sounded stupid to be talking to it like she was talking to the neighbor's Labrador but not knowing what else to do. "Good lizard. Nice lizard. You wouldn't want some of this fruit Struth left, would you? Here, boy. C'mon and get it."

The lizard stared, cocking its head, then took a cautious step toward her. A long, thin tongue whipped out from its mouth and disappeared again. "That's it," Jen said. "Good boy. Yummy fruit. It's all yours if you want it."

Another step, then a waddling quick motion: the lizard sniffed at the fruit. Jenny grimaced and held steady as the lizard's head darted forward, the mouth open. She was half expecting to lose some flesh, but the creature took only a small bite and then sat back, chewing and watching.

"Good, isn't it?" she told it. "Yes. You want some more? Sure you do. Here, go get it."

She tossed the fruit, underhanded, to the back of the enclosure. At first the beast refused to move, then it waddled quickly away—at the same moment, both she and Peter made a rush for the gate.

As quick as they were, the lizard was quicker. Jenny managed to reach the gate and swing it open, but Peter suddenly cried out behind her. Jenny turned to see the lizard with Peter's leg in its jaws. "Jenny, go on!" Peter cried, but the lizard was staring at her, almost daring her to do exactly that. It hadn't bitten hard yet; as Peter struggled to get away, it simply tightened its grip but didn't bear down. "Go on, Jen!" Peter shouted again.

Jenny took a step away; the lizard made a strange mewling sound around Peter's leg and shook its head like a dog shaking a bone; Peter cried out more from surprise than pain. "Jen!"

"I'm sorry, Peter; I can't. It'll hurt you if I do."

It was too late, anyway. A sleepy looking Struth had come from the nearest opening to the dinosaur compound, her spear grasped in her hand. Jenny remembered how quickly Struth had moved when the samurai had attacked them—there was no use in running. Jenny raised her hand in surrender, hoping that the gesture signified the same thing to Struth that it would to a human, and backed into the enclosure again. Struth followed her. When the gate was shut once more, the lizard released Peter's leg. He sat down abruptly, pulling up the leg of his jeans. Jennifer immediately went to check him. A row of angry red pricks stitched his calf, visible even in the moonlight. A few of them oozed blood, but the injury was minor. He'd have a nasty bruise, but nothing else— assuming, she reminded herself, that this lizard's bite wasn't poisonous. Assuming the creature didn't carry some disease. Assuming the open punctures didn't get infected. She couldn't even clean the leg with the water here.

Suddenly Jennifer wasn't so sure. Here, away from any medical aid, even a scratch could lead to complications. Jennifer pulled a tissue from her pocket and dabbed at the blood. "You're okay," she said as reassuringly as she could.

"Yeah," Peter muttered angrily. He jerked his jeans back down and got to his feet. "Well, that worked real well didn't it?"

Struth snorted at them. "Jhenini," it said, and waggled her spear at her. Jenny raised her hands again. "Okay," she said. "You win. Tonight, anyway."

Struth blinked slowly, the crest along the back of her head rising. She huffed, beckoned the lizard over to her, and stroked its chin, crooning to it softly. Then she left once more, closing the gate behind her.

"Well, Jenny?" Peter said.

Jenny sighed. "We might as well get some sleep," she said resignedly. "Maybe things will look different in the morning." She chuckled ironically. "Maybe we'll find out it's all just a bad dream, huh?"

THE CAPTURE OF THE FAR-KILLER

In the still-dim light of the new day, SStragh motioned Lhath, Caasrt, and Miadoa forward with her spear. Her companions nodded and moved out of the clearing and into the forest, following the faint spice scent of the trail SStragh had laid the previous evening. The large gland at the base of her tail still ached from that long exertion.

She wasn't certain whether she hoped it would be worth the effort or not. The youngling bipeds she'd captured the day before were puzzling; SStragh couldn't decide how she felt about them—not that her opinion would matter, she reminded herself.

For three days since the last slaying by the Far-Killer, SStragh had been searching for its spoor, driven by a shifting combination of guilt, anger, and the chidings of Frraghi, the OColi's Speaker. Those three days had seemed like an eternity, and returning with no news each day had been humiliating.

SStragh had finally happened upon the trail yesterday, a well-used trail which indicated that the Far-Killer moved through this area regularly. By the scent, by the condition of the grass, SStragh had guessed that this was a morning trail and that the Far-Killer would be found here not long after the sun rose.

A regular trail. A pattern. That had been a good omen.

Then, not a hundred breaths later, she and the others had captured the two Killer young-lings, just off the same trail. That was a better omen.

SStragh was also certain that it was an omen that one of the younglings could almost speak her name. She had thought that these bipedal creatures from the floating stones were simply too stupid to learn Mutata speech—not even as smart as the Gairk. The bipeds that had been seen most often, the ones with the hard metal scales over their bodies and the shining blades in their hands, never spoke at all: they simply attacked. Not that the younglings spoke *well*; SStragh had barely been able to understand her own name through the garbled noises the youngling Jhenini had made.

Stupid. *Definitely* worse than Gairk, who at least ate the bodies of those they killed. Neither the Scaled Ones nor the Far-Killer did *anything* with the remains of those they killed. Still, at least the Scaled Ones issued what was obviously a challenge and fought honorably, one against one. They used weapons that SStragh could understand. The Far-Killer had no manners at all. It killed without reason, staying hidden if it could. And its method made no sense at all.

SStragh had seen the last murder herself. The Far-Killer had pointed it spear, a horrible noise came from it, and a horrible, bleeding *hole* had appeared in Deaaio's chest. The Far-Killer was already gone by the time SStragh could react.

An insane thing. Not even an animal.

SStragh began circling around to the right. By now, her companions would have made their way to the other side of the hill and have begun working their way back, making far more noise than necessary and hopefully driving the Far-Killer toward SStragh.

In her mind, she was certain that this was hopeless. The Far-Killer would do to her what it had done to Deaaio and three others of the Mutata tribe so far: point the killing spear at her before she could get near enough to use her own spear. She would die horribly, her chest plate torn apart as if it were a leaf, the scales on her chest ripped open like some giant, invisible claw had slashed deep, her blood pumping out helplessly. The Far-Killer had magics that made a mockery of the OColihi—the ancient Path, the way in which things had always been done as far back as any of the Mutata Speakers could remember.

SStragh wondered what it would feel like to die. She wondered whether it was true that the All-Ancestor really came and placed your spirit within the World-Egg as the last breath left the body. She wondered if it would hurt.

She could hear the cracking of branches and the snorting of Lhath as they began moving

toward the clearing where SStragh waited. She
adjusted her chest plate and moved the spear
from her right hand to her left, then back, not
quite certain which was correct. Etiquette: one
killed an animal with the right hand, since there
was no spirit. Another Mutata, a Gairk, a Riilk,
or for any of the other dozen or so sentient and
half-sentient creatures, one must use the left
hand—the hand of self—for the thrust or risk
losing one's own spirit.

But no creature like the Far-Killer existed in
the Speakers' histories. There was no prece-
dent.

*Which hand? It's important—it determines every-
thing: where you stand, what you must say, how you
react.* Right-handed, she was permitted to throw
the spear from cover; right handed, she could
remain silent. Left-handed, the OColihi dic-
tated that she be visible; she must also challenge before she moved. She didn't question
that—it was simply the Path. It didn't matter
that the Far-Killer obviously followed no such
rules: it would pay for the mistake when the
All-Ancestor came for it. Adhering to OColihi
mattered greatly to SStragh. *No matter what
Frraghi may believe of me*, she added.

*Choose wrong, and you fall from the Way and
disgrace all Mutata.* There was no question how
Frraghi or even her companions would have
felt, but last night with the younglings had
changed the way SStragh thought about it.
Jhenini *had* spoken as a Mutata, however badly.
That shifted everything; changed everything.

SStragh reluctantly transferred her weapon back to her left hand.

There was a new sound in the noisy approach of her companions: a harsh, quick breath, a lighter tread that thrashed through the dead leaves on the ground like a scurrying branch swinger. The sound made SStragh's neck glands pulse; as was proper, she allowed the sharp, sour smell of fear to escape so that her opponent would be aware of her presence and her polite trepidation. The scent made her nostrils widen and twitch.

The Far-Killer. It was coming.

Right hand? You can still choose to move the spear . . .

SStragh hissed, warm breath whistling faintly through the hollow bone that ran the length of her snout. Her clawed fingers tightened around the haft and she stepped forward, facing the screen of brush from which the Far-Killer would emerge.

The creature blundered through a few breaths later, looking back over its shoulder at the dark shadows below the trees, running in that strange upright stance. It had taken several steps into the glade before it noticed SStragh. The Far-Killer stumbled to a halt, almost falling, its breath coming faster than seemed possible as it stared at her with its strange, flat face. Its tailless, skinny body was wrapped in strange leaves that covered most of the pale skin. The mouth was open, the round eyes wide and the oddest blue color.

As she had to, SStragh raised her head high and roared her challenge, shaking the spear in her left hand so that the Far-Killer could see it and know that it must submit or fight. The Far-Killer glared at her and brought up its own odd-looking weapon. It did the strangest thing with it, squinting at SStragh down its long, straight, and hollow length, holding it in both hands in the most impolite and confusing manner. The weapon was blunt, neither end possessing a point. SStragh felt a thrill of fright at that moment, not understanding why but shivering with the feeling nonetheless. For a breath, they stared at each other, neither moving.

Then Caasrt entered the clearing in a wild rustling of leaves. The Far-Killer spun on its thin legs at the intrusion—more strangeness, since no Mutata would have been so distracted while properly challenged. Caasrt halted, seeing the spear in SStragh's left hand, but the Far-Killer pointed its own blunt spear at Caasrt.

The weapon screamed—one barking, concussive sound full of death and smoke and stench.

Caasrt screamed at the same time.

SStragh leapt and thrust at the creature. A gash ran red along the Far-Killer's arm and it screeched and dropped the horrible death bringer. SStragh stepped on the weapon reflexively so that it couldn't be picked up again.

She was puzzled when it cracked underneath her weight, snapping in half. So fragile, for something so powerful . . .

The Far-Killer did something very odd then. Its legs collapsed and it went sprawling on the ground, its trunk upright but the legs folded underneath it in what would have been an impossible position for a Mutata.

It spread its arms wide.

SStragh snuffled at that, caught in mid strike. Why in the name of the All-Ancestor would the Far-Killer make a gesture of hospitality at such a time? Did it want her to eat—now?

The Far-Killer smelled of . . . everything and nothing in particular. Couldn't the thing even control its *odors*?

Strange. The Far-Killer's head was up, rudely staring at SStragh as if the challenge were still accepted and it would fight on empty-handed, but yet it was hunched down like a broken thing and it was asking SStragh to join it in a meal while the sun was still high in the sky and there was no offering in sight.

SStragh was confused. Too many signals, all pointing in different directions. The thing *was* mad. It was making nonsense noises now, odd bleats and garglings that sounded like a drowning mud walker. SStragh hefted the spear in her hand, but didn't cast it.

Lhath and Miadoa entered into sunlight a moment later. They glanced at Caasrt's body. The All-Ancestor had already borne away his spirit, so they gave it but a breath's notice. Lhath turned quickly to SStragh and the Far-Killer on the ground below her. "Wrong hand,

SStragh," Lhath said. "Use the right."

"The younglings—" SStragh began in protest, but Lhath's stance straightened slightly, indicating impatience.

"It doesn't need a challenge. Kill it and let's take it back to the OColi. He'll be pleased, and maybe the Gairk will stop their threats. The Far-Killer just killed Caasrt like a beast. Why treat it as more?"

The advice came with the warm odor of ripe grass, sweet and thick. SStragh was tempted, yet she could not. "We will take the Far-Killer as we did the younglings," she replied. "Alive."

"Why? Is SStragh suddenly so much wiser than the OColi? Do you know the Path better?" Lhath hissed. His crest rose balefully down his spine. Miadoa took an aggressive, wide-legged stance as well. "You're listening too much to Raajek," Miadoa told SStragh. "That's why Frraghi doesn't trust you. If anything, the floating stones are a sign that the OColi must be obeyed without thought. He was angry enough that you brought back the younglings alive."

"They didn't attack us."

"No. They were as mad as this one." Lhath hissed in amusement again, pointing his spear at the Far-Killer, who continued to make grunting sounds and stare challengingly from one of them to the other, though its hands were now clasped.

"It doesn't look dangerous at all now," SStragh said, and indicated the twisted fragments of the spear thing it had carried. "Why kill it? Maybe we can learn more about the floating stones from it."

"That was the OColi's decision to make, not SStragh's," Miadoa answered. "The Far-Killer probably didn't look dangerous when it killed Ghayi or Beadsi, either. But it did."

"I have pulled its sting," SStragh insisted. "The spear..."

"Maybe. But this isn't a decision we were asked to make, SStragh," Lhath insisted, and he released the acrid smell of displeasure to emphasize the word. "Kill it."

The tone, posture, and smell all caused the crest on SStragh's back to rise stiffly and her whole body to raise up slightly. She knew that Lhath wanted her to submit, to expose her neck. "No," she answered, in the same voice. Defiantly, she held his gaze.

"Then I will," Lhath told her. Moving his spear quickly to his right hand, he raised the weapon over the Far-Killer. SStragh bellowed in anger. Her tail held out straight to provide balance, she rushed forward, knocking away Lhath's spear with her own.

Lhath trilled in fury; SStragh answered in kind. The Far-Killer bleated in terror between them.

"You are disobeying the OColi," Lhath hissed.

"And you are disobeying *me*," SStragh answered. "The OColi gave *me* the task of finding the Far-Killer, and I have. The OColi also

agreed that I did right to bring in the younglings. He has trusted my judgment in that, no
matter what Frraghi has whispered in his ears.
Now, either pick up your weapon and ask me
for formal challenge or hobble our captive so
we can bring it back." SStragh pulled her head
up as high as she could, so that she was standing
nearly straight up. "Choose," she said.

Lhath hissed and growled; his scent was first
angry, then the odor softened and went apol-
ogetically sweet. He lowered his head, no
longer meeting SStragh's gaze directly. He
didn't move to pick up the spear.

"Good," SStragh said. "We'll send others
back to bring Caasrt later."

SStragh heard Miadoa's whisper as he helped
Lhath tie the Far-Killer's legs together, though
she pretended she didn't.

"You won't always be lucky, SStragh."

SECOND MEETINGS

It wasn't a dream, this world.

Morning brought an assortment of hunger, thirst, and strange sounds from the encampment, most of which were impossible to identify. Jennifer lay halfway between waking and sleep, hoping that her eyes would deny what her ears and body were telling her. She could smell the mustiness of the furs covering her, feel the coarse nap of the hairs, and her back was stiff from a night on the ground.

Despairing, she opened her eyes.

Peter was already up, sitting with his back to the rough wooden walls of their pen and scowling angrily at the guard lizard, which yawned widely at him, flicking a red tongue.

"Morning, Peter," she said. "What time is it?"

"What's the matter, Jenny? Afraid you've missed your wake-up call?"

Jenny scowled at Peter. The taste in her mouth made her want to brush her teeth, but she was about as far from toothbrushes as she could be. "What's the matter, Peter, you get up on the wrong side of the bed?"

"The wrong side of the ground." Peter gestured at the lizard. "Big and ugly here looks like he's getting sleepy."

"Are you thinking that now might be the time to make a run for it? After the fiasco last night . . ."

Peter shook his head. "Uh-uh. I set my watch to six A.M. at dawn; it's about ten now. Your Struth's already been in to check on us, just after the sun rose, and there're dinos walking around all over out there. We don't stand a chance of getting out right now." '

"How are you feeling, Peter?"

"I'm really hungry and really thirsty." He scowled again. "But I'm all right. I'm okay."

Jennifer nodded. The stubborn defiance in his voice told her more than the words. *He's really scared, but he's not about to let me know it.* That was okay, too. She was pretty scared herself.

She went to the outer wall, peering through the gap between the logs. The dinosaurs were up and active. Nearby, one was pounding something in a huge ceramic pot with a large stick; two other were standing alongside and occasionally adding water and a flourlike substance to the mixture. The breeze brought an odor of sharp spices that reminded Jennifer of how hungry she was. All around the encampment, the dinosaurs went about their business. They all appeared to be the same species, one of the kind that Aaron had told her were duck-bills. Though they wore various types of jewelry—pendants and arm bands and chest plates—they didn't wear clothing. Jennifer couldn't identify most of the tasks being performed, though she could see one planing a wood plank between two of the conelike buildings. The blade glinted in the sun, though Jennifer couldn't tell whether the implement was made of metal or not. Through an opening into the building, she could glimpse another dinosaur with its arms coated in clay hunched down in front of a spinning platform coated with slurry: obviously a potter.

This was a village, Jennifer decided. A permanent community.

A cacophony of hoots and trills erupted from the edge of the small town. Several juvenile dinosaurs went running in response; the adults all looked up curiously. Jennifer and Peter could see a band of spear-armed dinosaurs approaching the enclosure, but the scurrying of the juveniles and the wall between them made it difficult for her to see much.

There was a brief commotion at the gate. Struth entered the enclosure; behind him, hobbled as Jenny and Peter had been the night before, was a human—roughly bearded, his right arm bloody from a gash in his bicep, and not quite as thin as Jenny remembered, but very, very recognizable.

Eckels.

He stared at the two of them as Struth untied the hobbles and thrust the man toward Jennifer and Peter. Eckels stumbled and nearly fell as Struth closed the gate behind herself without uttering a word.

"Eckels!" Peter cried. "I've wanted another crack at you!"

Peter took a threatening step forward, but Eckels fell back, shaking his head. "Hey, kid, I don't know you," he said. "Back off. Take it easy." His voice had Travis's strange accent, the vowels produced deep in the throat.

"Yeah, right. You don't remember hitting me with the butt end of that rifle or tying us up last night in your cave, huh?"

"Last night? Cave?" Eckels licked his lips—they were dry and cracked, like he'd been out in the sun for some time. His clothing was tattered, frayed, and dirty. He looked and smelled like he'd spent the night in a swamp. "I'm sorry, but I don't know what you're talking about. I've been wandering lost around this place for the last week or so, most of the time being chased by these damn big lizards. I'll admit that there's some of it I don't remember—I fell down a cliff and hit my head a few days back—but if I did something to you two, I don't recall it. You understand me? Now, we don't need any violence, not between three people who are in the same difficulty." The man scowled at the two of them. "I don't have a quarrel with either of you."

"Eckels," Jenny said, and at the sound of his name, the man whirled around, his eyes wide and suspicious.

"How do you two know my name?" he said.

"You told us last night," she said. "When

you were raving. Besides, Travis told us everything.''

Eckels snorted at that. "*That* explains it. So you know Travis, huh? Well, Travis is an idiot. He's to blame for all of this."

"That's not the way we heard it," Peter answered quickly. His hands were still balled into fists.

Eckels's eyes narrowed. "What did he tell you?" He looked quickly from Peter to Jennifer, and Jenny didn't like the way his gaze lingered on her. She remembered what he'd said the night before. "For that matter, where did he meet the two of you? Where are you from?"

"We're from Green Town," Peter said. "From your past."

"Peter, I don't think—" Jennifer started, but Eckels's face rearranged itself into a smile. It didn't look like a natural expression to her.

"Please, I'm not lying to you," Eckels said. His voice was softer and gentler. He sat down and rubbed his ankles where the ropes had been tied. He didn't look dangerous at all, Jennifer had to admit. Not at the moment. He looked tired and hurt—*just like us*, she thought. Peter must have felt something of the same sympathy, for his stance relaxed and his hands dropped to his side. "I can understand how you two would be suspicious of me," Eckels said, grimacing as he massaged his legs. "I'm just asking you to be fair. I don't know you; you two don't know me—or if you do, it was a crazy, out-of-my-mind me that *I* don't remember either. I'm . . . I'm sorry if I did anything to hurt you.''

Eckels stopped rubbing and sighed, a deep weary sound. "All you have to go on is Travis's word, and he's far from neutral in this. Right now, the first thing I want to do is get out of here—and I'll bet you kids feel the same way, huh?" He reached down and picked up one of the fruits on the tray. "At least they gave us food.''

"Eckels—" Jennifer began.

"Don't worry about it," he told her. For a moment, his smile changed slightly. Jennifer seemed to glimpse *something* within it, some hint of expression that she didn't like—or maybe she just imagined it, for it was gone instantly. "I was pretty hungry out there, believe me. I've had these before—they're a little bitter, but you can eat them and keep them down. They don't make you sick or give you the trots. If you haven't tried them, go ahead. You both look pretty famished." He smiled, almost gently. "Trust me.''

Eckels tossed Peter one of the fruits, then Jennifer. Jennifer looked over the red-orange rind speckled with yellow. Her stomach growled insistently and her mouth was watering. Peter was already eating.

She took a bite. In her condition, the meat inside was about the most heavenly thing she'd ever tasted.

"You see, that's better, isn't it?" Eckels told them. He was sitting now, reaching for another one of the fruits. "We have to eat; we have to keep up our strength until we can get out of here. We all *need* each other. So—how did you get here?" There was an eagerness in his voice that bothered Jennifer. Peter was starting to speak, but she interrupted him quickly.

"What about *you*, Eckels? You said that Travis lied—so what's the true story?"

"Judging from the suspicious way you're acting, I'd say that Travis definitely lied about me, yes." Eckels's eyes were hard on her and the smile had gone, but then a veil seemed to come over his gaze and the smile returned. "Fair enough. Let's . . . let's do it this way. You tell me what Travis told you, and then I'll give you my version. You two can judge for yourselves afterward. Is that fair enough?"

"C'mon, Jen," Peter said.

"Hey, a couple minutes ago, you were ready to deck him, Peter."

He shrugged. "I was. I still might. But it isn't going to hurt us to listen, is it? He's in the same fix we are. Aren't you the one who's always trying to be fair?"

Jennifer shook her head. "All right," she said. "Might as well talk. What else are we going to do? Go ahead."

Jennifer sat down as Peter began the tale. For the next several minutes he told Eckels how they'd met Travis and how they'd stumbled into this world. Eckels's eyes narrowed as Peter told him about the paths; he nodded and grinned.

"That's *great*." Eckels laughed; Jennifer decided that she didn't like his laugh, though Peter chuckled along with him. "That's the best news I've heard. I've been looking for a way back since I stumbled into this time."

"Your turn, Eckels," Jennifer said. "Remember? We don't trust you."

Eckels looked at her, and though the smile stayed on his lips, it didn't touch his eyes at all. They glared at her. "Sure," he said. "Let me tell you about what *really* happened. . . ."

ECKELS'S TALE

I don't know what that fool Travis has told you about me (Eckels said), but I doubt that it's true. He's . . . well, I guess the best way I can say it is that Travis has the prejudices of his class. I could feel the resentment he had toward me from the moment we met.

I was everything he wasn't: I come from a rather wealthy family and I had the advantages of education and influence. Travis, well, he seemed resentful that I hadn't fought in the stupid war, though he never bothered to ask why or I would have told him about the medical problems I was having at the time. And I don't care how patriotic he pretends to be himself, *he* was never in the service either. No, not our Mr. Travis, he was too 'essential' at his job to be a simple military grunt—so he doesn't have much room to complain.

I'll skip all the gory details of our time safari—you already know them, in Travis's version, anyway. He probably told you that I cut and run, didn't he? I thought so. Well, that's not the truth. When the T rex charged, I stood there just like the rest. It was *Travis* who lost his nerve, not me and not any of the other people with the safari. That's a fact; I swear it is. We were along for the ride, after all. I know that they'd told us how dangerous it might be, but none of us really believed it. We had guns, we had experienced guides—there wasn't any *reason* for us to panic, even in the face of that monster.

I think Travis had made a mistake. I think he'd marked a creature that was just a little too big and too ferocious, and he didn't realize it until we were there facing it. Travis was backing up like he figured that the monster was going to get the people in front first and he wasn't going to be one of them. He plowed right into me and knocked me off the path into the mud. Travis went down too, but *he* fell on the path.

When the T rex finally went down a few moments later, I was just picking myself up. You should have seen the look on his face. I mean, he was terrified. He knew what he'd done, knew it very well. He was *scared*, really scared when he saw me sitting on my rear in the mud and ferns. He knew he'd broken his corporation's rules. Trouble was, no one else had noticed what he'd done, and he realized that at the same time. He was also a lot smarter than I realized.

His face went all tight and angry. He started shouting at me, calling me a blundering idiot and a coward, yelling at me about breaking their precious regulations and stepping off the path. I protested, but it didn't do any good. Travis and his assistants—well, they were all of a kind and they were going to back up their boss, not me. I can't even say I blame them. Most people would have done the same—it was just my word against Travis. As I said, in the confusion and noise, no one had really seen what happened. Everyone was shaken, everyone was still scared, and I was an easy target on which to place the blame.

I didn't make a big deal about it, though, because I didn't believe that there was anything to worry about. I figured that all those warnings and caveats and restrictions and regulations were just so much fluff. You know, the corporation protecting itself just in case something happened to go slightly wrong or they wanted a good excuse to kick someone off one of the expeditions. It couldn't *really* be that dangerous, I thought, or else they wouldn't let us do it at all. The worst that could happen was that I'd get some hand-slap fine and they wouldn't let me go on another trip—which I wasn't planning on anyway, since they were so damned expensive in the first place and they don't let you see any *real* history with ancient people and old civilizations.

So fine, I thought. Let Travis blame me if it kept his job. He probably needed it; maybe he had a wife and kids to support. I didn't really care. If his people started getting nasty, I'd tell them what actually happened, how Travis had knocked me off the path. If they wanted to push it, their high-priced lawyers could talk to my high-priced lawyers. No problem. I had as much money as they did. Maybe more.

But when we got back . . .

I—I wasn't prepared for that. I didn't want to believe what I saw there. It was our time but yet . . . yet it *wasn't* our time. The wrong man had been elected. A demagogue—a military adventurist. I remember screaming, I remember all of them just looking at me and the mud on my boots and seeing a butterfly there, all crushed and torn. Travis, he was thundering curses at the top of his lungs, and the lab people were looking at all of us like we were crazy. I suppose that to them we were, since as far as they were concerned the world was just the way it always had been. It was only for *us* that the future had changed, you see.

No one else could see it. We were the only ones who could remember the way it had been. We had been outside the stream when the river of time had changed its course.

I saw mingled fury and dread in Travis's gaze, and I knew that no matter what, there was no way he was going to admit his guilt now, not after this fiasco. It was going to be *Eckels's* fault, that spoiled rich snob's fault, that cowardly little so-and-so's fault. Eckels was going to hang.

Travis was also going to make absolutely certain that the truth never came back to haunt him. He snatched the rifle from one of his assistant's hands, and I was suddenly looking at certain death. He would have killed me, too, if his assistant hadn't knocked the barrel aside at the last moment. I felt the concussion, I heard the slug whine past my ears, and I did what felt like the safest thing at the time—I dove for the nearest shelter, which happened to be the open door of the time machine. Travis was looking angrier than ever, and everyone in the place was shouting. I saw guards with their guns out coming toward me, but Travis was ahead of them all. I figured that if I stayed where I was, I was going to live about another fifteen seconds at best.

I'd watched Travis run the machine. They'd set it up with a simple computer interface any idiot could use. I started up the machine as Travis barreled across the room toward me, waving that rifle.

I didn't know when the machine was set for; I just punched it back into the past. The room faded away like morning fog in a valley and I was safe. I looked at the controls. There was a listing of times and dates—I figured those were the times the machine had already visited. The one at the bottom was highlighted and blinking at me, so I guessed that was where I was headed.

I—I let it go. I had some vague notion of meeting my old self coming in and stopping the whole thing before it happened, of getting on their time machine and going back to the *right* future, the one I knew.

That was my mistake, I suppose. I vaguely remembered Travis saying something about the 'bumps' we'd felt when we were first heading

DownTime, and about how careful we had to be not to show up at the same time. I figured that there had to be some kind of automatic safeguard to prevent that from accidentally happening.

Guess I figured wrong, huh?

Alarms started whooping just as the prehistoric jungle started to take shape outside the windows. I didn't know what to do, and I didn't have much time to react. The machine howled louder than that old T rex, and then . . .

. . . then . . .

There was an explosion. All I remember is a feeling like someone had slammed a two-by-four hard across my chest. The front of the machine disintegrated into pieces like we'd materialized into the vortex of a tornado. An invisible giant's hand picked me up and tossed me like a baseball.

I don't remember anything else for a while.

I woke up to find myself lying on my back in thick mud. I was lucky; the mud had probably saved me a broken spine. I got up, really dazed—my memory is still fuzzy, like an old movie. I remember seeing a piece of the path hovering near me. I lurched toward as the only piece of familiarity around. I half fell, half stepped up on it . . .

. . . and landed here.

Wherever 'here' is, anyway.

A LOST PAST

16

Frosted mist dissolved from the windows like an April snow. Aaron stared through the glass into the world of 1992, trying to force Green Town to be there by sheer force of will. He imaged the feathery mist evaporating to reveal the familiar wooded hills of Illinois, the oaks, the creek, the long green hill leading up to the house with the weatherbeaten clapboard sides, all blue with white trim and Grandpa Carl on the big wraparound porch, a dewy pitcher of lemonade sitting beside him. . . .

There. They'd be right there, just beyond.

But no. This scene wasn't Illinois. It might as well have been Mars.

Wherever—*whenever*—they were, this was the same timeline Aaron and Travis had just left. Aaron could recognize the skirted cacti that had nearly killed Travis, though their dominance of the rocky, snow-sprinkled landscape was now challenged by sparse clumps of six-foot high grass whose blades were as thick and rigid as upright swords. The landscape wasn't exactly Green Town, either—they weren't sitting among hills but younger, steep mountains, their shoulders high in the sunlit sky and covered with bright, eye-glaring mantles of ice.

There were none of the huge snails here, though as Aaron watched, one of the sword blades fell like a small tree. A creature like a cat wearing plate armor trundled out from the base of the growth. It bit into the blade and began backing away with its hindquarters raised up, dragging its prize with it. At the same moment, a shape plummeted from a nearby cliff ledge: recognizably a bird, but one with a wing-span larger than the time machine and a head more like a ferret's than an eagle's. Its wings were covered with rust-red hair, not feathers. The thing landed on the cat creature, which struggled uselessly under the talons. With a shriek of triumph, the predator flew off, carrying the still-flailing victim.

Definitely, absolutely, *not* Illinois.

"I'm going out there," Aaron said. "I've gotta see, gotta make sure."

"You're crazy," Travis told him. "Don't be stupid, kid. That bird's big enough to take nice big chunks out of you, and remember what happened to me UpTime. This isn't our world. Not anymore."

Travis sounded so bitter and angry that Aaron turned to look at him. Travis's head was down; he was brooding again, half lost in dark thoughts. Aaron could guess at what Travis was thinking: he was reliving the whole tragedy again: seeing Eckels blundering from the path, going back to his changed future, Eckels fleeing in the stolen time machine. Travis was wondering what he could have done to stop it, what he could have said or how he could have acted . . .

Something clicked in Aaron's head, a nagging inconsistency in Travis's story that had jigged his subconscious like a burr until—now—it suddenly surfaced. He'd wondered at it before, but he'd been lost in the flow of the story.

"Travis," he said slowly, "these machines are pretty automated. How was it that Eckels managed to materialize at the same place and time as his past self? That doesn't make sense, not if your company was being as careful as you claim they were. Shouldn't there have been some automatic cutoff?"

When Travis glanced up, his eyes were bleak. His whole face sagged, as if all the energy had been drained from him. "No—" he began, and before the word was said, Aaron knew it was a lie. Then Travis shook his head and gave a laugh that was more like a cough. He clutched at his ribs and for a moment his whole face went pale and beads of sweat stood out on his skin. The man took a long, shallow breath. "What have I got to worry about? Who's going to blame me now, huh? Sure there was a safeguard," he said softly. "Of course there was."

With the words, Aaron knew what had happened. The guilt in Travis's face told him. "You turned it off," Aaron said, disbelievingly. "It wasn't working. You lied to us. It was *your* fault, not Eckels's."

"Wait a minute, kid," Travis said hurriedly.

"That's not true. I didn't leave the path, I didn't go stomping through the jungle like a crazy man, and I didn't take the time machine back. That was Eckels. Eckels. Yeah, sure I'd fiddled with the overrides. Every guide did that—it lets us fine-tune the safaris, makes it easier to find and mark the prey. The buffers the corporation builds in are way too conservative. They won't let us within a full day of another machine: do you know how difficult that would have made our job, how much longer it would have taken?"

"So you found a way to take out the safeguards entirely."

"It was just a software hack. That's all. And we were all careful. We knew what we were doing."

"Right. I can tell." Aaron looked out the window contemptuously. That explained a lot of Travis's anger—it was directed inward. Guilt gnawed at the man like a cancer, tearing at his guts. Funny how that didn't make Aaron feel very sorry for him, not when he looked outside at what this machine's instruments claimed was his home.

"You killed my family," Aaron said. "You killed *all* of it—friends, the town, everything."

"Eckels did it, not—" Travis began again, then stopped. He took a long, shuddering breath. "Yes," he said. "It's my fault, too."

Aaron didn't know what to say. He wasn't even sure how he felt right at the moment. He was confused and lost. He was stuck in a nightmare from which he wasn't going to awake. A certain disbelief still lingered in him despite everything, and Aaron knew that was simply shock, numbing him from the overwhelming loss.

Any minute now and this will all go away. We'll walk outside and Green Town will be back. Or Travis will laugh and tell me how this has all been just an elaborate stunt. It can't be real. I won't let it be real.

Defiantly, Aaron went to the door of the time machine and opened it. The acrid, frigid air buffeted him and made his breath a fog.

"Kid . . ." Travis said behind him. "Aaron . . ."

"Just shut up, would you?"

Travis groaned and started to lever himself painfully up from his seat. "At least let me come with you." Fresh blood from the allosaurus' wounds were soaking the bandages Jenny had wrapped around his chest and arms.

Jenny. With the thought, a new fury rose in Aaron. He wanted to pummel the man, wanted to make him cry out until he wept the way Aaron wanted to weep. Instead, he ignored Travis. He walked outside, not caring whether the man followed or not.

Carefully, avoiding the cacti and the clumps of grass and watching the cliff ledges around him carefully, Aaron clambered up the nearest slope, panting in the thin, freezing air. He ignored the stinging touch of the snow and frozen rocks on his bare hands, climbing higher until he stood on ledge that overlooked a valley to the west. The sun was sinking below the jagged teeth of the mountains, casting purple and black shadows over the land. Far down in the valley, a river carried broken ice floes toward some distant, unseen sea. As far as Aaron could see, there was no sign of anything human at all. Nothing matched his memories in the slightest. He couldn't believe this was Illinois or Green Town or anything close to his time.

His teeth were chattering. He still wanted to shout and rage and cry. But he didn't. *The tears would just freeze on your cheeks, Aaron. And it wouldn't change anything.*

Aaron stood there a long time in the cold. After a while, he heard Travis groaning and puffing as he made his way slowly up the incline to him, his rifle in one hand, the other helping him over the broken landscape.

"You gonna stand out here until the cold gets you, kid?"

"Does it matter?"

Travis sniffed. He had a jacket with a fur collar over his bloodied shirt. "I guess not. It isn't like you and I are going to repopulate the world again, is it? You're right—I have food for about a week. No more. The time machine will give us shelter and mobility until its batteries are gone—maybe a few months, a little longer if we don't move it much in space; much, much shorter if we start jumping around in time. Then we're on our own."

Aaron stared at the landscape revealed before

him. *Nothing familiar. Nothing that I can recognize.* As he mused, he saw a dusty swirling in the dirt at his feet. He crouched down to look. A cone-shaped depression had appeared, a hole in the center a few centimeters in diameter. A few sandy granules slithered down the slope and disappeared. Aaron looked closer, his finger just touching the edge of the hole.

A whiplike appendage lashed out and coiled around his forefinger. The small tentacle pulled at him, almost taking him off balance with surprising strength; immediately, the hole yawned open like a mouth. A snakelike head appeared and struck at him. Aaron had a quick impression of blind eyesockets, a frill of jellylike, writhing things like anenomes on either side, and jaws bristling with needled teeth. He twisted and pulled backward.

The first strike missed. As Aaron yanked his arm back, the tentacle holding his finger resisted and then reluctantly let go. He fell backward; the snake head slid back down again and disappeared. Dirt swirled, and there was nothing there to show the creature had ever been there.

The ledge was quiet again. Peaceful.

Aaron scrambled to his feet. The attack made up his mind. "We're going back," he said to Travis. "This place . . . we don't belong here. It's isn't ours. The Mesozoic isn't home, but it's more like home than this."

Travis scoffed. "What's the difference? Here, there—who cares?"

DINOSAUR WORLD SKETCHBOOK

A Record of My Adventures
by Aaron Cofield

Pages 2 and 3: The Mutata village, as seen from the main entrance. That's Struth in the foreground.

Page 4: A portrait of Travis, time safari guide from the future, and my traveling companion through many strange worlds.

Page 5: The time machine, as best I can remember it, with a piece of the path. Also, pterosaurs—which turned out to be stranger animals than I could ever have imagined.

Page 6: Travis's very impressive, loaded-for-death rifle.

Page 7: A confrontation that was related to me—a Mutata killing a Samurai warrior.

Pages 8 and 9: A Gairk warrior in full battle regalia; the fiercest fighter I've ever seen.

Pages 10 and 11: An overview of the late Cretaceous.

Pages 12 and 13: A typical Mutata warrior and its "house." Primitive by our standards, perhaps, but state-of-the-art in its own world.

Pages 14 and 15: The old Cofield family homestead, and a most unusual visitor.

Page 16: A Mutata "guard dog." I wish I had one of these back home.

THE MUTATA-VILLAGE

BUILDINGS ARE SCATTERED
WITHIN STOCKADE WITHOUT ANY
SENSE OF URBAN PLANNING.

BUILDINGS ARE STONE BASED
WITH UPPER PORTIONS EITHER OF
MUD OR ADOBE.

NO WINDOWS, GLASS, DOORS OR
BUILT FIRES TO BE SEEN.

2

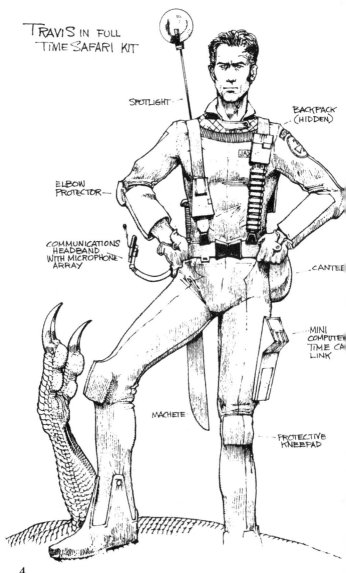

TRAVIS IN FULL TIME SAFARI KIT

SPOTLIGHT

BACKPACK (HIDDEN)

ELBOW PROTECTOR

COMMUNICATIONS HEADBAND WITH MICROPHONE ARRAY

CANTEE

MINI COMPUTE TIME CA LINK

MACHETE

PROTECTIVE KNEEPAD

4

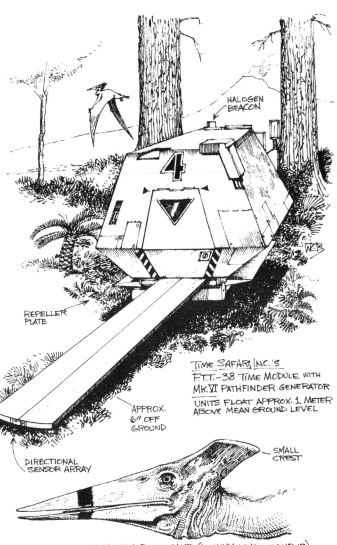

HALOGEN
BEACON

4

Time SAFARI, Inc.'s
F.T.T.-38 Time Module with
Mk. VI Pathfinder Generator

UNITS FLOAT APPROX. 1 METER
ABOVE MEAN GROUND LEVEL

REPELLER
PLATE

APPROX.
6" OFF
GROUND

DIRECTIONAL
SENSOR ARRAY

SMALL
CREST

HEAD OF A PTEROSAUR (I THINK NYCTOSAURUS)
8' WINGSPAN
VERY LITTLE HAIR

5

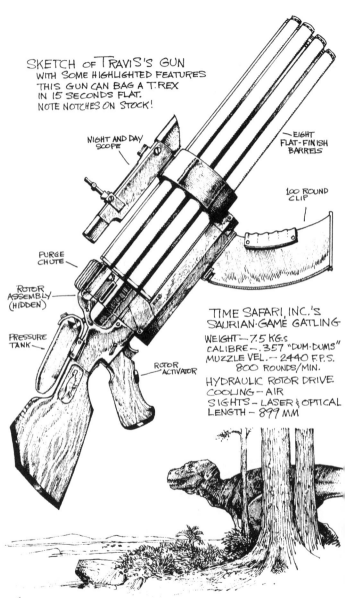

SKETCH OF TRAVIS'S GUN
WITH SOME HIGHLIGHTED FEATURES
THIS GUN CAN BAG A T.REX
IN 15 SECONDS FLAT.
NOTE NOTCHES ON STOCK!

NIGHT AND DAY SCOPE

EIGHT FLAT-FINISH BARRELS

100 ROUND CLIP

PURGE CHUTE

ROTOR ASSEMBLY (HIDDEN)

PRESSURE TANK

ROTOR ACTIVATOR

TIME SAFARI, INC.'S SAURIAN·GAME GATLING

WEIGHT — 7.5 KG.s
CALIBRE — .357 "DUM·DUMS"
MUZZLE VEL. — 2440 F.P.S.
    800 ROUNDS/MIN.

HYDRAULIC ROTOR DRIVE
COOLING — AIR
SIGHTS — LASER & OPTICAL
LENGTH — 899 MM

6

THE MUTATA KILLS A SAMURAI

H. BARLOW 91

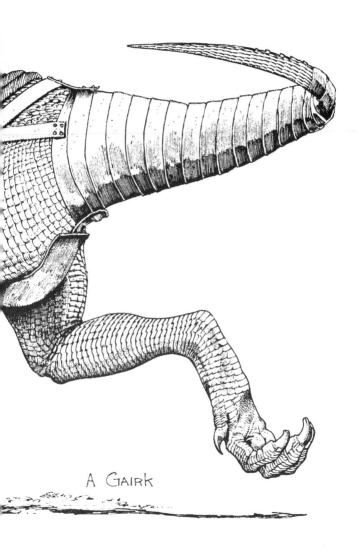

A Gairk

THE LATE CRETACEOUS,
FLORA AND FAUNA

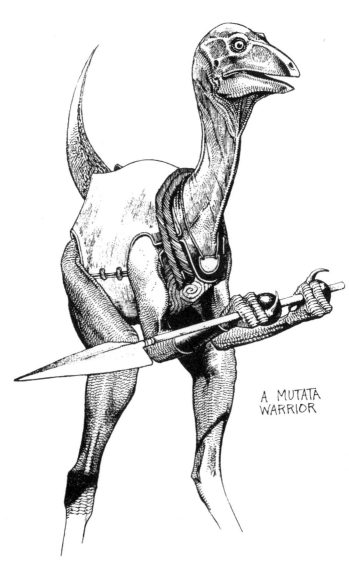

A MUTATA
WARRIOR

12

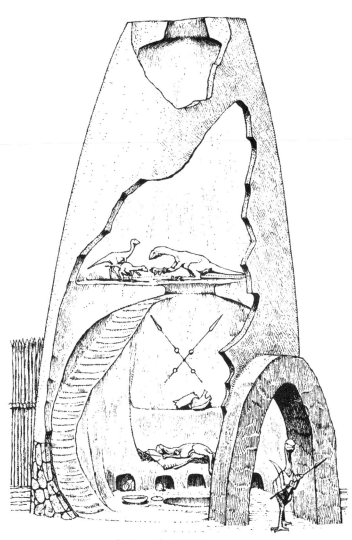

A TYPICAL MUTATA
DWELLING

MY FIRST SIGHT OF A
LIVING DINOSAUR—
IN OUR BACKYARD.

15

MUTATA
SENTRY
LIZARD

————

2 METERS LONG

" 'Cause I'm not giving up, Travis. There has to be something we can do, something we haven't noticed, some mistake that's been made."

"Yeah, there's been a mistake all right. His name is Eckels. . . ." Travis's voice trailed off. Aaron looked at him: the man was staring into the distance but he wasn't seeing anything here at all.

"What are you thinking?" Aaron asked. Then, when there was no answer. "Travis?"

Travis started. He looked up suddenly. The pained veil over his gaze was gone, replaced by a new alertness. Aaron knew he was holding back something, either because the man still didn't trust Aaron or because he hadn't crystallized the idea in his own mind yet.

"Just a thought, kid. Nothing important." Travis scuffed at the dirt where the whip snake had appeared, prodding the frozen earth with the butt of his rifle. "I think you're right. Let's go back. C'mon."

With that, he turned to begin his painful way back down the mountainside. He stopped with a gasp. Aaron gaped as well.

The time machine wasn't there.

PLANS MADE

SStragh lifted her head so that the long, graceful length of her neck was exposed, especially the soft, purplish folds just under the throat where the OColi's claws could easily tear through the skin and rip out the windpipe. Quite often this gesture of complete submission caused her to tremble all over—the OColi had been known to take advantage of his underlings when he was irritated. As the PastVoice said: "An OColi is the wind: as gentle as a zephyr, as fierce as a storm. And like a storm, its wrath will find whoever stands in their path."

Such an action was certainly within the OColi's rights, of course. Not one of the Mutata would complain if the OColi exercised his right as Eldest and killed SStragh immediately, here and now. In fact, some of them would have welcomed it, since much of the blame for the horrible omens lately had been placed upon SStragh.

Today, SStragh's submission was entirely ritual. SStragh could smell that the OColi was in a fine mood—the zephyr whose touch was fragrant and cool. Frraghi, the OColi's Voice, motioned SStragh back with an irritable wave, then bent down to listen to the OColi's whispered, ancient voice. SStragh looked away politely, deliberately placing her attention elsewhere. The room's pale walls, knobby and pocked, deadened all sounds. SStragh could not hear the OColi's voice at all over the sound of her own breath, which was as it should be. The OColi's voice was the Mutata Voice. Except on rare occasions, it wasn't proper for anyone but Frraghi to hear the OColi. SStragh could taste the OColi's scent, though, and his fragrance was sweet.

Even if Frraghi's wasn't.

Frraghi glared at SStragh as if she had personally made the floating stones and called forth the creatures from the other side. *It wasn't my fault that I found the first floating stone after we returned from the last Nesting. I didn't create the ugly intruders who came through the path. It isn't my fault, nor was it the fault of OTsio Raajek, no matter what they say. The floating stones are just an accident, a whim of the All-Ancestor.*

But then blame was like the OColi's temper: capricious.

"The OColi has said that he is pleased to find that SStragh has at last captured the Far-Killer," Frraghi said, although *he* didn't seem very pleased by the words at all. "He would like to know whether it was difficult."

"We were all surprised at the ease of it," SStragh answered, looking carefully into Frraghi's eyes. Behind the Voice, she could see by the cocked, aged head that the OColi was listening intently, but SStragh pretended not to notice. The OColi didn't like to be stared at; the rumor was that such attention made him very conscious of his maimed appearance; many Nestings ago a Gairk spear had taken out one of the OColi's eyes and left that side of his face a mass of scar tissue.

Instead, SStragh closed her eyes to better recall the scene. She spoke as truthfully as she could, holding back none of the details.

"Why did you use the left hand?" Frraghi said afterward. "That was stupid. It is an animal. Only an animal could have killed Caasrt in that way."

"I was asked to kill or capture the Far-Killer because it had murdered three Mutata and two of the Gairk," SStragh answered flatly and carefully. "I did as I was instructed. The younglings we found are intelligent, so I felt I must treat the Far-Killer the same way."

"It's *your* contention that the younglings are intelligent," Frraghi retorted scornfully. "You say that only because the female can mimic your name—very badly, by the way. In the meantime, while you've been floundering around trying to capture the Far-Killer, who was so 'surprisingly easy' to catch once you finally got around to it, the Scaled Ones came from the floating stones and killed two more Mutata. The Gairk also tell us that there are strange winged beasts attacking them from yet another floating stone further down the valley. The Gairk OColi blames us. He says that there wouldn't be floating stones if the Mutata hadn't done something offensive to the All-Ancestor. They may yet attack *us*."

Frraghi snorted a long, loud, and derisive note as he drew up to his full height, his head nearly touching the roof. "This is what comes of listening to you and your OTsio Raajek, SStragh. That's what comes of claiming that the old path is not longer valid."

"I *found* the floating stones; I did not make them, as the OColi knows," SStragh replied patiently. It was the same old tiresome explanation. "The Mutata have done nothing to offend the All-Ancestor, as the Gairk OColi knows. As for OTsio Raajek's teachings, this has nothing to do with them, either. The omens only make OTsio Raajek's advice more imperative than ever."

"Phaah!" Frraghi snorted. From behind the Voice, the odor of the OColi had gone sour as well. "Then let Raajek come back and speak for herself. She will have just as much success as she did before. As for the Gairk, they've never been patient or smart. Truth has never stopped them from violence, has it?"

SStragh shrugged. Her complacency seemed to disturb Frraghi, who (as SStragh was well aware) preferred that visitors to the OColi be visibly frightened. Frraghi hissed in displeasure, showing his tongue.

"Why are you so anxious to save these young-lings and the Far-Killer?"

"I . . . I'm not certain," SStragh answered honestly. She ignored Frraghi, directing her plea to the figure behind the Voice. "Forgive me, my OColi, but something inside me insists that they are somehow important to us."

"So we should listen to an imaginary voice inside the useless and unlucky SStragh rather than do as the Mutata have always done," Frraghi scoffed.

"The Mutata rarely do anything that is new," SStragh answered. "That is the problem."

Frraghi ignored that. "I have counseled the OColi to dispose of the Far-Killer and its young-lings," he said. "I feel that SStragh wastes the time and efforts of Mutata with her insistence on keeping them captive. We risk offending the All-Ancestor, and if the Gairk should learn of them . . ."

Frraghi paused, and SStragh chose her next words carefully, knowing that the OColi was listening to their discussion. "Then I'm pleased that the OColi has had the wisdom to ignore your counsel so far, Frraghi," SStragh replied.

Frraghi recoiled in irritation, his chest widening, his crest engorged and widely spread. His acrid smell overpowered all the other odors in the room; his tail whipped around threateningly. "They are dangerous animals," he hissed. "They should be treated as such."

"How can you say that?" SStragh answered. She kept her stance carefully docile, not giving Frraghi an excuse to strike. "They speak a language of their own. Jhenini is beginning to learn ours. They wear coverings that they have made. They don't act like animals."

"I say it," Frraghi said. "Are you saying that I'm unwise to do so, SStragh?"

SStragh hesitated, risking a glance up at Frraghi's eyes. She knew then that if she said more, Frraghi would use the provocation. He would roar his challenge, and she'd die under his spear. Frraghi's skill with weapons was unmatched among the Mutata, which was part of the reason that the OColi, the eldest of them all and thus frail, had chosen him as his Voice.

Yet the words had to be said, as dangerous as that was. *Yes, you are unwise. They are not animals. I don't know what they are, these bipeds, but they're more than animals. They are part of OTsio Raajek's new path.* SStragh opened her mouth to speak, but a delicate, husky voice from the back of the room interrupted: the OColi himself.

"An animal will not follow the OColihi," he said. "That makes them dangerous. My Voice has spoken correctly, SStragh. Dangerous animals must be removed."

Frraghi had turned to gape openmouthed at the OColi. SStragh didn't dare look up at him. The OColi only rarely spoke to anyone other than his Voice. His speaking now awed SStragh, even while his words caused her to despair.

The OColi opened his ancient, knobby-jointed hands, the arthritic joints unfolding slowly. The OColi mewled with the pain of the movement. It was many breaths before he spoke again, but both Frraghi and SStragh waited patiently. "We will give Caasrt back to the All-Ancestor in three days. Bring the younglings then," he said, bringing hope back to SStragh. "We will see if they act as animals or as Mutata. We will see if they know the OColihi."

SStragh started to speak, stopped, then began again. "OColi," she said, "forgive me for my boldness, but that is hardly a fair test. The younglings know nothing of our rites."

"All rites differ," Frraghi countered. "We know that. Yet any Mutata could assist at a Gairk Giving. Their OColihi is not that different."

"Yes, but—"

"Yes," Frraghi interrupted. "Yes. Listen to your own words, SStragh. Yes. We are not animals, so we know the Gairk ways. Both the Mutata and Gairk know the All-Ancestor. If your strange creatures know the All-Ancestor also, then they'll show us. Even your OTsio would say that."

"At least let me teach them the rites," SStragh asked.

"No," Frraghi answered.

"Ask the OColi," SStragh insisted. Frraghi snorted, but leaned down to the OColi. When he straightened again, his scent was spiced with smugness.

"The OColi gives you one boon. You may continue to teach the younglings our language, if they can learn it. But of the Giving rites, SStragh, you must say nothing. Nothing."

From the corner of the room, the OColi snorted in agreement.

SStragh hissed; Frraghi gave a satisfied huff. SStragh knew then there could be no more argument. She felt a deepening despair, but there was nothing she could do now.

"Thank you, OColi," she said. "I will do as you ask. I will bring the younglings to the Giving in three days. I will teach them our language. I will tell them nothing of the Giving."

She bowed, exposed her neck once more, and turned to leave the chamber.

"SStragh," Frraghi called. SStragh halted. "If they show themselves to be animals, I will kill them there in the Giving Hall. Immediately."

Jennifer was running, panicked and gasping, through the forest of fern trees. The leafy fronds snatched at her, their sharp edges lacerating her skin like a thousand small knives. Unseen things hissed and struck at her feet, her head, her hands. Behind her, the dinosaurs of Struth's tribe hooted and snorted as they pursued her, their feet pounding a rhythm of wild drums.

"Jenny!"

The voice was like the shock of cool, sweet water on an August afternoon when the sweat burns in your eyes and makes a dripping tangle of your hair. Jenny stumbled, catching herself as she turned to look back. Aaron was standing in the middle of the trail, grinning at her with his arms out.

"Aaron! Ohmigod—"

She ran to him, clasping him to her. Her mouth found his; her kiss was frantic and desperate. He was laughing and crying all at the same time. "We have to run," she told him. "The Mutata . . ."

"They're nothing," he whispered in her ear, hugging her fiercely. "Nothing at all. Haven't you figured it out yet, Jen?"

She could still hear them, though. The sound was close on them, their trumpeting shouts shivering the leaves. "Aaron, we have to run!" she insisted, breaking away from his grasp and pulling at his arms. "Please—"

"No, Jen."

"Aaron! Hurry. Can't you hear them?"

He shook his head, looking puzzled. "I don't hear a thing."

Branches cracked like dry fire, the duckbills blared their anger. She could see them now, shapes materializing like dark ghosts from the shade of the trees. Aaron didn't react, didn't seem to notice them at all.

"Aaron—"

He shrugged away from her. At the same moment, Struth rushed screaming from behind, her spear upraised and pointed at Aaron's back.

She cast the weapon like a big-league pitcher. Jenny screamed, seeing that the blow would not miss, could not miss. The weapon seemed to move in aching slow motion, yet

Aaron still didn't react; though Jennifer was leaping toward Aaron at the same time, the air had turned to thick molasses around her. She could see that bone-white needlepoint tip spiraling as it arced closer to Aaron, destined to slither its deadly length into Aaron's body. . . .

Jennifer sat up gasping. The echo of her scream still seemed to ring in her ears. Her breath was fast, shallow, and loud in the quiet night, and she could smell the musty rankness of the blankets across her lap.

"Aaron . . ." she whispered, but he was gone with the rest of the dream. She realized that she must have cried out. Across the enclosure, the guard lizard was looking at her.

So was Eckels.

His eyes were open, staring at her from his bedding across the enclosure. Near him, Peter was snoring.

"Bad dream, Jenny?" he said in his thick accent, so much like Travis's.

She pulled the furs up around her shoulders and tried to slow her breath. She didn't like him looking at her, didn't like his sympathetic smile or the way he called her Jenny as Peter did or the fact that his words sent the dream memory of Aaron to bitter dust.

"Yeah," she said, because she had to. "I guess." She lay back down, pulling the furs over her and turning her back to him, hoping that he'd leave her alone.

"Want to talk about it?"

"Not really."

She heard him starting to get up, and she turned around quickly. Her glare made him stop. "Hey," he said. "I just thought you might like—"

"Don't think. Just stay where you are, Eckels."

"You don't like me much at all."

"That's very perceptive of you. I'll bet you have a degree in psychology."

"I'm sorry you feel that way. I'm also sorry that you're stuck here and that you seem to blame me for it. I wish I could change things. I *will* make a change if I get a chance. I want to get out of here as much as you do. Why don't you let me help you?"

"I don't want your help, Eckels."

He didn't answer. Instead, he threw aside the furs covering him and stood up. Moonlight threw a soft cloak of light over his form. He took a step toward her.

"Eckels—"

"Peter's right there asleep, Jenny." Another step.

"I don't care."

"I'm not going to hurt you, Jenny."

"I told you—"

Step. "I'm not going to touch you."

"Damn it, Eckels—"

Another. "You can always yell for Peter, can't you, Jenny? What's the problem?" Eckels took advantage of her confusion to cover the rest of the distance between them. He sat cross-legged on the ground too close to her. "We might as well try to be friends, Jenny. How about it?"

She couldn't see his face. He was a darkness against the backdrop of moon and stars.

"I don't want to be your friend, Eckels. I don't want to know you at all."

He laughed softly at that, a quick, surprisingly deep chuckle. She could see his eyes, a liquid sparkle in the inky well of his face. "You're not in much position to have a choice."

Jennifer didn't like his tone or the superior amusement in his voice. "What do you mean by that?"

"Oh, just that I've been talking with Peter while your dinosaur friend's been teaching you how make her kind of noises, and I know that you and Peter aren't exactly real close anymore. You hurt him with Aaron. You hurt him a lot. He still has a big load of anger toward you because of that."

"That's none of your business, Eckels."

"Maybe not. I'm just mentioning these things, you understand. And then, *everything's* my business as long as we're stuck here together. We can't get away from each other, Jenny." He paused. She could hear him take a long breath. "We need each other, too. You two know where that vital little piece of road is that can get us back to your time; *I* know these dinos and how to deal with them." He aimed an imaginary gun at the guard lizard and curled his index finger. He quietly mimicked the sound of a gunshot.

Jennifer went cold with the sound. "Eckels,

they're intelligent beings. What we need to do is learn how to communicate with them.''

"That's your opinion. It's not mine. What we need to do is get out of here any way we can. As for as the dinos, if they get in my way, I'm not going to cry about what I have to do to them.''

"Is that the way you deal with everything?''

"Not quite *everything*," he said with an odd inflection that she didn't understand. He leaned forward quickly. His hand brushed her cheek, his fingertips brushing the skin lightly and then withdrawing before she could move or react. "Not everything," he repeated. He rose to his feet, looking down at her, and began to walk away.

"Eckels.''

He turned, a shadow in the night.

"Don't ever touch me again. Never. Or—'' She stopped, not knowing what she was going to say. She wondered what she'd do if he called her bluff.

But he said nothing at all.

He didn't need to.

It was a long, long time before she could find sleep again.

THE RITES OF DEATH

The next few days were more horrible than anything Jennifer could imagine. She felt constantly filthy. Struth had brought in very little water for the three of them.

She also decided that there was nothing to like about Eckels. She didn't like the eye contact that he always seemed to make if she glanced in his direction, didn't like his smiling, smug friendliness or the way he acted as if they shared some hidden secret. She didn't like the closeness into which they'd been thrust. She especially didn't like the way Eckels seemed to quickly gain Peter's trust. Worse, there wasn't any way to discuss her feelings without Eckels overhearing the conversation.

"Peter, I just don't know about him," she said on the third evening after Eckels's capture, trying to whisper. Eckels was at the edge of the enclosure, staring outward at the village while the guard lizard padded back and forth between them. Eckels could hardly avoid noticing the two of them talking, but he gave no outward indication that he was listening or was interested in the conversation.

"He's okay, Jenny. Really. Hey, I'll take him over Travis. I didn't like the looks of that guy."

"Peter, Eckels hit you in the cave, remember?" Jennifer tried to keep the exasperation from her voice. "He tied us both up."

"So he was a little paranoid. Wouldn't you be if you were in the same situation? Let's say you're all alone in your house and some stranger barges right in without knocking. Would you have just said 'Hey, how ya doin'? Can I get you something to drink, maybe?'"

"Peter—"

"Well, you wouldn't, would you? So don't go blaming Eckels for doing what you would have done in his place. He's okay, Jenny. In fact, I think he kinda likes you."

"Peter, I . . ." Jennifer stopped. The words were there, but she couldn't say them: *He looks at me like I'm his property. I don't want him to like me. He scares me.*

"What?" Peter said. "What's the problem?"

If he'd said it some other way, if Peter had sounded halfway sympathetic or if the irritation he was feeling wasn't so obvious from the squint in his eyes and the tight-pressed whiteness of his lips, she might have said something, might have confided in him. But she knew there wasn't much sympathy there. *What's the matter, Jenny?* he'd say, his voice overinflected with sarcasm, emphasizing the words far too much. *Is it* Aaron? *You too much in* love?

"Forget it, Peter. Forget I said anything. I'm just . . . I don't know. Just forget it."

Peter shrugged. That was worse than anything he could have said. "Look, Jenny, Eckels has a plan for getting us out of here."

"What? What plan?"

Peter just grinned at her, infuriatingly.

"You'll see," he said. "You'll see."

Jennifer stayed close to Peter as Struth escorted them into the building—not that she had any choice. The rough fiber of the hobble scraped her ankles, the bindings tied to the loops around Peter's legs. Her heart was fluttering like a frightened bird against the cage of her chest.

Struth and two other dinosaurs had come into the enclosure this morning, their fourth day now in this world. One had prodded Eckels away from Peter and Jenny with his spear while the two teenagers' legs had been tied, then Struth had herded them from the enclosure. Eckels had been left behind.

Jennifer's first thought was that any plans to get out of here didn't matter anymore. She wondered just how long she still had.

Neither of them had said anything. Neither of them wanted to voice what they were thinking. Jennifer had asked Struth (in her halting, baby-talk Mutata) what was going on, where they were going, what they might expect, but Struth had only answered "Ghe odo."

Cannot.

She would say nothing else.

"Pete—" Jenny whispered as they passed the high archway leading into the building, but Struth tapped her shoulder with the butt end of her spear and glared at her hard and unblinkingly.

Jenny shut up.

They moved from sunlight to gloom. In the false twilight of the building, there were distant, echoing voices—a massed chorus singing in long, low tones like a hundred bassoons, a thousand cellos. The sound was primeval, ancient; it throbbed in Jenny's blood, awakening ancient, unknown resonances deep within her. Shivering dissonant tones pulsed and vibrated in the bass voice; a multivoiced baritone chant flowed in and around that foundation, weaving and crisscrossing. The composition was a dozen Gregorian chants performed by giants and played back simultaneously on an agonizingly slow tape recorder. Always quick at languages, Jenny had learned a substantial vocabulary from Struth, but if there were words in this slow, mournful song, they were lost in the droning.

Her eyes adjusted quickly to the dim light, which was fortunate since the floor of the building was not at all level. The interior was one large open area with strange dips and hills and ledges and arches set at random intervals. The conical walls came together far above, though the very summit opened like the mouth of a volcano, admitting a bright shaft of dusty sunlight that shimmered against the sand-colored walls and splashed diffuse light around the room. Here and there, rocks were set in the material of the wall—chunks of mica gleaming darkly, small forests of quartz crystals, flickering knobs of schist and granite. Jennifer might have been walking through the middle of a huge geode.

Struth led them through the twisting interior landscape and into a dark tunnel that connected to another dome. The droning, eerie song reverberated strongly here, louder and more insistent. The deep tones vibrated in the very walls; Jennifer could feel it through her fingertips as she groped her way along the curving tunnel, trying not to fall.

Light blossomed ahead; the song became louder and more insistent. Struth prodded them from behind, hurrying them until the hobbles yanked at their legs. They walked out into a blaze of light, a fury of sound, and the overpowering scent of a charnel house.

Jennifer tried hard to breathe through her mouth.

They entered another huge room. The walls curved up and in, ending abruptly thirty feet or so above the ground level, as if they stood inside a large crater, the edges of which were in shadow but whose center stood in brilliant sunlight. In that natural spotlight was a circular platform rising half as high as the walls and flanked by earthen ramps at the compass points. A dinosaur's body lay atop the platform. Scattered haphazardly around the base of the platform were bones glaring white in the unrelenting sun: dinosaur skulls leering toothily, leg bones sprawled helplessly, great barred cages of ribs, arm and hand and finger bones strewn like confetti. The skulls and skeletons all looked like those of Struth's kind, as far as Jennifer could tell. The bones were all picked clean of flesh, but the stench of them had remained.

Along the roof, birdlike carrion eaters perched, their black feathers like bedraggled formal clothing, waiting.

All about the room—on ledges, on great boulders thrusting up from the earth, on the ramps leading up to the platform—the dinosaurs had gathered, their heads raised to the sky. From their long snouts issued that uncanny singing: throbbing, mournful notes that could only speak sorrow. Struth, alongside them, had stopped. She too lifted her head to join the dirge with a wail like a fog horn pulsing in the night.

Jenny huddled alongside Peter. The feel of him was comforting. His voice husked in her ear. "We'll be okay, Jenny. Really."

He sounded as if he were trying to reassure himself more than her.

One of the dinosaurs moved from the ramp toward the tunnel opening where they stood. This one wore a wrapping of lustrous azure feathers attached to a papery cloth around his shoulder, and he carried a short, dull bar of metal as if it were a sign of office. He approached Struth. His glance made Jenny shiver; it was malevolent and cold and angry.

Struth had gone silent, raising her head so that her snout pointed to the roof. The other dinosaur seemed to regard Struth's long, taut neck with amusement, his long fingers twitching around the metal bar. For a second, Jenny thought he might swing at Struth. She could well imagine that a blow to the throat from the bar would collapse the windpipe and kill Struth. But the dinosaur only grunted; Struth lowered her head. They locked gazes, then Struth's bright stare dropped.

They conversed briefly in low tones. Jenny could hear them through the continuing drone from the other dinosaurs, but even though Struth had been diligently teaching her Mutata (while showing absolutely no interest in learning Jennifer's language), they were speaking too fast for her to understand anything of it. Once she heard Struth's name and—several times—her own. In the midst of their conversation, the male pointed significantly to the body on the platform.

"This one's definitely Struth's boss," Peter whispered to Jenny. "I don't like him, either."

"Neither do I," Jenny admitted. "What I'm wondering is why they dragged us here."

"Yeah. I really *hate* funerals."

Struth came back to them and nodded toward the male. "SStragh," she said, pointing at her own chest. Then: "Jhenini"—pointing at Jennifer. "Frraghi," she said finally, nodding in the direction of the caped male, the two syllables linked by a nasal snort.

A name, then. Jennifer tried to imitate the sound. It came out more like "Fergie," but the male seemed to understand. With a sighing rustle, Fergie turned to them. His coppery, vertical-slit eyes regarded Jenny, ignoring Peter. She stared back, and the male uttered a rumbling hiss that sounded angry. Jenny remembered Struth's initial behavior.

"I'm not supposed to look at you yet, am I, Fergie?" she said. "You great ugly thing." She slowly lifted her chin. With her throat bared, the significance of the gesture was immediately apparent to Jenny. She felt exposed and very vulnerable. This creature could kill her instantly if he chose.

But he didn't.

Fergie sniffed and said something. "Jhenini," Struth snorted beside her. Jenny lowered her chin. When she could catch Fergie's gaze, she did so, holding it for a long, challenging second before dropping her eyes downward. "There," she said. "Peter, did you catch the routine?"

"Yeah," he said sullenly, "but *I'm* not about to act like a slave. I'm not going to do it."

"Peter, don't be stupid." That was exactly the wrong thing to say. Jennifer knew it the moment the words came out. She tried to soften the rebuke. "Please. They have different customs."

"Then let them learn ours," he said stubbornly.

Jenny started to argue with him, but then Struth gave her the *harrumph* that she'd learned was a warning. Jennifer watched as Fergie moved over to Peter. Their gazes locked in defiance before the male gave a disgusted trill and spoke again to Struth. They both then endured Fergie's rough touch as he plucked at their clothing and examined their hands and faces. Finally, he grunted a long sentence to Struth in which Jennifer caught the phrase "clever animal"; he motioned imperiously and walked away. Struth herded them along in his wake until they stood blinking on the platform itself.

Here, the dinosaurs' song found a locus, the shape of the building acting like an acoustic dish to funnel the sound to them. The voices were incredibly loud; they dinned in Jennifer's ears, hammered at her body, vibrated through the very soles of her feet. Jennifer was untied from Peter, her hobbles cut so that she could move her feet freely. Peter was escorted to the edge of the platform, another dinosaur set to guard him; Jennifer was ushered inward, toward the body.

Up close, the corpse stank worse than she could have imagined. The body was frozen in a contorted position, the mouth open and the eyes staring blindly upward. Whoever it was, its death looked as if it had been a painful one.

For good reason. With a start, Jennifer realized that the creature had been shot. Nothing else could have ripped a hole through the crude metal chest-covering or ripped out the gaping hole beneath.

Eckels. It had to be Eckels who'd shot it. Struth's

people don't have the technology. Is that why we're here—because this was done by a human?

Fueled by that realization, her imagination conjured up several reasons why the dinosaurs might want her and Peter here, in what was obviously a memorial service to their slain companion. None of those scenarios was pleasant to contemplate. The fear choked her, squeezing the air from her lungs until she gasped.

Another dinosaur awaited them on the platform. This one was old and wore no ornaments at all. Folds of skin hung from his emaciated frame like a father's clothes hanging from a child's body; his right eye was the blue of the sky but the other was gone, only the cratered of the socket remaining. The ear tympani on his left side was scarred and useless, the tooth ridges in the open mouth were missing in places. His breath sounded like that of an asthmatic dragon.

Yet both Struth and Fergie exposed their neck to the old one, and she noticed that they did not look directly at him. So this was the one Struth called the OColi, she decided. The Eldest and leader.

She dropped her own gaze then, and lifted her chin as well. As she lowered her head again, Fergie bent down close to the old one's mouth. The OColi husked and snorted faint words to the younger male. Jennifer could feel the old one's gaze on her, but she kept her own eyes lowered as the chant buffeted her, as the oppressive sun beat down, as the stench of the body filled her nostrils.

Fergie straightened, lifted his snout, and trilled a high note that floated above the low rumble of the singing. Struth and Fergie stepped away, leaving her briefly alone with the old one. Another dinosaur approached quickly, bearing a shallow bowl. The jade green, slick glaze shimmered with the reflection of the knife laid across its rim. The sight of the dull, sharpened metal made Jennifer's blood pound in her temples in counterpoint to the rhythm of the chanting. She wanted to bolt, wanted to run blindly away since Struth's cutting of the hobble had allowed her that freedom, but the blade mesmerized her.

"Jennifer," Peter called from behind. "Go on! Run!"

She didn't. Somehow she stood there, feeling her entire body tremble as the knife came nearer, as she felt the dinosaur's hot breath on her, as he placed bowl and knife at her feet and backed away.

The song of the dinosaurs ended, as if severed.

The shock of silence nearly staggered Jennifer. Her ears still roared with remembered sound. Disoriented, she looked from the knife and bowl to the dim, multitiered room. The dinosaurs sat like statues, motionless except for a slow blink or a twitching of the hands. Jennifer realized that she was holding her breath; her inhalation seemed impossibly loud.

So did Peter's whisper from the edge of the platform. "Jennifer—"

"Be quiet," she whispered back. Then, more softly: "Please, Peter." Hair whipped her shoulders as she glanced back at him. Flanked by Struth and Fergie, he was tensed, ready to lash out at anything that seemed a threat.

They were waiting. Jennifer was certain of it. This was some ritual, a death rite, and they were testing her. The old one especially was watching and evaluating. Jennifer looked back at Struth, but she refused to meet her eyes. Still . . .

Was she looking at the bowl more than she needs to?

Confused, Jennifer turned desperately in the middle of the platform. Fergie was hissing like an old steam kettle beside Peter, and his spear was clutched tight in his hands. Nothing there but malevolence.

From above, a carrion creature shrilled. Jennifer glanced up at the open circle above her. Several more of the beasts had gathered, looking like sullen, scaled vultures. They milled and fought among each other, but none descended into the room itself. Like the dinosaurs, they too seemed to be waiting.

Waiting for what?

Jennifer looked at the bowl again. It was empty, though below the knife blade, at the very bottom of the bowl, there were flecks of brownish red.

Blood. Old blood.

Jennifer dared a glance at the OColi. He was staring placidly at her. She dropped her gaze quickly down again.

Blood and a knife, and bones all tumbled down around the base of this pedestal. Were they planning to kill her? Why the silence and waiting? Did they want her to kill herself? That was certainly possible. She'd studied Japanese culture; seppuku, a ritualistic and honorable suicide, was part of their cultural heritage. The body beside her had been killed by a human, possibly Eckels. Was that it? Had they been brought here to atone for this death? Was she to be a sacrifice?

Jenny stooped to touch the knife. A collective sigh came from the dinosaurs watching. The carrion eaters on the roof cawed hoarsely and ruffled ragged tuxedo feathers. Peter uttered a quick "No!", only to have Fergie place the point of his spear at Peter's chest as he tried to leap forward toward Jennifer.

Jennifer picked up the knife in one hand, the bowl in the other. Yes, it had to be blood trapped in the cracked glaze. But still—why? What was expected here?

She glanced again at the figure of the old OColi, not daring to raise her gaze to his own this time, but simply ranging over his sagging body for a clue. Above, the vulturelike watchers were squabbling again.

Blood. Bowl. Bones.

She had it, suddenly—at least she hoped so. Jennifer set the bowl down once again. Taking the knife and holding her breath, she placed the tip of the weapon against the inside of her elbow. She was trembling, the sharp point dimpling the skin without breaking it. Jennifer closed her eyes—*just do it, girl!*—and with one gasping, choking cry, sliced her arm.

For a second, the short, ugly wound gaped white, then a bright, thick stream of brilliant red began rolling down its length. Jennifer choked back a cry at the pain. The dais did an impossible lumbering dance around her, and the world went hazy and dark. She forced herself back.

No! You can't faint. Not now. No matter how much it hurts.

Jennifer inhaled deeply through her nose, her eyes closed, then held her dripping, gory arm over the bowl. Warm scarlet rained from the thundercloud of her fingers, pattering into a deepening puddle in the bowl.

As the bowl slowly filled, she dared to look around. They were all watching her. The intensity of their stares told her that—so far—she had passed the test. Peter's face had gone white, whether from anger or shock, Jennifer couldn't tell. Fergie's spear had dropped to his side, unnoticed. Struth was watching, her mouth open. The OColi was making a sound almost like humming, as if singing to himself.

The bowl was nearly half full. Jennifer knew that she couldn't afford to lose any more blood, not if she intended to walk away from here. She used the knife to cut away the bottom of her T-shirt, then wrapped the cloth tightly above the wound, knotting it savagely with her teeth and good hand. She wrapped another piece around the wound. The blood soaked the cloth, and she knew that she would need to watch the cut for infection, but the flow ceased.

Now what? she wondered. None of the dinosaurs had moved, though the carrion eaters were cawing and screeching excitedly, their bulbous eyes fixed on her. Jennifer stooped to pick up the bowl. Her left hand was trembling and she couldn't quite seem to force the fingers to grasp well. The bowl's contents sloshed turgidly. Hoping that she had guessed correctly, she took the bowl and upended it over the stiff body of the dinosaur.

It was either the stupidest or the bravest thing Jennifer had ever done—she wasn't quite sure which.

Jennifer waited for death. She waited for the cold feel of the spear in her back. She waited for the howl of outrage from the assembled dinosaurs as they rushed forward to take revenge on the blasphemer.

None of it happened.

Instead, the OColi's humming turned louder, recapturing the sound of the previous chant. One by one, the others joined in, even Struth, and finally Fergie. The carrion eaters descended from the roof in a shrieking black cloud, set their claws in the newly blooded flesh, and began to feed. As the dinosaurs crooned their lament, hooked and savage beaks tore deep into the body, ripping out strips of gray meat. The smell of corruption intensified.

Already weak from the loss of blood, shock, and three days of nothing but fruit to eat, Jennifer suddenly found herself sitting on the platform. She struggled to her feet as Peter half ran, half shuffled to her. She leaned against him, and then pushed away as he started to guide her from the platform. "Just a minute," she said.

Facing the old one, Jennifer bared her throat for him. The one-eyed, ancient OColi husked three slow words: "Ghreyi thyasiisey Oyid."

Jennifer had no idea what he had said. She risked lowering her head, looking at the old one for just an instant as she did so. His head was cocked at her appraisingly. They held eye contact for a moment, his eye glaring, then Jennifer ducked her head and backed away with Peter's help.

No one stopped them.

Bone was beginning to show through the dead dinosaur's flesh as Struth escorted them from the platform, as the dinosaurs sang, as Fergie glared in obvious irritation. Jennifer gave him a gaze of defiance in return, shook away Peter's helping arm, and walked ahead of Struth out of the chamber.

She managed to stay on her feet until they stepped outside.

THE BEAST OF THE AIR

A wild dervish tornado spun madly over the rocks where the time machine had been, a wind devil cloaked in dust and twigs. The apparition danced and swayed like a live thing, bending and twisting and leaping, carrying its load of debris eight feet or more in the air. The creature should have been attached to a low roof of black clouds, a storm flail sent down from an Illinois thunderhead to punish the earth, but it existed alone and unchained under a cloudless, frigid sky. There should have been sound, some frantic, breathy howling, but there wasn't. Aaron felt nothing but a slight breeze from his vantage point. The small cyclone had come from nowhere; it was as if the time machine itself had undergone some odd metamorphosis, shedding its cocoon of steel to become a beast of air.

Travis was half running, half limping toward it, shielding his eyes with his hands.

What Aaron saw then was, flatly, impossible.

The whirlwind seemed to lean down and pluck the rifle from Travis's hands. The weapon was caught up in an arm of wind that protruded from the main body and moved with it, around and around. As Travis approached, the twister swooped down toward him. The rifle cut like a staff behind Travis's knees, taking his legs out from under him and upending him. The barrel broke away from the stock with a sound like a length of bamboo being snapped, both ends pinwheeling into the distance as Travis crumpled with a groan.

The whirlwind swayed at Travis's feet, its long funnel seeming to regard the man as Aaron watched, helpless. Then it began its sinuous ballet once more, this time dancing toward Aaron. The tornado did impossible Nureyev leaps from rock to rock up the steep slope toward him.

Aaron was certain of one thing. Whatever it was, it was moving with definite intent. Unfortunately, the thing was far faster than he was, and there was no place to retreat unless Aaron wanted to jump from the high cliff at his back.

Feeling very foolish, Aaron picked up a fist-sized rock, ready to throw it. He cocked his arm back.

The whirlwind hurdled a boulder and halted, swaying as if to some unheard music, a few yards away from Aaron. Tendrils of wind stroked Aaron's face and ruffled his hair. He could hear the sound of it now, a soughing wind chorus that rose and fell in no pattern he could detect.

"Aaron!" Travis cried downslope.

"You okay?" Aaron didn't dare look at Travis; he watched the dervish in front of him.

"Yeah. Watch it. That thing . . ." A pause; from the edge of his vision, Aaron saw the man struggling to his feet. "That thing *hit* me."

"I know. I—"

The whirlwind lurched into motion. It darted forward, and Aaron—more from reflex than anything else—heaved the rock at the same time. The rock struck the swirling mass, bobbed within it for a moment like an apple in a tub of water. A burst of angry wind erupted, hurling the rock back at him. Aaron ducked; the chunk of granite grazed the top of his shoulder and went clattering over the cliff edge.

The whirlwind swayed forward. Aaron could feel the harsh, gritty touch sandpapering his cheeks. He squinted, trying to keep his vision clear. The funnel was directly in front of him now, backing him up until one more step would take him over the precipice.

It stopped. The wind chorus moaned with its hundred voices, the fingers of air caressed him. Aaron only had two options open to him: run directly through the thing or stand there. So he stood—as it dipped and bowed before him, as an arm defined by twigs and dust emerged from the main funnel to encircle him.

A presence touched his mind.

That was more frightening than the physical threat. The intrusion lasted only a few moments, but in those brief seconds, Aaron's thoughts were opened like a book and examined. Unbidden, his own memories went racing past, like someone flipping through a mental photo album at an impossible pace.

Worse, the intruder was as open to Aaron as

he seemed to be to it, and the creature rummaging through the attic of his memories was entirely alien. Aaron found himself utterly lost within it. Vast, cold, an impossibly immense matrix of which the whirlwind was only the slightest extension: there was no comprehending the being. The presence didn't have language or a fixed locus of self or even a great deal of intelligence—it was a mixture of emotions and inborne reflexes. Curious, it snatched at Aaron's self, stole it all, and retreated.

Aaron gasped. The whirlwind had moved a few yards back. Inside it, the debris was coalescing, forming a shape: a mouth. The lips moved; air pushed past dirt larynx and twig tongue. The word was breathy but recognizable.

"Aaron . . ."

"Who . . . who are you?"

The mouth dissolved as if struck by a hammer, then the pieces flowed back together again in the midst of the storm. "Who?" it moaned. "Name name name name . . . Words are so fragile and useless. . . . You have so many of them. . . . I *am*, that's all. No name. No name for me. Not an us. Not a them. Not an it or he or she."

The mouth was swept away again, and the whirlwind leaned. A new mouth appeared at the summit of the thing. "You . . . fear me? Yes, fear. That is word. This shape not pleasant to you. I will change."

The mouth shattered, the whirlwind collapsed into a zephyr and was gone. Where it had been rooted to earth, suddenly rocks and stones exploded upward. Aaron cried out, raising his hands to protect himself. Further down the slope, Travis yelled as well. Chips and fragments of stone pelted Aaron as he hunched into a ball. When the hard rain ended, he glanced up cautiously. Travis was staring as well.

Where the whirlwind had been, there now stood a woman.

"Hi, Aaron," she said. "Call me Jennifer."

Everything was *almost* right: her soft, long hair; the brilliant, laughing eyes; the husky contralto voice; the way she put one arm on her hip and smiled at him, the tanned, muscular legs and long-fingered hands. Aaron hurt, looking at her. Jennifer stood there as if she belonged under that alien sun, in front of that surreal landscape.

"Stop it!" Aaron said angrily. "You're not Jen. You're just a thing."

"You fear this too?" it said. "I'm sorry, Aaron. . . ." The voice was perfect, an exact imitation of Jenny's. It sounded sad and almost wistful, and it tore great wounds in his soul. Jen—no, *not* Jen—shrugged and her features started to run like a wax figure in a fire. "No—" Aaron started to cry, then stopped himself.

It's not Jenny. Be cool. It's okay.

Travis had struggled back to where Aaron stood transfixed. They watched the thing carefully as Travis limped past it to stand next to Aaron. The fluid body solidified once again. It was an old man this time. With a start, Aaron recognized it: the wizard from the cover of a fantasy book he'd read earlier that summer. Caleb Mundo, the character's name had been. There was something else, too, and he suddenly realized that the face was a clever amalgam of the book cover's wizard and Grandpa Carl.

"This is the way you saw me," the figure said. "This was in your head. Does this please you better? Call me . . . Mundo. Yes. Mundo would be good."

"Where's our machine, Mundo?" Travis asked.

Mundo seemed to contemplate that question for a moment. "It's where it should be," he said at last.

"That's not much of an answer."

"It's all I'm prepared to give at the moment," Mundo replied, and smiled. It was an eerie gesture. It seemed to affect no other part of his face, which remained slack and expressionless, like that of a marionette.

"Stop that," Aaron said.

"Stop what?"

"That smile—that's Grandpa Carl's smile. You stole it."

"You like that smile," Mundo said. "That's why I used it. I thought . . . I thought you'd like it." Mundo sounded disappointed—like a child, Aaron thought. Like a four year old who doesn't quite understand how to talk to an adult.

"Well, it doesn't. It makes you look like a ghoul."

"Ghoul?" Mundo's huge white eyebrows furrowed in bewilderment for a moment, then relaxed again. Like the smile, it was a puppet's movement, touching only that one part of his face. The eyebrows looked like a pair of dove's wings glued to a blank forehead. "Ahh, a ghoul," he said. "Oh, that's not very flattering, is it? You really shouldn't insult me."

"I don't even know who or what you are," Aaron replied heatedly. "You stole our vehicle, you attacked Travis and me, and you stole your shape and language from my mind. Well, *use* what you took from me—how would you expect me to react?"

Mundo laughed. "You are such trivial things," he said. "I, me, us—all these words just for you, as if you were all there was."

"So who or what are you?" Aaron insisted.

"I . . . am," Mundo said. Confusion blurred his words, as if he were searching for the right description but couldn't find it. "I don't have the strong sense of identity that's in your mind, Aaron. That concept wouldn't make sense for me. In fact, I wonder . . ."

Mundo raised his hand. A flickering blue phosphorescence enveloped Travis's head, shimmering there for a few seconds like an aurora. As Travis stepped back with a cry, the light faded. Mundo nodded. "Yes, you are the same, Travis. Isolated, alone, only here."

"Only here?" Travis repeated. "Where the

heck are *you* if you aren't here?"

Mundo smiled again, that childish, dead smile. His mouth no longer looked like Grandpa Carl's, Aaron saw. The lips were fuller and longer, almost feminine. Aaron wondered whose they were—they too seemed familiar.

"Let me try to tell you," he said. Mundo pointed to the distant mountains. "You see, I'm here talking with you. I am also there, where two . . . well, I don't use names for them and you don't possess the words, though I suppose you might call them scavengers . . . are feasting on carrion. I'm in the great sea, where creatures larger than your whales are swimming in the depths. I'm wandering in the darkness below the ground, sensing the world only through sound and feel and pressure. There's only a small, small part of me here, speaking these strange symbols which seem to be more real to you than the world itself."

Aaron looked at Travis, who shrugged.

"Why did you take our vehicle?" Aaron asked. "We hadn't harmed you."

"You don't understand, do you? Can't you imagine how I felt when I realized you were here? You—or, rather, the thing you call a 'machine'—moved and made noises and touched me just as if it were a living thing, but yet . . . I couldn't *feel* it. I couldn't see through its eyes. Then you emerged, like chicks from the shell. But you were dead and silent too, just like that 'machine' that I thought was your parent. You were . . ."

Mundo paused, and that smile hovered on his face, alien and out of place. Dove-wing eyebrows fluttered dust. "The word you would use is 'new,' I think." His voice went back to a childish singsong prattle again. "I have never experienced 'new.' I don't think I enjoy it."

"Nothing is ever new to you?" Travis asked. "What are you?"

"I'm—" Mundo's head tilted like a marionette's "—all," he said finally. "All. I told you that once already."

"Look, you had to come from somewhere. You haven't been here forever, *can't* have been here forever."

"I awoke, once," Mundo admitted. "There were centuries of slumbering where odd dreams stirred me, decades of slow awareness while glaciers drew cold white blankets over my rest, untold years while the jagged teeth of birthing mountains pierced the sky and then were worn down again to pebbles by persistent rains. I saw through a million sets of eyes at once, I birthed and hatched and lived and loved and died a thousand times in every second, experiencing it all and remembering how it felt. But—" smiling—"There was never anything here that wasn't me. There never had been, not in all the endless cycles of the seasons."

"Until us?"

"Yes. I touched the machine first, because it was the largest of the three of you and because you two had come from within it. I found nothing there: no mind, no feelings. It was simply made of earth things, so I placed **it** where things of the earth should be. And then I came to investigate you. Now I've found that you think and feel, but you think and feel *apart* from each other. You see, but I can't see with you. You touch, but can't share the sensation. You think with words that mean far too many things and yet are paltry vehicles for what you're trying to say."

"Then try to understand this," Travis said. "We came here"—he glanced at Aaron—"to see this time and place for just a moment. We never intended to stay or to bother you, Mundo. Why don't you just let us go? Give us back the machine."

"No," Mundo said. "I can't let you leave."

"Why not, Mundo?" Aaron pleaded. "You've already said that we don't belong here. Give us back our machine and we're gone. You'll never see us again."

"I can't do that because I've looked into your minds. I've seen much there that I don't understand, but I've also seen your memories, both of yours."

Mundo paused and blinked. The eyes narrowed with inner puzzlement but the furrows in the brow didn't deepen. "There is nothing of me in your minds." A strange sadness welled in that voice now. "I am not there."

"Mundo," Aaron began, but the being sliced off the plea with a wave of his hand.

"It's tiring for me to hold this form," Mundo said. "It feels wrong." With that, the smile collapsed as if the puppet master had cut all the strings. His clothes grew great moth holes of decay and fell away like funeral shrouds. Eyebrows fluttered down from their perch. Flesh dried and cracked like old papyrus, peeling away in fragile tissue paper strips, crackling like dry fire. Muscles shriveled, tendons loosed their tenacious grip, bones clicked like old ivory dice and clattered to the icy ground, becoming a white flour that the rising wind scattered with a breath.

Mundo was gone.

The world seemed to laugh at them.

It was suddenly very, very cold.

OFFERINGS

The jhiehai were still gathered around Caasrt's corpse, though the ceremony of the Giving had ended long ago. The OColi was still watching the slow consumption of the flesh when Caasrt's OTsio, last of all, left. Such attention on the part of the OColi was unusual and some of the departing Mutata speculated why the OColi would so honor Caasrt. Many of the jhiehai, fat and sated, had gone back to the roof, where they sat and preened their hairy feathers. There was no one in the Giving Hall when SStragh arrived except for the OColi and Frraghi.

Both ignored SStragh as she approached. SStragh performed her polite submission and then watched the jhiehai for a time with them, remembering Caasrt as he had been when alive as she prayed to the All-Ancestor to send him back soon in another form. The sun was nearly down and the Giving Hall was entirely in shadow, the white bones seeming to glow in the twilight. SStragh was struck by weariness in the dim light; she wanted nothing more than to lie down herself in her own room, but the OColi had summoned her and she couldn't leave until dismissed.

SStragh inhaled deeply and moved onto the platform. The three stood there in silence for many breaths. Finally, the OColi leaned toward Frraghi and spoke.

"The OColi says that your Jhenini surprised and pleased him," Frraghi said, though there was no pleasure in *his* voice. "I suppose you are going to say that you expected her to behave so well."

"No." SStragh could not lie. No Mutata ever lied to the OColi—that was not part of the Path. The OColi must always know the truth, or else he or she could not keep the Mutata on the OColihi. But then there *were* times when it was safer to answer only the question asked, no more and no less. SStragh knew this was one of those times, but she spoke her feelings anyway.

"I was as surprised as the OColi. I thought that this test was unfair and prejudicial. I expected that Jhenini would fail. Instead, she demonstrated that she's even more intelligent than any of us knew. Ekils, Jhenini, and Peitah are not simply animals, OColi, Speaker. No matter what you would like to believe."

"Be quiet, SStragh," Frraghi bellowed.

"They came from the floating stones," SStragh persisted. "They can tell us more about them, maybe show us how to get rid of them forever. Don't you understand? By insisting on following the OColihi, you'll destroy the ancient Path entirely."

Frraghi hissed in displeasure at that, drawing

back and raising his crest in irritation, displaying his claws in an open show of anger. The OColi snorted and glared sidewise at SStragh. With the sudden motion of the two, the jhiehai fussed and made leaping hops away from the corpse before settling down again to feed. SStragh took that as a bad omen.

"You will be silent!" Frraghi roared. The Speaker's Rod was trembling in his hand and SStragh knew that the desire to use it as a weapon burned in Frraghi's chest. "We have had enough of your disrespect, your prattling about Raajek's new path, your interference with what the OColi would have us do. I tell you now—"

"Frraghi." The OColi husked the word. Frraghi gave a last glare at SStragh and bent down to listen to the old one's words. When Frraghi straightened again, the color of his scales had gone brilliant with fury and his smell was like a Gairk just before it attacked.

"The OColi has given you a small reprieve despite your impertinence," he said. "The OColi wishes to think upon what he has witnessed today. While Caasrt's bones stand, Jhenini and Ekils may live. When the bones fall from the platform to join the others, the OColi will make a decision. You have until then to prove their worth, SStragh. That is the OColi's ruling."

"You mention only Jhenini and Ekils," SStragh said. "What of Peitah?"

Frraghi moved closer, until SStragh had to

step back or have Frraghi collide with her. The nearest jhiehai complained and then moved grudgingly away to pick at the strips of flesh still hanging from Caasrt's bones. "The OColi does not care what happens to the other youngling," Frraghi said. "He did nothing to impress the OColi or me. Jhenini is spared because of what she did here. Ekils is the Eldest, the OColi of the floating stones, so he is spared also. The fate of Peitah is my decision to make. That is what the OColi has said," Frraghi husked out. The smell of challenge was nearly overpowering; SStragh's nostrils flared with it.

"And this is what I say, SStragh. After the last Nesting, your OTsio Raajek made a choice to leave this community because none of us would listen to her. That choice probably saved what little life she has left. There are many of us who would like to see you make that same choice. There are many of us who are tired of hearing Raajek's words still coming from you, and who feel that the floating stones and the plagues that come from them would never have been found unless the All-Ancestor was angry with the Mutata because of Raajek and you. I will tell you the same thing I told Raajek before she left: I am the OColi's Speaker. My duty is to the OColi and OColihi, and I take it very seriously. Be extremely careful, SStragh, because if I find the slightest excuse, I will personally make it my pleasure to see your bones next to Caasrt's on the Giving platform."

SStragh glanced at the OColi. If the Eldest

was paying attention to Frraghi, he gave no indication of it, though he had to have heard. Only his blind eye faced them, and his snout was pointed toward Caasrt and the feeding jhie-hai. He was humming the song of Giving to himself. The significance of that wasn't lost on SStragh.

Alone. She was alone in this. The OColi spared her now only because of what Jhenini had done.

SStragh found herself trembling. She wanted nothing more than to be away from the hall. She forced herself to stare back at Frraghi. "And Peitah? What about the male youngling?"

"Dispose of it. It is an animal and it has no manners. If it weren't already evening I would have you kill it now. Instead, you will bring me its body before the sun sets tomorrow."

SStragh sighed, but there was no bending in Frraghi or the OColi, and nothing SStragh could say to change it. She raised her snout, as formality demanded.

"As you wish," she said.

After the strangeness of the Mutata funeral, Jennifer wanted nothing more than to sleep. After Struth had returned them to the encampment, Peter had made a fire ("Never thought this old Scout stuff would actually come in handy," he'd said as he'd carefully made a pile of tinder around the two sticks) and they'd boiled water in one of the clay pots Struth had given them. Jennifer had carefully cleaned the wound and then rebandaged it. Then, while Peter told Eckels about what had happened, she'd slept.

Struth had awakened her what seemed minutes later. "Go away, Struth," she said, and then noticed that Peter and Eckels were just crawling out from under their blankets.

"You were sleeping so well, I just let you go on," Peter said. "I thought you needed it."

"I guess I did." Her arm throbbed, a reminder of yesterday. Jennifer forced herself to unwrap a little of the bandage and peek underneath. The cut looked angry and red and it hurt to move her arm, but the wound had scabbed over well. *No infection, yet. Just hope it stays that way* . . .

"EHei," Struth trilled. It was a word Jenny recognized. *Out.*

"Aii?" *Now?* Jenny tried to give the word the nasal trill, as well as the falling end tone and glottal click that Struth had told her indicated an interrogative. Jennifer had found Struth an excellent and patient teacher. Both of those were necessities. Jenny was used to languages coming quickly to her, but the Mutata language had been designed for a horned nasal tube and an entirely different larynx. Jennifer struggled with the sounds and concepts, and she knew that to Struth she must have a horrible accent and the worst speech impediment in the world. "Daiisoo," she added. *A few minutes.*

Struth gave the snort that was an affirmative.

"What's going on, kid?" Eckels asked.

"We're going on another field trip," Jennifer told him. "All of us this time, I think. Struth is giving us a few minutes to get ready."

When they'd finished their morning ablutions, Struth hobbled them together—leaving enough slack to walk comfortably though not to run—and led them from the enclosure, taking one of the guardian lizards with them. A half hour's brisk walk brought them to a meadow on the crest of the surrounding hills. There, Struth led Jennifer aside, leaving Eckels and Peter to the care of the vigilant lizard.

Jennifer sat in the field of waist-high, bristly flowering plants, none of which she could recognize. There was no grass at all, though underneath the taller plants, a few cloverlike patches covered the dirt with soft, fragrant nubs. There were flying insects, all larger than Jennifer would have liked them to be. Well away from them, smaller dinosaurs of several species were browsing. None of those wore clothing or carried weapons—Jennifer assumed they were the unintelligent cousins of Struth's people.

For all the strangeness, it was an oddly pastoral scene.

Struth hunkered alongside her, the thick, muscular neck craning from side to side as she watched her charges. She touched Jenny's bandaged arm with soft, almost reverent, fingers.

"Jhenini," she rumbled with her great bass voice. "Werata Oei." Werata was "pain" or "anguish," Jennifer had learned, though it seemed to have several other meanings as well; Oei was a modifier indicating a large amount: *Much pain*.

"Gahedo," she answered with a lifting of her chin. *Yes*. It took both the word and the head movement to indicate the affirmative, as she'd learned in one particularly frustrating session. The way one stood changed the way the words were understood; she knew that. Jennifer also suspected that odor played a part, since Struth's scent changed radically and often while she spoke. The posture Jenny knew she might mimic, however awkwardly, but scent was hopeless. She was never going to speak or understand this language well.

"SStragh Ogharidao reiyi keieso OColi jieei Peitah werada Equee."

That took some time to decipher; she didn't know all the words.

Struth[something]   [something]   ordered by the OColi[something]Peter's death[something].

When a glimmering of what that might mean came to her, Jennifer suddenly gasped, her skin prickling as if the temperature had dropped thirty degrees in an instant. She could hear the blood pounding in her temples. She replayed the words in her mind, hoping that she had misunderstood, that there was some mistake or trick of intonation that had caused her to misinterpret.

"Jhoii," she said. *Again*.

Struth repeated the statement, more slowly this time and using simpler words. Jennifer tried to rearrange them, thinking that maybe the strange Mutata syntax had garbled the meaning, but the basic translation still kept coming out the same.

The OColi has ordered me to kill Peter.

"No," Jennifer protested in English, then went silent as Struth spoke again. From the long torrent of words, most of which she only half understood or didn't understand at all, she tried to grasp as much as she could. It was all a horror: the OColi had ordered Peter's death. Today. Peter was only an animal. Struth intended to fulfill that order now, right here. There was more, something about a god/spirit called the All-Ancestor, and how Jennifer shouldn't worry since this decision didn't affect her.

Without realizing it, Jennifer had risen to her feet. "No!" she said again, her face flushed and hot. "You can't do this. I won't let you." She frantically searched through her pidgin Mutata for words. "Khiisoo yeie," she shouted. *I won't obey.* "Khiisoo yeie!"

"Jenny?" Peter was looking toward her from across the meadow. He was already walking toward them.

"No," she said loudly. "It's okay. Leave us alone, Peter. Please."

He kept coming. "What's going on?"

"Just stay away." She waved him back. Peter glared at her, irritated, and put his hands on his hips. Eckels was shuffling toward them also. "Look, would you both just please leave me alone for a few minutes?"

Peter sniffed. He gave her a look he might have given a child. "C'mon, Eckels," he said. "She wants to play with her pal all alone."

Jennifer closed her mouth to the angry retort she wanted to make. Peter and Eckels, talking together, moved away a few yards.

Struth was watching Jennifer carefully, her huge eyes calm but puzzled. She held her spear carefully in her left hand. As Jenny turned back from Peter, Struth's fingers flexed around the rough shaft. "Jhenini?" she said.

She didn't have the words for her, not in the Mutata language. *What do you want me to say?* she wanted to ask. "Khiisoo yeie," she repeated to Struth. She didn't know how else to say it.

"Khiisoo," Struth said, with a gentle emphasis that could only be a scolding. Struth released another barrage of Mutata as Jennifer struggled to translate and make some sense of what was being said. It was something about duty and obedience, about death being necessary, or did she mean that death was simply a natural process and nothing important? Jennifer shook her head, bewildered and lost.

"Neeeo," she told Struth: *stop.* She wanted to cry and shout to Struth. *Don't you see that I can't sit here and let you do that? Don't you understand that you can't just watch calmly while someone kills your friend? I don't care why you have to do it or who it's supposed to benefit or that death is something we all will experience. I don't care. Could you let Fergie murder your best friend?*

Maybe Struth could, she told herself. Maybe the Mutata were that different. Maybe Struth could even do the deed herself if old One-Eye told her to. Maybe she could live in the same village with Fergie forever afterward and speak politely to him and laugh and joke like nothing had ever happened.

"Jenny," Peter said. He was starting to walk toward them again.

"No, damn it!" she shouted at him. "Just go away, would you? Don't you listen to what I'm telling you?"

"Hey—"

"Go *away*, Peter!"

"This is important."

"So is this."

Peter shook his head at her and shuffled through the high weeds toward Eckels again.

Jennifer was adrift. The gulf in distance and time and culture between this world and her own suddenly seemed very, very wide. She could feel the tears running down her cheeks. Struth had seen them too, for she reached out with her spindly arm and long fingers and gathered a drop of the moisture on her fingertip, gazing at it curiously.

"Khiisoo yeie," Jenny said again. It was the only thing she could say. "I'm sorry, Struth, but it's khiisoo yeie. I can't let Peter be killed, not without trying to stop it. I know you can't understand a word of what I'm saying, but I have to say it. If you attack Peter or Eckels or me, I'm going to fight back. I'm not just going to sit here and watch."

Jhenini was babbling in her own tongue and talking to Peitah. SStragh ignored it, looking instead at the wonderment of the water that ran from Jhenini's eyes. She had never seen an animal that let loose water from that orifice before. SStragh sniffed the droplet on her finger and smelled the faint salt odor of the sea. Very strange.

The youngling's agitation disturbed SStragh. They were all so unpredictable. Did they have no rules in their own culture or did everyone simply do as he pleased? Jhenini had been so smart in the Giving Hall; how could she be so stupid now?

It seemed almost *too* obvious to SStragh. Didn't she see in which hand she was holding the spear while she talked about killing Peitah? Didn't she see the dichotomy contained in that choice and know to look below the surface of SStragh's words?

All this eggling prattling of "obey not" did no good, and made no sense besides. SStragh was using the imperative form of the word. For Jhenini to add the negative was to speak an impossibility. SStragh needed Jhenini to act, or Peitah *would* die. SStragh must obey.

Patiently, because there were still hours before the body had to be delivered to Frraghi, SStragh tried again. "Jhenini," she said. "The OColi has told me that I must kill Peter." She

proferred the spear held in her left hand again
to emphasize what she was saying beneath the
words. "This must be done before the light fails
today." SStragh said the next very slowly. "As
long as Peitah is here and I am capable of it, I
have no choice in this. I must obey the OColi."

There. How more plainly could she put it?
Holding the spear in the left hand rather than
the right to show that she disagreed with the
OColi's and Frraghi's assessment of Peitah as
only an animal; sitting down before Jhenini
rather than standing as she should; making certain that her scent glands exuded only the sweet
citrus aroma of peer talk rather than the heavy
spice of superior to inferior; telling Jhenini that
there were still hours before the deed must be
done; bringing them here out in the open and
away from the enclosure where there would
have been no chance; saying that she must obey
as long as she was capable of obedience:
SStragh had already gone far beyond the
bounds of proper behavior doing this much. She
couldn't say more without utterly breaking the
OColihi.

Jhenini must be able to understand what
SStragh was saying beneath the words. She
must understand.

"Obey not!" Jhenini said again.

SStragh snorted in confusion. She wasn't *asking* Jhenini to obey—following the OColi's order was SStragh's burden. Why did Jhenini
keep saying that? Certainly she wasn't asking

SStragh not to obey—that would be extraordinarily rude.

Admittedly, SStragh hadn't been certain how Jhenini would react. If Jhenini's response had been properly subservient, SStragh would have simply gone ahead and given Frraghi the body and been glad of it. SStragh wasn't quite certain exactly how Jhenini, Peitah, and Ekils related to each other, but she was certain that none of them were animals. If they had to be killed, fine, but let the Giving be done in the proper way, then, not like this.

If letting the humans live meant that SStragh must let Jhenini kill her, then fine. The only trouble was that it didn't seem that Jhenini was going to accept the gift of life SStragh was offering.

Slowly, SStragh said the words one last time, as slowly and simply as she could. "Jhenini, if Peitah stays here, I have no choice. None. I must obey the OColi. Unless something happens to me, Peitah must die by my hand."

There. SStragh carefully held the spear out where Jhenini could easily grab for it. That was the way of the OColihi: SStragh must make the appearance, the shell, of obeying the OColi or the All-Ancestor would turn Her back on her. SStragh could not herself allow the younglings and Ekils to escape. But *if* Jhenini would take the spear, *if* Jhenini would give SStragh the dignity of a proper end, then Peitah could live.

SStragh opened her fingers so that the spear

leaned loosely in her left hand. All it would take was a quick movement by Jhenini. . . .

It was almost as if Struth were mocking her. She was saying again how she was going to kill Peter. At the same time Struth kept waggling her spear at Jennifer. The dinosaur smelled like rotten orange peels and stared intently with those golden brown eyes at Jennifer as if she were daring Jennifer to do something. Jenny had a sharp feeling of déjà vu, of standing on the platform with the bowl and knife and wondering just what it was that the Mutata were expecting of her. Her arm throbbed with the memory.

Unless something happens to me. Peter must die by my hand.

What in the world did *that* mean? If Struth was supposed to kill him, why hadn't she just done it back in the enclosure or earlier in the day while they were all hobbled. Why come here, why wait?

Why tell me?

Struth moved the spear closer, holding it even more loosely than before. The sharp edges of the bone white blade swayed mockingly near her. "Struth—"

"Jhenini, maioia Peitah werada Equee."

The spear tip was nearly brushing her nose. Jenny snatched at it with her good hand in irritation. To her surprise, Struth immediately let go of the weapon. Jennifer held it awkwardly, her eyes narrowed in puzzlement.

Struth had closed her eyes, lifting her snout slightly so that her chest expanded and the soft hollow of her throat lay exposed. The dinosaur's hands were down, the long fingers closed.

She's expecting me to strike her. She's allowing this to happen.

Everything was suddenly clear to Jennifer: Struth's strange words, her decision to bring them up here, the way she told Jenny about the order to kill Peter . . .

Jennifer gave a quick laugh of disbelief. "No possible way. Struth . . ." She searched for the Mutata words, couldn't find them.

Struth's eyes opened quizzically. Her head cocked to one side. "Jhenini?" The eyes closed again, the head lifted a little further.

Jennifer didn't do anything. She stood there, the spear a strange weight in her hand. She was paralyzed with indecision. She could no more strike at the defenseless Struth than she could at Peter or Aaron or even Eckels. It wasn't in her.

"Hey, Jenny . . ." Peter was staring at her also. Eckels had come up next to him; they were both looking at her. Eckels may not have understood what was going on, but he took in the situation quickly.

"Kid, *use* the spear," he said. "Then we can get the h—"

She never had to make the decision. From between the trees girdling the meadow, Fergie and a squad of Mutata soldiers appeared. Struth heard them also. Even as Fergie gave a trumpet bellow of hello in their direction, Struth had snatched back the spear from Jennifer. Holding it firmly in her left hand, she turned to hail Fergie herself and went over to meet with him.

"Jenny . . ." Peter sighed. "You had it in your hand. . . ." Eckels had turned away with a look of condescending disgust.

"So what, Peter," she said. "What would you have done?"

"I wouldn't have stood there, that's for sure."

"Well, I did, okay? I guess I'm just not the big brave hero type like you."

He sniffed at her mockery. "No, I guess you're not," he said. "We could have been *out* of here. You could have been back with your darling Aaron."

Struth's return with Fergie ended the conversation. Struth spoke to Jennifer slowly in Mutata.

"We must return to the village," she said. "The Gairk have sent an emissary who insists that he must see the OColi human and his younglings."

NEGOTIATIONS

"Here, kid," Travis said. "You better take my coat."

Aaron was still staring at the bare ground where Mundo had stood only seconds ago. He looked up to see Travis holding out his parka. Underneath, the man's shirt was bloody and torn. He coughed, a sound that rumbled deep in his chest, thick with phlegm. Travis spat; what hit the rocks lent the snow a pink tinge.

Aaron knew then that Travis's condition was deteriorating and if the man didn't get help soon . . .

There isn't any help, he reminded himself. *Nowhere. Not anymore.*

"The coat's yours," Aaron said. "Keep it. I don't need it."

"I'm not being a social worker here, just reasonable," Travis replied. "You can see what's happening as well as I can. You need the warmth. Only one of us has a chance to live here for very long, and that's you. So what I want you to do is take the coat. Then we'll go down and see if that rifle of mine's repairable. If it is, it's yours too. Only . . ."

Travis paused, long enough so that Aaron knew before he spoke what he was going to say. "If we fix it," he continued, "I want you to use it. You understand me?"

Aaron understood. He understood all too well. Travis exhaled depression, smelled of despair. He was a dead man standing there in front of Aaron. The icy fog that came from his mouth was the cold of the grave. "I can't do that," Aaron said. "Travis . . . I just can't."

The dead man eyes stared unblinkingly at him, like hard copper pennies. "Then you'd rather leave me to die slow, is that it? You'd rather I cough my lungs up, let the blood seep out until I choke or these cuts become infected and put out dark fingers of poison gangrene. You'd let the legs swell like a peddler's balloon, the skin getting all tight and shiny until it looks like a touch will cause it to burst. Or maybe I'll die because I can't run from some predator, only stumble along or maybe crawl with broken fingernails on these godforsaken frozen stones. Is that the fate you want for me, Aaron? Is that the kind of mercy you have for me?"

Each word was a hammer blow, staggering Aaron. "No," he said. "It's just . . . You don't . . ."

"Or would you rather I do it to you, and then use one last shot on myself?" Travis said. His haggard face leaned toward Aaron, the skin hugging the skeletal cheekbones, veins like a snarl of ropes under his eyes. "If you want that, I can do it. We're lost, don't you understand that? We're lost forever. There is nothing to hope for."

Travis tossed the coat toward Aaron. The heavy cloth hit Aaron and then slumped like a lifeless torso to the ground. "C'mon, pick it up. There isn't any sense in both of us freezing to death." Travis was shivering, goose bumps pimpling his arm under his short-sleeved shirt. His lower lip trembled. "Please, kid . . ."

Now that the fury was gone, now that Aaron was just standing in the cold and wind and snow, still in the jeans and T-shirt that had actually been too warm back home in Green Town, Aaron felt the cold, no matter how much he protested to Travis that he didn't. It would have been easy to take the coat, to let himself slide down the same mental well that had swallowed Travis.

But Aaron refused. Some part of him denied the reality of what was happening. Not twelve hours ago, everything had been normal: Green Town slumbering in an August afternoon, Jenny beside him, the last dregs of that eternal pause between high school and college just trickling down summer's throat. How could he believe that the universe had altered itself entirely in half a day?

It was a dream. He'd wake up. He *had* to find the way out of this—had to. It was insanity to believe anything else.

The optimism gave him slow warmth.

"Pick up the coat," Aaron said. "Just pick it up, Travis. Mundo said the machine was safe. All we need to do is find it."

Stomping his feet, trying to get circulation

in his sneaker-bound toes, Aaron clambered down the slope to where the time machine had been. The remains of the rifle were frost-covered on the ground. Aaron looked back up to where Travis stood. The man's eyes were fixed on some unseen, bewildering distance. The coat still lay where Aaron had dropped it.

"Travis!"

The man started, his eyes moving in confusion to find Aaron. Aaron picked up the rifle, whose barrel had a distinctive bow. He showed it to Travis, then gave the broken, useless weapon a great, sidearm heave. It went whirling off with a sound like a dying helicopter, landing with an unmusical clatter on the rocks fifty yards away, kicking up dirty ice. Something birdlike and large cawed in irritation and flapped away.

"There, Mundo!" Aaron yelled to the air and the retreating bird. "Something to remember us by."

The warmth of anger faded like the quick, false spring of March fading back to winter. *It was made of earth things, so I placed it where things of the earth should be*—that's what Mundo had said. Aaron could only think of one meaning for that.

Mundo had buried it.

Somewhat sheepishly, Aaron retrieved the rifle barrel he'd so melodramatically heaved, using it to dig into the frozen ground where the time machine had once been. If nothing else, Aaron thought, the activity would keep him warm. Travis watched, sitting morosely on a nearby boulder and occasionally moaning.

Two hours later, Aaron had nothing to show for his efforts but a hole three feet wide and about the same depth. The ground was like flash-frozen concrete, strewn with fist-sized rocks. There was no sign of the time machine yet, the sun was bending lower, shadows were lengthening, and the sweat Aaron had worked up dried to ice in his hair.

Aaron threw the rifle barrel—bent even more now—to the ground in disgust and climbed out of his shallow hole. He clasped his hands over his chest and shivered. Travis just looked at him with a lost, bewildered gaze.

"I'm sorry, kid," he said and coughed. "I really am."

"Yeah. I am, too." Aaron looked around, stamping his feet. "Travis, I wonder if there's a cave or something around here. We need some dead wood, something to make a fire. . . ."

"Kid—"

"We could start digging again tomorrow. . . ."

"*Aaron!*" The shout cost Travis. He coughed again, a racking spasm that left him doubled over. He wiped his mouth on the back of his hand finally and looked up. "Aaron," he said more softly. "This is not going to do any good."

"It is," Aaron insisted. "It *has* to. We need to talk to Mundo again—"

He stopped. A creature was peering out at the two of them from a long crack in a screen of rock to his right. Aaron could see a triangular, furry snout with a row of six eyes set in behind it. Several Aarons were reflected there, silvery versions of him all distorted and elongated. *I am . . . all.* Mundo's words. *There was never anything here that wasn't me.*

Mundo, or the group mind that Mundo claimed to be, was watching him.

Assuming that Mundo was telling the truth. Assuming that Mundo had the standard curiosity of most intelligent creatures.

The thought gave Aaron an idea. "Travis, every living creature has certain common traits, right? We all breathe, we all eat, we reproduce."

"We all eventually die, too."

Aaron grinned maniacally. "Yeah, and we all try to avoid that as long as we can. Fight or flight—isn't that the reflex? Well, Mundo should have it too."

Aaron spoke to the animal. "Mundo, can you hear me? If you can, let us know. This is important."

Nothing happened for a moment. Aaron's shoulders sagged. Then the mouth of the thing opened to show a gullet lined with lacy stalks rather than teeth and a long whip of a tongue. "Essss," it said, the tongue flicking and coiling, the stalks in the long throat vibrating. "I lhissssen."

"Then listen to this. You're putting yourself in danger. You looked into our minds, but I don't think you can understand what you saw there. I don't think you really know what will happen."

"Nhhhoooo," the beast crooned slowly. It sounded like a stretched and garbled tape played on a weary deck. "Dooon'ttt unnnnerstannnnn. Toooo ssstrannnnj. Nhhhoooo unnnersssstan alllllhh. Jusss sssooooome. Wwhhhhaaait. . . ."

There was a sound behind them. The sixeyed creature pulled its head back into the crevice of its rock as Aaron turned. A monkeylike biped with thick dirty gray fur and a leathery, wrinkled face loped toward them with a rolling, side-to-side gait. It stopped a few feet away from Aaron and Travis and sat. Long, triplejointed fingers with webbing between them began prowling the fur on its chest. It plucked something unseen between thumb and index finger and popped it into its mouth.

"Is this better?" it said. It chewed and swallowed. "The utter one coul'n' speak your words well, and its min' kep' wandering. The mout' was all the wron' shape. This one is easier—closer to your kin'. I brough' him here."

"It's better. Some, I guess."

The creature gave a giggle that was half shriek. It echoed shrilly among the rocks. "Bu' it still isn' righ', eh? Okay, wai'."

The ape stood upright, snow and ice matting its fur, and bounded off. A whirlwind formed where it had been, gathering dust and snow until Aaron and Travis had to shield their eyes. When the howling wind died, Mundo—in his wizard incarnation—was present once more.

"There, are you satisfied now?" Mundo raised a hand and faint lightnings crackled forth; Aaron felt the being's touch on the surface of his mind, like a feeling of nagging déjà vu. "The two of you are such a marvel—you have no interest in the larger scheme of things. You're frightened but you don't think of how your death might feed a thousand insects, a pack of scavengers. Aaron, the glories that will rise from your decomposing body, the wonders that you will be responsible for . . . and yet you feel nothing for it. You worry only about the loss of your own thoughts."

"If you've read my mind, then you know that that's the way it is for every creature in my world."

The eyes rolled, the lips stretched, the forehead wrinkled, but none of the movements worked together. The effect was like bad animation. "So you say. Though I wonder if you would know. Until I came to you, you had no idea that I existed, did you? Maybe your kind has just never met me." Mundo chuckled his dead chuckle and smiled his empty smile. "Besides, your world doesn't even exist. This is— was—your time, remember, Aaron? Green Town, your family, Jenny. This is where they should be, but they're gone. You have no home, not anymore. Why shouldn't I let you die here?"

"Mundo, if you don't give us back the time

machine, what happened to us will happen to you. Think of that.''

The fingertips wriggled with their pale blue firefly fire, and Aaron felt Mundo's mind wandering over his once more. Travis grimaced a moment later, and Aaron knew that Mundo had done the same to him.

"You both believe that. I'm surprised," Mundo said, and though his voice was now touched with uncertainty, the smile remained on his lips like the ruin of a tumbledown castle on a hilltop. "I will grant you the possibility that you're even right. But still . . . I can remember ancient century upon century and nothing has changed in the way that you're saying that things will change. The world's never shifted around me. It still has not.''

"You'll *never* notice," Travis said wearily from his boulder. "That's the danger, Mundo. When your history changes, you'll feel nothing because you're an integral part of this timestream. The change will be like a dam bursting far downstream, a tidal wave of brand-new history crashing century by century forward, tearing at the entire landscape of the past and tumbling down the ages, roaring its way UpTime. But you'll never notice the uproar, because that's your past and your memories that have been eroded or silted over or even washed away entirely. The wave may even take you out, if it's big enough and if it's gathered enough momentum.''

"But I *remember.*" Mundo's face shifted; the

wizard's ancient features merged and became a face that Aaron didn't know at all, someone younger, thin, and hollow cheeked. Travis must have known him, for he hissed with an intake of breath.

"You will always have memories, Mundo," Travis said. "But those memories will alter too. They may have already changed. Do you understand?"

"I understand that neither of you have any interest in me except that I'm standing in your way. You're not going back to save me. That's not why you want your machine." The voice was a whine, a pout. The lips pressed together into a white, harsh line.

"You're wrong—" Travis began, but Aaron interrupted the lie before it began.

"Yes," he said. "That's true, Mundo. But this is also the truth: if we don't go back, you'll die. The evolution that made you is as precarious as the one that brought us into existence. Eckels's presence in the past will change everything again. He's back there, so change is inevitable. But if *we* go back . . ."

Aaron stopped and looked at Eckels. Until now, he'd simply been talking without any real plan, trying to find an argument—*any* argument—that might convince Mundo to return the time machine. He'd been thinking that if *he* were Mundo, he'd be laughing at Travis and him. After all, Eckels might well be dead, and if *that* were true, then Mundo was entirely safe. In some ways, gambling on Eckels being dead was better odds than letting Aaron and Travis return to the past and muck around.

Except . . .

Mundo *did* laugh then, as Aaron felt the whirling disorientation of the being's mind touch and saw the sparks shimmering in the twilight. "I agree, Aaron. Those *are* better odds."

Aaron shook his head and smiled back at the death's head grin of Mundo. "No—you're not looking deep enough, Mundo. I just realized two things. First, right now my bet's that Eckels is still alive. We were just in your future, remember? A mere skip ahead, and you weren't there. You weren't there at all."

"You just failed to notice me," Mundo said smugly.

"No. We saw animals; they noticed us. Yet you never arrived. You're curious, Mundo. You like to see new things, don't you? Yet we never met Mundo or a whirlwind or anything like you—only a few centuries forward. That's just a breath, a gasp, a moment for you, right? You've lived for millennium upon millennium." Aaron paused, and Travis spoke up haltingly, his voice suddenly animated.

"The kid's right, Mundo. Two centuries from now, you're not there. Maybe you died somewhere in the meantime; or maybe you had never existed at all. Somewhere in the space between our leaving there and arriving here, Eckels stomped on another world-changing butterfly or slapped dead a mosquito that held the fates of a dozen other species. When he did that, he made you possible and you popped into existence—the whole long history of you—all at once."

Mundo said nothing to that. Instead, he bent impossibly from the waist like a broken puppet and reached down. Where his hand met earth, the frozen dirt boiled. When he straightened again, his hand held a dinosaur egg. The elongated, mottled white spheroid looked exactly like the egg Aaron and Jennifer had discovered, the egg that had started this whole insanity.

"You said you had realized *two* things, Aaron," Mundo said. "What's the other?"

Suddenly, everything crystallized in Aaron's mind—the nagging little inconsistencies, the questions. Aaron blinked and drew a long breath. He knew that some of what he was thinking must be wish fulfillment, that he just so badly wanted this to be true that he was grasping at any straws in the wrecked timestream. But—if this could be right . . .

"There's an experiment I'd like to make, Mundo. It wouldn't put you at risk, or very little. I want a few minutes of your time." Aaron laughed. Travis was staring at him through pain-wracked eyes. Mundo's grin seemed painted on. "A few minutes and a few million years of time, more precisely. Read my mind, Mundo. Go ahead. Please. That'll be the easiest way for you to understand."

Mundo handed Aaron the egg with a stiff flourish. Aaron took the offering. At the touch, hissing blue sparks arose from the surface, arcing between Mundo's head and his own. This time the mind touch was harsher and more complete. Aaron felt the dizzying impact of Mundo's world mind, the intricate, distant webbing that linked the being inextricably to the world. The scope of the network was beyond comprehension, yet Aaron realized that Mundo was as naïve as a child. He was also as confused by Aaron and Travis's minds as they were by his.

Then Mundo pulled back and the vision of the world web receded. "Yes," he said slowly. Above the mouth, Mundo's features were shifting, as if the very bones of his skull were twisting underneath the skin. "I understand. You'll let me go with you? To make sure?"

"Yes," Aaron said.

Mundo's form sagged into dirt and dust. For a moment, Aaron thought Mundo had abandoned them altogether, but then the stones underneath them began to dance. The earth shook itself like a dog trying to rid itself of fleas. The mountainside rippled and cracked. Travis and Aaron retreated as the ground opened up, a gaping, widening mouth that screamed with a granite voice. They shielded their eyes from the dark hurricane that erupted at their feet, falling helpless. Stones and pebbles rained down, a curtain of choking dust waved over them.

Then, abruptly, the earthquake subsided.

Aaron brushed dirt from his clothes and hair.

He knuckled his eyes and spat gritty sand. "Travis—"

The time machine sat there on unbroken ground as if it had never been gone. Aaron helped Travis to his feet, then watched as the injured man limped to the vehicle and stroked the cold flanks of steel as if the machine were a lost child. Travis touched the contact; the door shushed open as the apelike biped came bounding up to them.

"Le'ss go," it said. "I always wan'ed to see where I came from."

THE STORM OF DREAMS

The wind had picked up. Even though the sky was mostly clear with only a few clouds above, Jennifer felt the premonition of a coming storm. A little bad weather seemed to be the least of their problems.

Jennifer didn't like whatever it was that was standing in the middle of the village when they returned. The beast must have stood ten foot high, looking like a miniature version of Godzilla dressed in someone's copper cooking ware. A helmet of beaten metal covered the wide head and dinner-plate tympanic ears. A flap trailed down the top of the long snout but did nothing to hide the snaggled crocodile teeth bristling from under black lips. A heavier metal covering protected the wide chest but left the back bare. From the bottom of the copper plate, where the short, muscular arms could reach them easily, hung two large wooden bludgeons, the heads studded with obsidian spikes. Both weapons displayed bloodstains in the cracks and crevices. The creature's legs were like tree trunks, and his tail was banded with a leather strap studded with nodules of raw ore.

Worse than the sight of this war beast were the two bodies that lay at its feet. One was a crumpled, man-size kite: a pterodactyl with its thin neck bent backward and broken, the great glider wings torn and ripped.

The second was human—a man with skin the color of an old oaken desk, wearing a loose, white cotton loincloth splattered with blood that was still wet. The man had a large pectoral medallion hung around his neck with a leather thong. The jewelry seemed to be carved from one flat piece of greenish stone: a stylized, squarish face leered out at Jennifer, with intricate smaller symbols tracing the edges of the piece. A headband with similar but much smaller carvings wove its way through tangled, shiny black hair. The face, with soft, wide features, stared empty eyed at the sun. Jennifer saw immediately that one side of the skull was crushed as if from a heavy blow.

The beast exhaled violence and implicit threat. The atmosphere around it seemed somehow clouded and dark. When he spoke, his voice was the deep rumble of a distant storm. The words had an impatient choppiness. Even though Jennifer knew that the language was the same as the Mutata's, the harsh, abrupt edge made the words even more difficult to understand. Jennifer caught nothing beyond the OColi's name. The rest seemed to be one long litany of complaint.

Jennifer stared at the body of the human as the Gairk spat out his speech. "Where'd the man come from?" she whispered to Peter and Eckels.

"It sure isn't a samurai this time," Peter said. "He almost looks Amerind."

Eckels said nothing. When Jennifer glanced at the man, his hair moving in the freshening breeze, Eckels's thin face was white and drawn. He refused to look at the dead man. "Eckels, what's going on? Do you know something about this?"

Eckels shook his head, then shrugged. "No . . . well, maybe. There's a whole city of those monsters further down the valley, and I once saw them fighting a squad of people like this guy, waving those nasty clubs and howling like mad—"

Eckels stopped. The Gairk had turned and that huge head swiveled down toward them like a smooth-geared killing machine. Tiny wide-set eyes regarded them coldly; sun glinted red from the metal head covering. He spat out a word—"Keeio"—and its breath descended on them with the smell of the grave as it displayed a cavern of stalactite fangs. The three of them looked into living death. Hobbled, they couldn't run; unarmed, there was nothing they could do to resist. All it would have taken was a snap of those powerful jaws, a flick of the awesome neck. The Gairk's fetid atmosphere enveloped them and the rising wind did nothing to blow it away. His solemn, cruel gaze held them helpless.

Then he looked away, and each of them let

out a breath that they hadn't realized they'd been holding. The Gairk bellowed some staccato order; Fergie snorted and stamped his feet in an emphatic no.

At that, the Gairk seemed to go insane. It wheeled around and the massive armored tail flicked like a bullwhip an inch from Fergie's snout. Amazingly, Fergie didn't move. The Gairk screamed his order once more, and this time he pointed his weapon directly at Peter. To Jennifer, the implication was obvious. The Gairk wanted one or all of them. After Struth's unexpected offering in the meadow, this seemed utterly insulting, even if it seemed that Fergie was refusing the request. Jennifer found herself moving forward against the hobble, actually pushing Fergie back as she interposed herself between the Mutata and the Gairk.

"No," she told him. "Khiisoo yeie." The phrase seemed to be all she'd been saying today. "It's not going to happen."

The wind gusted suddenly, a burst so hard and unexpected that Jennifer had to step back to keep her balance. The Gairk was staring at Jennifer as if she were a roach in a five-star restaurant. His expression, the way the black lips were lifted around the snaggled canines, made her think that she might be joining the pterodactyl and Indian at the carnivore's feet.

She didn't care. Jennifer pointed her finger at the Gairk, ready to shout her defiance to him.

She didn't have to. A flash of lightning arced over them from the placid sky, as if Jennifer had loosed the bolt with the gesture. Jennifer gasped and blinked, trying to see through the skittering afterimages. She rubbed at her eyes. "Oh, *yucch* . . ."

The Gairk had toppled to the ground like a dead tree—or rather, half of it had. The creature had been sliced cleanly from the top of its head down, armor and all. One gory section had fallen, spilling steaming entrails; the other just wasn't there. Neither was the ground on which it had been standing.

In its place was a perfect circle of banked snow several inches high and perhaps ten feet in diameter. Inside that circle, in a smooth column extending straight upward, a blizzard was raging.

Jennifer followed the impossible snowstorm upward to where it met a scudding wall of gray cloud and her eyes widened, for where an instant before there had been a perfect summer sky, there was now an ugly mass of boiling clouds all around.

All of them had backed away from the vision of the snow and the dead Gairk. All except Peter. He was leaning forward, reaching out to touch the drifting flakes. "Peter—" Jennifer shouted in alarm.

Peter drew his hand back. Another lightning stroke, utterly devoid of any accompanying thunder, lit the Mutata village like a flare in the night. Distorted, giant shadows raced and flowed over the domes. With the flash, the winter landscape disappeared.

Behind Jennifer, Struth snorted in alarm.

Just beyond the Mutata village and out in the high grass, a building had appeared. A tower of stone with a shorn wall, it looked like a corner torn from a castle and thrown down here. As they stared, a man appeared high up on the ramparts. He wore chain mail and a steel helmet. He shouted down to them; to Jennifer, the words sounded like French.

Another flash. The tower vanished with it. Gone, as if it had never been there.

Fergie was pointing to Jennifer's left. She followed his gesture. Near the enclosure where she, Peter, and Eckels were being kept, there was the front end of a streamlined vehicle. The glass canopy atop it was being opened, and the person trying to scramble from the cockpit had too many arms and a chitinous shell.

Flash, and the apparition was gone.

Jennifer spun around, trying to see what other nightmare had risen. She almost missed it, for the rocky landscape fifty yards to her right wasn't so horribly out of place until a blue-shelled, overgrown snail slithered over the slabs of granite.

Flash. The wind kicked up sand (*sand?* she thought) and Jennifer had to cover her eyes.

Flash.

As quickly as it had arisen, the surreal storm passed. The sky cleared as if wiped by an invisible hand. There was nothing left to witness to the strange sights they'd seen. No snow, no sand. No tower, no French knight. No blue snails and no sand.

Just the half body of the Gairk.

Everyone was staring at Jennifer. Fergie said something; Jennifer instinctively turned toward him, and Fergie nearly fell over trying to back away from her. Behind her, Peter laughed. "Yeah, Jenny. Give it to him."

"Peter—"

"Hey, if they're stupid enough to believe it, take the advantage. What else do we have?"

Struth and Fergie were having a heated conversation, far too fast and low for Jennifer to understand. Around them, other Mutata were emerging from their buildings to stare at the Gairk's corpse and gaze around them.

Jennifer watched Fergie, wondering what the Mutata would do next. What actually happened was anticlimactic. Fergie hooted something to Struth and—keeping his gaze on Jennifer—disappeared into the complex of domes. Struth, almost gently, herded the humans back to their compound.

Jennifer noted that Struth was very, very careful not to touch her.

The OColi was furious, though he was pretending to be calm. SStragh could smell the anger wafting from the corner of the room, where the OColi rested on rocks glowing warm in the sunlight from the open roof. SStragh knew that the OColi's uncertainty was due to Jhenini and the Far-Killer—the human's

OColi. They had both been summoned here along with SStragh. The OColi was as disturbed as everyone else by what had just occurred. SStragh knew this because SStragh felt the same strange reluctance to be near Jhenini, who had brought on the storm of ghosts and the Gairk's odd, honorless death.

There was another underscent to the OColi's miasma, something SStragh couldn't quite identify among the stronger odors. The OColi didn't acknowledge SStragh and Jhenini's obeisance.

Frraghi, however, made no pretense at all. The Speaker's Rod quivered in his left hand as he turned from listening to the OColi's whisper. SStragh noticed that even Jhenini smelled the violence in his manner.

"The OColi asks the human's OColi why Jhenini destroyed the Gairk without provocation," Frraghi snapped. He snorted angrily, towering over Jhenini with the rod of his office dangerously close to her head. Jhenini returned Frraghi's gaze without flinching, which made SStragh perversely proud, even though Jhenini smelled of absolutely nothing.

Then, without saying anything at all to Ekils, she spoke in her atrocious Mutata. "Jenny asks the OColi why Peter must die," she said.

Even SStragh hissed at that impossible rudeness. The question had been asked of Ekils, as the Eldest of the huimans, not Jhenini. She should have performed as Speaker for her

OColi, not answered by herself. That was the least offense. Even worse was the insult of responding to the OColi's direct question with one of her own.

Scales flicking wild highlights, the OColi whipped his head up, glancing sideways with his one good eye at Jhenini. Frraghi trumpeted fury and brought back the rod, ready to strike. The Far-Killer was bleating something in his own language; he smelled like an eggling being berated by its OTsio. SStragh was humiliated for Ekils; no OColi should behave so badly. She waited for the blow that must come, wondering if the OColi would allow Jhenini to have the proper Giving.

But Jhenini raised her hand, the same gesture she'd used when the Gairk had been struck down, and Frraghi hesitated. The slight delay was enough.

The OColi shouted: "Yeie!"

The rod swept down, making the sound of death, but missed Jhenini's head by an eggshell's thickness. Frraghi was breathing heavily and exuding a thick odor of mingled hatred, frustration, and rage, along with the taint of fright. He made a noise of disgust, trying to negate the unbidden fear Jhenini had raised in him and not succeeding, for all of them could still smell it.

"OColi, I am sorry," he said, but the OColi ignored him.

"SStragh," the OColi said, and SStragh was simultaneously awed, worried, and pleased that the OColi would address her directly, "you will ask the youngling Jhenini if she brought the storm that killed the Gairk."

The OColi's voice was weak. SStragh knew that speaking aloud hurt the OColi, whose throat (it was rumored) was lined with ugly growths. The pain underscored the importance he attributed to the question.

Jhenini had not understood the OColi; SStragh rephrased the question for her, using the simplest terms she could. Jhenini shook her head. The simplistic huiman gesture lacked all the nuances that should have been in the answer. Jhenini spoke something to Ekils in her own language, words which upset the Far-Killer. He argued briefly with Jhenini.

Jhenini turned from Ekils while he was still speaking—another strangeness, one SStragh had seen many times before but which she knew bothered the OColi, whom no Mutata youngling would dare to contradict or interrupt. "No," she said—to the OColi, not SStragh; a minor rudeness—"I didn't cause the storm. I scared *him*, though," she said, pointing at Frraghi. "I think—"

"That is all I wished to know," the OColi husked out, speaking pointedly to SStragh without looking at Jhenini. "Tell it I am not interested in its thoughts. Stay here, SStragh; I will have one of the others take the human's OColi and Jhenini back."

"What about Peter?" Jhenini said.

SStragh stamped her feet at the incredible

affront; only the OColi's previous admonition seemed to be holding back Frraghi. "Jhenini, you have been dismissed," SStragh hissed at her. "I ask you, be quiet."

"No," she said. "I won't. Not about that."

The OColi refused to look at her. He gazed at the patterns the sun made on the wall. "SStragh," he said, "ask her why the animal's life is so important and hers so useless that she would throw it away by her behavior."

SStragh could see that Jhenini was trying to puzzle that out; again she repeated the OColi's words. Jhenini's face had gone red; she wondered if the color had some significance. Jhenini glanced once at Ekils and then began speaking. She stumbled over many of the words, often looking to SStragh for confirmation or help. Slowly, the meaning became clear.

"OColi, Peter and I know how the floating stones were created. We also know someone who at least understands how the floating stones work. Maybe he can tell you how to close the paths. The cost of that knowledge is Peter's life."

The OColi refused to even answer that insult.

"Frraghi," he grumbled, and the Speaker hurried over to listen to the OColi's whisperings. Whatever the OColi was saying, Frraghi seemed pleased to hear it, for his scent changed and his crest lowered. He gestured sharply with the Speaker's Rod to the Mutata who had appeared at the opening to the OColi's chamber.

"Get the humans out of here," Frraghi ordered.

"I want an answer," Jhenini insisted, and Frraghi ignored her entirely. They were swept out of the room with Jhenini still protesting. SStragh watched them go, helpless, shaking her head at Jhenini in a vain attempt to bring her back to reason or even minimal politeness.

"Your huimans are showing their true nature," Frraghi said as Jhenini's continuing protests echoed faintly and then faded away. "The OColi has had enough of them."

"It is my fault," SStragh apologized, though she knew it would make no difference. "I was a poor OTsio to Jhenini. I didn't teach her well."

"True enough," Frraghi said. Behind the Speaker, the OColi's claws clattered on rock as he settled slowly into a more relaxed position. SStragh's spirit sank; it was obvious that a decision had been reached. It was also obvious what it must be. "The OColi has instructed me to tell you that to cage the humans as we do is an insult to the OColihi."

"Then let me release them. Send them back through their floating stones."

"They are to be Given. The Gairk OColi will come tomorrow to watch."

SStragh had expected such. She allowed her disapproval to show in her scent, and Frraghi's crest engorged slightly. "You have no support anywhere within Mutata, SStragh," he said. "Not one Mutata other than you would say that the OColi is wrong in this. The signs are clear to the OColi. The floating stones have to be continually guarded against the things coming from them, and now Jhenini has brought on the ghost storm."

"She didn't do it. She's said that."

Frraghi snorted. "I was there. I saw her point, I saw the Gairk emissary die."

"Jhenini said that this other human knows how the paths were made, that he might be able to close them off. Won't that restore the OColihi?"

"And maybe she lied, as she did about the ghost storm. The OColihi will be restored when we give them to the All-Ancestor."

"Is the OColi frightened that the Gairk might attack us because of these ghosts? Is—"

"*Enough!*" Frraghi bellowed, flourishing the rod. He snorted in disgust. "The humans have infected you with their disease of rudeness," he said. "Or you have been listening to OTsio Raajek too long. Leave us, SStragh. Leave us and go back to your humans for the brief time they have. The OColi is tired of you."

STORM ABOVE
THE TYRANT

Travis had set the time machine to return them to the Mesozoic, adjusting the controls so that they'd arrive exactly an hour after he and Aaron had left for his own time. That buffer prevented them from stumbling upon themselves, with the results that Aaron already knew too well.

Travis then leaned wearily back in his seat. He directed Aaron in the procedure for setting the rest of the coordinates, showing him how to avoid drifting in space as well as time, so that they'd arrive in the same location rather some random place that might be half the world away. The entire process was extremely simple—in fact, Aaron found it to be almost insultingly so. As Travis had once said, the controls and computer interface had been designed for the novice, not the technician.

They'd strapped Mundo into a seat, buckled their own restraints.

"Activating..." the computer said.

Mundo's world shattered, tore, and disappeared.

The time machine shuddered and bucked.

Aaron's teeth chattered with the shuddering motion. Whatever interreality lurked outside the windows was darker than black. The sight of it hurt Aaron's eyes whenever he looked at it, like staring at a slightly out-of-register color television screen through someone else's glasses. The cold that rolled off the front glass of the machine was more intense than anything he'd ever felt before. He could imagine placing his hand on the glass and having it flash freeze to the pane.

Travis slumped in the chair alongside Aaron, the ape that was Mundo sat wide-eyed behind them. He was moaning softly, as if in some pain. As the chronometer on the panel hit the targeted coordinates, a more violent jerk than usual rocked the cabin and the utter darkness outside the machine began to dissolve and run with streaked traces of green.

Mundo suddenly screamed.

"I's gone! I's all gone!" the ape gibbered, and then lapsed into incoherent shrieking, thrashing in the seat restraints.

"Mundo, what's the matter?"

"I's gone. Everythin's quie' in my hea'. All tha's lef' is a whisper. I'm *alone*." The last word was a sob.

"You're in your past," Travis said. He looked at Aaron, then back to Mundo, his eyes dull with his own pain. There was no compassion at all in his voice. "You're in a time eons before you existed as an entity. There's no world mind here; there won't be for a long, long time. All you're hearing is the echo of your future. I expected that, even if Aaron didn't." Travis shrugged, coughed, and hugged his ribs. "I wasn't even sure you'd make it back here at all. I didn't know if something like you could survive the trip and the loss of all the other parts of you. I figured that maybe you'd just be an ape, nothing more."

"Take me ba'," Mundo pleaded. "Travis, Aaron . . ."

"No," Travis said. "Not a chance. You'd pull another stupid trick and leave us stranded again."

Mundo surged against his seat restraints, snarling like a dog and showing his teeth. "You promise'," he hissed at Aaron. "You tric'ed me. You sai' that you wan'ed to do the essperimen'. You sai' you would hel'."

"I do want to try the experiment," Aaron answered. "We will help." He looked at Travis. "I *do* promise that. Mundo—"

"I' *hur's* to be alone!" Mundo shrieked. "All I have is this bo'y." He struggled against the straps, then lapsed back, gasping. "No energy, no power. I wan' to be the wind, I wan' to move from being 'o being, but i' won' le' me. I can' leave this form, can' even ma'e myself Mun'o again. I am dea'."

"You're not dead," Aaron told him. "You've just become like us, that's all. No worse. I'll keep my promise, Mundo. I will. All we have to do is find the path that brought me here. Out there in the jungle is a bridge from this

time to mine. . . ." Aaron stopped and grimaced. "Well, I guess it's not my time anymore, is it? It's yours. Anyway, it'll get you back
easier than the time machine."

Aaron touched the door contact. The mech-
anism sighed and folded back the door. The
three of them were hit with the scent of the
jungle: steaming, earth-black mud and lush humidity. "Come on," Aaron said, undoing Mundo's seat belt—the ape didn't seem to be able
to comprehend how to operate even the simplest technology. "Travis?"

"Coming."

The world was as they'd left it. A pack of
new scavengers—dromaeosaurs, Aaron decided, one of the fastest and fiercest dinosaurs,
standing waist tall to him and Travis—were
slicing fiercely at the tyrannosaurus corpse. The
dromae, luckily, scattered at their approach.
Mundo was staring at them, the wrinkled ape's
face a mask of concentration; Aaron knew that
Mundo was trying to put himself in their bodies, trying to link with them as he had with the
animals of his own time. From the frantic gri-
mace of his mouth, he wasn't succeeding.

The rex's body was burbling and sighing,
liquids settling and shifting inside the great
leathern bag of its flesh. One saucer eye stared
at them accusingly, the frozen mouth snarled.
Close by, the remnants of the floating path hovered scant inches above the ground. To the left,
Aaron saw a bushy fern whose branches were
still bent from when he had originally found

this clearing. The opening led into darkness under the trees. Somewhere back there was a piece of the floating roadway.

The scene was exactly as it had been: the time machine had rematerialized in the space it had once occupied. They might never have left.

Travis came from the machine last, limping and wheezing. He'd taken the time to rearm himself from the weapons rack in the vehicle. "This is a dangerous place, kid," he said to Aaron's skeptical look. "You ought to do the same. That pack could tear you apart in a few minutes if they decided you looked tasty."

"Later, maybe."

Mundo had eased past Travis and Aaron and was standing in front of the T-rex corpse. Aaron watched him; the ape was standing slump shouldered and slack jawed, his hands touching the ground. "Mundo?"

There was no response.

"Mundo?"

"This is wha' happens?" Mundo said suddenly. He looked at the dinosaur, not the two humans. "I never knew. When something die' in my worl', I don' feel i'. I jus' fall ou' of that bo'y and don' hear i' anymore. I didn' un'erstan'. Didn' un'erstan' . . . ."

Mundo shuffled close to the fallen dinosaur. One trembling hand stretched out, a tentative forefinger stroked the bright orange scales of the creature's flank, then withdrew as if the touch had burned him. Mundo gasped, sobbed.

Suddenly his hands came up fisted and he began to beat on the side of the body, wailing. Aaron rushed forward and pulled the ape away. Mundo collapsed into Aaron's grasp, pulling at him desperately.

"Please! Take me bac'. Le' me go home. I'm frigh'ened. I don' wan' to die here an' die alone. Please!" Mundo was tugging at Aaron's shoulders, plucking at his T-shirt, pulling and clutching at him desperately.

"Mundo—"

"If I die here, I die forever! No one shoul' die forever, Aaron. You tric'ed me; now sen' me ba'."

"All right, all right," Aaron said, pulling the hands away. Mundo was surprisingly strong for his size. "Travis, come on. I pretty much know where the piece of roadway is. We're here now; we have the time machine. Let's get Mundo back to his place."

Travis shrugged. "Go ahead. I don't have any interest in seeing that time again. I'm going to start looking for that idiot Eckels."

Aaron looked at Travis, who stared back at him blandly. A sudden suspicion nagged Aaron, a feeling of distrust. Travis was hiding something. He started to question the man, then closed his mouth again. What did it matter? Aaron's own time had already been destroyed, altered forever. There was no way to get that back. Let Travis do whatever he wanted to do—the probability was Mundo's future would be altered, too—if not already, then sometime soon. Better to return Mundo now, while he still had something to go back to. When Eckels (or, he admitted, Travis or himself) did something to radically change history, Mundo would be in his proper place in the timestream and would never notice the change, not even if it meant that he himself faded from existence forever.

That would be better. That would be better than what I'm experiencing now, knowing that everything I once had is gone. Now I can understand Travis's rage and frustration.

Aaron looked at Travis. The man's jaw was knotted with either tension or pain, and he was clenching the rifle as if it were his only support in the entire world. Maybe, Aaron decided, it was.

"All right," he said to Travis. "You start looking for Eckels. I'll take care of Mundo." He glanced slowly over the clearing again, orienting himself and remembering. "It's over this way," he said. "C'mon, Mundo."

They had barely taken a few steps away when some premonition made Aaron lift his head. His eyes narrowed in puzzlement. He wasn't sure what had made him stop. He saw nothing unusual, heard nothing out of the ordinary. He noticed that the leaves far above their heads were swaying in some wind that they could not feel on the jungle floor, though the sky was an unbroken, cloudless blue. As Aaron watched, branches and fronds further down began to sway and bob, as if the unseen storm were descending. They could all hear an ominous, low murmuring.

What happened then was impossible and instantaneous. The sky arced brilliant, glaring white; the afterimage of an immense lightning strike burned behind Aaron's eyelids, clamped reflexively shut an instant too late. The jagged tendrils faded slowly through the spectrum. He waited for the thunder and heard nothing. He dared to open his eyes.

Where there had been open sky, there was now a roiling, green black surf of storm clouds. The wind hit an instant later, making the tall plants bow before its dominance. Near the time machine, Travis was huddled in a crouch.

"Mundo, are you doing this?" Aaron began, but Mundo was screaming in terror. Aaron shielded his eyes from a fierce gust, leaning into the gale. He waited for the rain, the swaying curtains of rain that would drench them at any second.

Instead, the clouds released a second stroke of lightning, a strange, gigantic blue green spark that illuminated the clearing with an underwater glare. Aaron expected the percussive kick of thunder, but none followed. Again the lightning was eerily silent, even though the strike seemed to have come from directly overhead. The wind howled and shrieked through the branches of the trees; somewhere close by, a branch tore away from its snare of vines and went crashing through the foliage. A herd of small dinosaurs streaked past Aaron, heading for the cover of the jungle; strange cries and calls sounded from deeper in as the denizens of the jungle darted for shelter.

Another stroke of silent lightning threw harsh-edged shadows everywhere. Aaron gaped in astonishment at what the light revealed.

Some strange building or temple had erected itself between Aaron and Travis. It was truncated, bisected at an acute angle as if some divine chain saw had hacked it off and flung it down here. A steep ramp of painted stone stairs led to a platform high above them, where a doorway carved like the mouth of some monster yawned. The scrolling was intricate and nearly abstract, like some primitive cubist's idea of a nightmare, and the stone was painted in bright reds and yellows. As Aaron gaped upward, a man stepped from within the doorway: an Indian, perhaps, with ruddy, dark skin. He wore a loincloth and a belt hung with brilliant cowry shells. On his head was a tall headdress with blue and yellow feathers; a necklace hung with jade faces decorated his chest. He stared down at them with equal astonishment. His mouth opened as if he were about to speak, and blood drooled from the corners of his mouth.

Then the lightning came again and the temple was gone as if it had never been there. Aaron could see Travis, his eyes wide. "Travis," Aaron shouted against the wind's clamoring. "Did you—"

The wind buffeted them. Another lightning strike came, and then another in its wake. Visions marched across the clearing with each flash, like quick mirages gone with a blink, each appearing in a new location: behind, to one side or the other, yards away or nearly on top of them. They passed in but a few seconds:

A huge block of stone standing canted on a meadow of tall grass. Two white-robed workers halted in the midst of carving the soft sandstone, their wooden mallets drooping in their hands as they looked in awe at the sudden jungle which surrounded them. The workers weren't human but large bipedal lizards ...

A foggy landscape in which something huge and steaming moved. For a moment, the fog parted and Aaron glimpsed dark scales spotted with yellow and a flank like an armored hill ...

A group of what had to be samurai warriors looking like scaled monsters themselves in their armor, long bright swords drawn and ready. They stood on the summit of a grassy knoll which not been there a moment before. They saw Aaron and Travis and shouted a challenge, running forward to the bizarre interface between their patch of world and Aaron's. Travis raised his rifle, ready to fire, but then the lightning came again and they were gone ...

Parsley's Grocery from Green Town, or at least the southern quarter of it, with a jagged section of pavement from Clifton Avenue set in front of it. Mr. Parsley himself was standing there, a broom in his hand and a white apron across his potbelly, goggling at the clean cut-away of his store and the half of a Honda Accord parked in front. Aaron could see groceries stacked on the shelves and a customer stopped in the middle of an aisle with cans spilling out from a grocery cart that was missing its front end. "Aaron! Aaron Cofield!" Mr. Parsley said. "What's—". . . .

And he was gone too.

The wind howled one last time as a final lightning stroke blinded them. When Aaron could see again, the jungle was as it had been. The sky had returned to pristine blue, and the T-rex lay there as if nothing had ever disturbed its final rest. Mundo was gibbering insanely. Travis had collapsed against the side of the time machine as if needing the solidity of metal against his back. Aaron took a tentative step forward, almost expecting the earth to collapse underneath his feet after the unreality of the quick storm. "Travis, what was that?" he called across the clearing

"I . . . I don't know. I've never seen anything like it. I—"

"What?"

Travis shook his head. "Nothing. Nothing, kid. Whatever it was, it's gone now. You and the ape okay?"

"Yeah. I think so, anyway." Aaron glanced at Mundo, who was crouching with his long arms hugging himself. He glowered accusingly at the two humans. Aaron started toward Travis. Halfway to him, he stopped. He bent down and picked up something from the grass.

He took it over to Travis, proferring it to the man silently.

A can of Campbell's chicken noodle soup. A pricing label printed with "Parsley's Grocery" was stuck to the top.

"It was real," Aaron said wonderingly. He hefted the can. The solid weight of it was a joy. Aaron laughed. "In the middle of that— that time storm, Green Town was here, for just an instant. . . ."

"It's gone now."

"But it was here. Maybe . . ." Aaron tossed the can into the air and caught it again. Holding that familiar shape made the Mesozoic backdrop in which he stood seem like a movie set. Such a simple, ordinary thing, yet it centered and anchored him, made him feel almost optimistic again.

If Green Town can come back once, then I can find it again. I know I can. . . .

"Mundo," he said. "Come on. Let's find that path."

CHALLENGE AND DEFEAT

The glade was as SStragh remembered it, alive and vibrant. Weed hoppers ticked and chattered noisily, leaping acrobatically from leaf to leaf; small growlers shrugged their odd, furry shoulders and ambled reluctantly toward cover; the nimble but small-brained cousins of the Mutata looked up and scurried out of her path. The clearing was all green leaf and blue sky, dappled shadows swirling on the ground as the breeze toyed with branches of the trees and made the tall grasses bend down in worship.

Alive. Exhaling a fresh, rich air that caused the sunlight to dance in SStragh's eyes and her nostrils to widen. She honked and snorted like a youngling.

"It is a wonderful place, isn't it?"

The words came with the faint miasma of rot, mingled with a sweet acidity. Shadows flowed and swarmed over a body moving under the trees on the far side of the clearing. SStragh glimpsed pale-colored scales and white scars along that flank, and the forward-leaning head had the anemic look of age. The apparition's eyes were fixed on SStragh, but there was no sight there. Milky white, devoid of pupils, they were blind, dead things.

"Yes, OTsio Raajek," SStragh said. "It's always beautiful here."

"There are times when I wish I could see it," Raajek said, moving slowly out into the sunlight. Her odor grew stronger: a hoary scent, holding the approaching death of the body and yet surprisingly energetic, still. "Lower your head, SStragh; there's no need for you to be so formal with me. Haven't you learned that yet?"

"What I haven't learned is how you see so well without your eyes."

Raajek's crest rose slightly with the praise, so SStragh knew that she was pleased even though her stance and smell revealed nothing beyond a careful neutrality. The flesh along the rippled spinal summit was torn and riddled with small ulcerations—worse than SStragh remembered from her last visit.

"One doesn't need eyes to see," Raajek said, her voice trembling with age. "I can still hear the way your voice tightens as you lift your throat, and the difference in the angle of the sound. I can still smell your submission—you never have learned all the subtleties contained there."

"I was a poor student."

"You were a good one. It's just that we all have our unique strengths and weaknesses. You can't learn what you can't sense. And I've known you for too long, SStragh. *That's* what tells me more than anything. I can feel the way the OColihi, the Ancient Path, moves within you. I couldn't have been your OTsio for so many Nestings without coming to understand you."

"How are you feeling, OTsio Raajek?"

Raajek snorted in amusement at that, a surprisingly young and vital sound from one so old. "I'm feeling the end of this part of the Path, approaching me like a fast-moving storm. I'm feeling the corruption and rot stealing through this body like niijeks burrowing into the grain stores. I'm feeling each joint turning slowly to stone until I think that one day there will be nothing here but an unmoving statue of a Mutata. I'm feeling almost angry that my body is betraying my mind this way, since I am still learning and still coming to an understanding of things. I can feel the OColihi shifting and turning, and I wonder at the cause and where it will lead. These are strange times, SStragh, as you will learn if you live."

"I wish you were OColi, OTsio Raajek. You could lead us on your OChiihi, your New Path. Then I wouldn't worry so much about what is happening."

"But I'm not the OColi. Tiafer—old One-Eye—is older than I by a Nesting, so he is OColi. I can't do anything about that, SStragh. Neither can you."

SStragh trilled her reluctant acceptance of that fact. She said nothing else for a time. Raajek waited patiently, as always, standing still and silent. "Caasrt was sent on the path four days ago," SStragh said at last.

"I knew someone had died; the jhiehai weren't making their usual noise around the water, and later I heard the death song echoing. Caasrt was young, just out of the egg when I left, as I remember." Raajek raised her head slightly. The blind eyes stared at SStragh. "This is important to you," she said. "Why?"

SStragh told her: from the time SStragh had found the first floating stone to how Jhenini had almost taken SStragh's own life in the meadow. At that, Raajek grumbled deep in her throat. "That would have been a waste of you, SStragh. This Jhenini was indeed intelligent if she knew not to take your offer."

"When we returned, OTsio, Jhenini . . ." She found she couldn't speak, still not certain of what she'd witnessed then. "The Gairk had sent an emissary who wanted to meet the huimans, but then there was a strange storm, full of ghosts and visions. . . ."

"I sensed the storm. I could smell the lightning and feel the wind, and the odors that came with it. . . . There has been nothing like that in the OColihi."

"Yes," SStragh agreed. "The OColi has taken it as an omen. He has ordered the huimans to be Given. That is a mistake, OTsio. I know it."

"So . . ." Raajek's knobby-jointed fingers twitched and she lifted her body slightly. "You're going to ask me to go back," she said. "That's what you came here to do."

The surprise of Raajek's statement drove away all the arguments SStragh had carefully prepared. She'd arranged them all, ready to refute any of the arguments that her OTsio might have used. But the words had hurled them away like wind-driven pollen. SStragh gaped.

"You do know me too well," she said at last.

"I do."

"Then . . ." SStragh began, stopped, and then began again. "Then know that I wouldn't ask if I didn't need your help. I'm alone in this, OTsio Raajek. And I'm very much afraid that I won't be enough. The OColi will lose patience or the OColi will order all of these huimans to be killed. Jhenini is just learning our language—"

"I will come."

"And from what Jhenini has hinted, she knows why the floating stones have come. After the storm—" SStragh stopped. "You'll come?" she said.

"Yes."

Relief spread through SStragh like the warm sun on the way to Nesting grounds; guilt followed in its shadow. "OTsio Raajek, it's not fair of me to ask. The OColi—he may order me to be Given as well. Or you."

"Old One-Eye and I have had many disagreements." Raajek snorted. "I long ago stopped worrying about when my Giving might come. If I die, I die. And I probably have been sitting here alone too long already. I need to follow the Chiihi myself, as you have."

Raajek groaned as she lumbered fully into the sunlight. She seemed to be looking around her grove, as if trying to fix the memory of the sounds and smells and taste of the air in her mind. Then she sounded a full roar, like a new adult on her first mating. "Lead me, SStragh," she said. "I want to meet the Far-Killer and Peitah. I want to hear this Jhenini speak."

All three of them were startled by the hubbub. Jennifer ran to the fence and peered between the saplings. Struth was entering the village not fifty yards away, a second Mutata hobbling along beside her. The sight of them had caused a stir. A dozen or more Mutata had gathered near the enclosure gate, nearly blocking the humans' view; several dozen more were peering from the dome entrances. Jennifer caught a name repeated in the excited chattering: Rajek.

She knew the name from Struth's talks with her—Rajek had been Struth's mentor or patron. There'd been something about her leaving the Mutata due to some political disagreement, Jennifer thought. From the reaction of the crowd, the disagreement must have been a serious one.

"What's going on, Jenny?" Peter said. "God, do these animals *stink* or what?"

She ignored that. "Struth's coming, with her old teacher."

"Doesn't exactly look like a welcome homecoming," Eckels commented. He was standing too close to Jennifer, his shoulder just brushing hers; she moved away a step.

The gate opened and Struth entered, Rajek following. Mutata faces crowded the entrance as Struth closed the gate behind them. "Jhen-ini," Struth said, "this is my OTsio Raajek."

"Hey, the dino's blind," Eckels said.

He was right, Jennifer saw. The eye sockets were open but the pupils there were the blank, soft white of cataracts. She saw now that Rajek's gaze was fixed a little too high and to one side of the group, and that she snuffled the air as if searching for them by their odor. "Jhenini," she said, and the voice was that of an ancient, quivering and soft—like the OColi's, but higher pitched. "Geiree." *Come here*.

Jennifer approached. The Mutata looked worse close up. There were open, ulcerated sores on her body and she stank of disease, yet there was a sweetness to her as well. Rajek's long fingers found Jennifer, examining her hair, her face, her body as it made *hmmm*ing noises and Peter snickered behind her. Jennifer had raised her head as Struth had taught her, but Rajek gently brought her head down, and her mouth opened in a Mutata smile. "There's no need for that," she said.

Rajek crouched down as if weary and spoke to her in slow, soft Mutata. "I like your smell," she said. "And the touch of you is pleasant. I hear two other breaths and one is harsher than the other—your OColi is here? The Far-Killer? The one called Ekils?"

"He is here, yes," she answered in Mutata. She found it hard not to like Rajek. There was something about her, an instinctive trust and gentleness that attracted Jenny. "He isn't my OColi, though. He's from . . ." She paused, deciding how to phrase it. "He's from a different tribe. . . ."

"Like a Mutata from another valley." Rajek nodded. The hand which had been touching Jennifer was trembling with palsy. Jennifer impulsively reached out and grasped it, stroking the leathery, finely scaled skin. Highlights of blue green and gold glittered in the hot sun. After a moment, the dinosaur closed her own hand around Jennifer's and then gently moved it away. "If you don't obey the Far-Killer, which of you then is the eldest here, Peitah or yourself? Which of you is OColi?"

"We . . ." Jennifer began, stopped, then shook her head. "We don't do things the way you do," she said. "We just don't."

Rajek's head lifted with that and she gave a sigh that almost seemed to be relief. Jennifer's nose wrinkled, for the odor of both Struth and Rajek had changed at the same time. "Yes," Rajek said, and satisfaction was obvious in her voice. "There are more ways than the OColihi. I've always said so."

The gate to the enclosure opened. Fergie stalked through. He glared at Rajek as if she were something vile and disgusting left on the ground. Struth started to move toward Fergie, but Rajek lifted a hand and Struth halted. "I smell you, Frraghi," Rajek said. "I smell your excessive pride."

Fergie let loose a great exhalation that raised dust. "You should have stayed away, Raajek," he said. "The OColi will see you. Now."

"Yes, he will," Rajek said. "He very much needs my help."

"Tiafer, my OColi, you smell of age and wisdom."

Raajek lifted her snout only slightly, as befitted her own age. From where he crouched on the heated rocks, the OColi sniffed and peered at Raajek with his one eye. Frraghi waited alongside him, leaning down to catch the OColi's words, but the OColi spoke directly to Raajek.

"And your words are as sweet and weightless as ever," he said. His claws scratched rock as he levered himself up. His crest rose stiffly in display, his chest widening. For a moment, the OColi looked as young as ever. SStragh, behind Raajek, found her head rising in unbidden response to the OColi's majesty.

"You should have stayed in your self-imposed exile, Raajek," the OColi said. "No one wants to hear any more of your OChiihi. Everyone sees now where new paths lead. Your OTsioiue SStragh has shown us that."

"There was a time when you were glad to have me here, Tiafer," Raajek answered.

"Most OColis have to worry about those almost as old as they. I never wanted to be OColi. I would have taken the burden if you had died, but I would never have challenged you to get it, as many would have."

"The OColi has me," Frraghi said. "I protect him."

Raajek's head swiveled in Frraghi's direction. There was contempt in her smell and insulting nonchalance in her stance. "Strength without thought is useless. You protect him from others, perhaps, but you're nothing to me," she said. "Tiafer gave my eggs life once. You were borne of that Nesting of mine, Frraghi—remember? The OColihi protects me from you in the same way it protects the OColi. Those of my eggs may not directly harm me: that is the OColihi."

"So have you come back to challenge the OColi now, Raajek?" Frraghi snorted in derision, his scent a mocking imitation of an eggling's mother-find odor. Even the OColi joined in Frraghi's laughter. Raajek let the amusement fade, letting her own soft chuckle mingle with theirs. When there was silence again, she spoke.

"Yes," she said.

It was the answer that SStragh had somehow known was coming.

"I challenge the OColi," Raajek continued, "if he will not see reason and let SStragh's humans live, at least until we find out whether they can help us or not." Raajek turned back to the OColi and spoke formally, her stance wide and her odor rich. "I, Raajek, invoke the OColihi and ask the All-Ancestor to stand in judgment of us."

Frraghi hissed rudely. "This should be entertaining. The OColi can at least *see*, Raajek. Where do you wish to die? I'll gather the Mutata in the Giving Hall. . . ."

"Wait a moment, Frraghi," the OColi husked. His crest had risen again with the issuing of the challenge, and the green of his chest scales deepened to the color of the darkest forest. "Raajek, I don't want this. It was enough that you were gone. I don't need your Giving, also."

"Then change your ruling."

"No," the OColi said flatly.

"Then I demand the privilege I've asked for."

"Raajek . . ."

"I insist upon my rights under the OColihi."

The OColi snorted and took a step forward. There was vigor in his step that SStragh had not seen in years. "Then you'll have them," the OColi answered.

He held out his hand; Frraghi snatched up the OColi's spear from its place on the wall and placed in the OColi's hand. His ancient fingers closed around it. "We'll go the Giving Hall. Raajek, I'll give you time to rest and ready yourself."

"I would prefer that the judgment happen here and now," Raajek said. "SStragh and

Frraghi are witnesses enough."

The OColi's mouth opened in irritation, his scent—so formal a moment before—went sour. "Fine," he snapped. "Frraghi, give the fool Raajek a weapon."

Frraghi brought a spear to Raajek. She fumbled for the shaft until Frraghi took her hand and—radiating scorn—guiding it, closed her fist around the wood. Raajek took the weapon in both hands and snapped the long shaft a bare hand's length below the head over her knee. She tossed the broken stick aside, keeping the small barbed end.

"What are you doing?" the OColi demanded. SStragh was as confused as the OColi. The OColihi laid out the procedure for a formal challenge in detail: the way the two must stand; the proper way to hold the spear; the various forms of thrusts which were allowed, and so on. But Raajek shuffled forward, her right hand out until she found the astonished OColi's own weapon. She placed the glassy head of his spear against her chest, directly over her heart. Then, with a sudden motion, she reached out and pulled the OColi close to her by the loose skin of his throat.

"There," Raajek said. "I don't need to see you, Tiafer. Blindness doesn't matter now. As soon as I feel the tip of your spear move, I'll grasp you and plunge this into your own heart. Both of us will die."

"This is not the OColihi," the OColi hissed. Frraghi and SStragh had not moved, too astonished at the breaking of the Path.

"No, it's not the OColihi," Raajek answered loudly. "It's a new way, and we're locked into it now. If you strike or if I feel or hear Frraghi start toward me, I'll finish it. Tiafer, you are OColi. You should be OColi because you know the OColihi best. Who will be OColi after you're Given to the All-Ancestor? Is there anyone else you can trust in this strange, dangerous time? Like any smart OColi, you've eliminated all the true rivals near your age. Who does that leave as Eldest? Frraghi? Anyone competent, or just those who pray every morning that you continue to live so they don't have to become OColi? If I'm wrong, then finish this now. What do we two have to fear from the All-Ancestor, Tiafer? We've lived too long already. Do it. Do it and we'll go together and let our bones mingle at the Giving. Do it or admit that this is a time when the OColihi must bend for the OColihi to prosper."

The tableau held for several breaths, the two old ones' breaths loud in the room's stillness, locked into an embrace of death in the glare of the sun. Raajek's blind eyes stared into the OColi's ruined face. Frraghi snarled, his muscles tensed as if to spring, the Speaker's Rod ready in his hand. SStragh was waiting herself, wondering if she could reach Frraghi before he struck Raajek down.

Cinnamon doubt spiced the air. Saffron desperation lent its oppression. A citrus tang touched them with soft fingers of resignation.

"Let me go," the OColi grunted.

Raajek's fingers loosened and released him. She stepped back. A small droplet of blood welled where the OColi's spear tip had punctured her skin.

"Such a shame," Raajek said. "You sentence me to life, Tiafer. That's the worst you could have done."

"I *know* it's around here somewhere. I know it. . . ."

Aaron was muttering as he thrashed through the leathery leaves of the ground plants. Muddy water soaked his sneakers. Rubber boots and a machete would have been useful, he decided. "Mundo, you had any luck?"

The ape was several feet away, walking stoop shouldered through the thick tangle of jungle with his head down. "No, Aaron. Please, le' me use the 'ime machine."

"I can't do that, Mundo. You know that. I promise that the roadway's close to here. I remember that lycopod, the one with the white cut on its side. I fell through and landed not twenty yards from it. . . ."

Aaron moved aside a screening fence of horsetails and saw the small section of roadway, hovering innocently above the marshy ground. Aaron reached out to touch it. The movement was reflex, but he stopped himself, drawing back his hand. The slick plastic surface gave off a faint shimmer of cold, a tingling he felt on the skin of his palm.

"Mundo," he said. "I've found it."

Mundo scurried over, splashing through a shallow pond, the hair on his legs matted and filthy. "This?" he said. "This? How 'oo I use i'?"

"Just step on it—or fall on it, like I did." Aaron grinned. The euphoria that had followed the time storm still infected him. Everything suddenly seemed a little brighter, a little funnier. The soup can that he'd left sitting on the time machine had changed everything.

Mundo didn't share his humor. "I's a tric'," he said. "You're lying. This doesn' go anywhere. I can see tha'."

"No, you can't," Aaron said patiently. "I'd've thought the same thing. The roadway looked exactly the same in my world. But when I hit this thing while I was rolling down that hill, all of the sudden I was here. I don't know how or why it works, but it did. That's how Travis moved from this time to my time and back, too. It should do the same for you."

"I don' tru' you." Mundo's eyes glowered at him under the mop of ruddy brown hair. The tufts on his cheeks wriggled as he scowled. "You go firs'."

"I haven't got the slightest interest in seeing your time again, Mundo."

Mundo sniffed at that, mockingly. "You tric' me once," he said. "No' again."

"I'm *not* tricking you. Won't you get that through your head?"

"Then you go firs'. You can come righ' ba'

jus' by steppin' on the roa'way from my 'ime.''
Mundo's stance was a comical parody of a challenge, the arms crossed over the chest, the feet
wide apart. He looked like an overgrown chim-
panzee imitating a five-star general.

"Mundo, really..." Aaron took a deep
breath and tried again. "There's no trick. It's
just... well, I don't want to take the chance.
I just saw Green Town. Here. Your time's too
strange, and I don't want to risk getting stuck
there. If you don't want to use the roadway,
that's your call. There's your doorway back—
use it or not. But I'm staying here."

Aaron started to move away from the roadway. Mundo screamed, a banshee wail, and
leapt at him. The sudden attack startled Aaron;
Mundo's weight, hitting him in full in the
chest, knocked him backward. Aaron lost his
balance as his arms came up to tear Mundo from
him.

He fell backward.

He remembered the sensation, the horrible,
freezing disorientation. He felt for an instant
that he was falling helplessly into some vast,
unseen pit, and then the ground came up to
wallop him on the back. All the air went out of
his lungs as he was pancaked between the
ground and Mundo's weight on top of him.

He couldn't see anything. He spat Mundo
hair from his mouth. Somewhere nearby, a bird
was calling.

A bird...

With sudden, manic energy, Aaron flung

Mundo aside and scrambled to his feet. He started to laugh and cry at the same time.

He was standing halfway down a hill, the roadway covered with dirt and leaves that had evidently fallen from further upslope. The air was hot and summery, and oaks, maples, sycamores, walnuts, and buckeye trees crowded around him, squirrels playing tag through their interlaced branches. He could hear a creek not far distant.

"All *right!*" Aaron shouted, and his glee echoed through the forest.

And then he was hit from behind by something heavy and muscular. Aaron rolled into the carpet of dead leaves, skidding a little further downslope before he could catch himself. Mundo was gathering himself to leap again. "You lie'!" the ape screeched. "You lie'! This isn' my worl'!"

"No," Aaron said, and he couldn't stop the laughter. "Mundo, don't you understand? This is *my* home. Green Town! It's still here!"

"You lie'!" Mundo hollered back. "You and Travis always lie." The ape flung himself forward again. This time Aaron turned with the motion, catching Mundo's outstretched arm and adding the energy of his own motion. Mundo was catapulted forward, crashing through the bramble ten yards away. The ape rolled and thumped hard against a tree. Mundo screeched and rose shakily to his feet, holding his head. His eyes had gone red and fierce, and Aaron was certain he would come at him again.

"I hate you!" he hissed.

"Mundo, I didn't expect this. That's the truth. I really thought this would be your world."

Mundo only snarled. He picked up a tree branch from the ground and hurled it at Aaron. Aaron ducked the pinwheeling length of wood; when he glanced back, Mundo was running away, moving quickly down the hill toward the creek. "Mundo!"

". . . hate you . . ." was the only reply, the words cast over the ape's back. In a few seconds, he was lost among the trees.

He probably should have gone after the ape. That's what he told himself. He didn't. He probably should have gone back through the roadway portal to get Travis, but he didn't do that either.

Aaron had no interest in leaving this time, this world, again. Not when he had finally found it again.

"Jenny!" he called to the air. "Grandpa Carl! Hey!"

He scrambled up the hill and through the familiar stands of trees. He emerged from a thick nest of blackberry bushes and onto sun-baked grass. There on the hill above him was the house, *his* house, and on the back porch was Grandpa Carl.

"Hey!" Aaron shouted again. "Grandpa! You're never going to believe this!"

The figure on the porch turned and waved back. Aaron, laughing, ran toward him.

GLOSSARY OF MUTATA TERMS

The Sounds of the Mutata

The sounds made by the Mutata (a race of sentient dinosaurs most similar to the duckbills of our prehistory) are produced through their long nasal horns. In the novels, they are omitted for the most part. However, the most common sounds are a nasal bleet, a snort, a full roar, and a trill.

Pronunciation Key

The Mutata language has been transcribed into an approximation of phonetic English. Most consonants are pronounced as they would be pronounced in that language. In most cases, "a" is pronounced as the 'a' in cat; "e" as the 'e' in met; "i" as the 'i' in dim (though an ending "i" is pronounced as the 'ee' in meet); "o" as the 'o' in solo; "u" as the 'oo' in moot; "ai" as 'i' in ride; "ei" as the 'ea' in heaven; "ah" as the 'a' in tall. Some of the Mutata sounds cannot be adequately reproduced by the human larynx. In those cases, the closest English sound has been used, as in "jh", which for the Mutata is glottal stop much like a very rapid "jeh-eh", the last syllable being a quick aspirant. In some cases, a literal translation of the Mutata word has been substituted, as in "Speaker" or "Giving." There are also subtle posture and scent aspects to the Mutata language which, unfortunately, must be lost in the written form and which humans can never imitate. Any human must always be partially mute and deaf to the Mutata language as spoken by the dinosaurs.

aii   An imperative: to be performed immediately.

Baosiot   Unintelligent predatory dinosaurs—the allosaurus, possibly.

bhieye   "Thank you."

broaii   The Gairk war club, a massive wooden mallet tipped with several protruding blades of obsidian. The Gairk will usually carry two, one for the right hand, one for the left. Like the Mutata, the left hand is used when striking another sentient creature; the right is for 'non-intelligent' lifeforms.

chodoe   "Follow me." An imperative, used only by a superior Mutata to his or her social inferiors.

ciosie
A demand for satisfaction. Ciosie means literally "The decision of the All-Ancestor"—in other words, letting the right or wrong of an issue be decided by combat, with the All-Ancestor's influence supposedly determining the outcome.

daii soo
Literally, "Pause (or wait) several breaths."

ehei
To go outside a dwelling. Also, to wander.

Eikels
Eckels.

Floraria
Unintelligent predatory dinosaurs, possibly the Tyrannosaurus family.

gaedo
An affirmative given by a younger to an elder. "Yes."

Gairk
The racial name for a species of sentient, small allosaurs.

geedo
"Yes." As spoken by peers.

geiree
"Come here," or "Approach me." An imperative form.

gheodo
Literally, "I cannot do that," with the added emphasis that the refusal is based on a superior's orders.

Giving   Translation of the Mutata phrase meaning "The time when the spirit is given to the All-Ancestor." The funeral rite for Mutata.

jhaka   The village in which Mutata live, each under the rule of its own OColi.

Jhenini   Jenny.

jhiehai   Scavenger proto-birds—these are deliberately enticed to feed on the bodies of dead Mutata.

khiisoo   A demand for obedience: "You must obey!"

LongDay   Or oGhielas. The summer solstice. As with almost all human cultures, the Mutata and Gairk also mark the solstices for religious celebration and ceremony.

Mutata   The racial name for Sstragh's species of sentient dinosaurs.

niijeks   Mouse-like rodents which feed on the stored grains within the Mutata encampments.

OColi   Literally, the Eldest. The ruler of a particular Mutata tribe is nearly always the oldest among them. Can be either male or female, though the males generally live the longest.

OColihi
The Ancient Path. The code of ethics and behavior which govern the Mutata. This code is handed down via a verbal tradition through the OTsio. The beginnings of the ritualized OColihi are lost in the long centuries of the Mutata past.

oei
A modifier. When used in conjunction with other words, it indicates "many" or "a large amount."

OTsio
Teacher. Each youngling Mutata, when the tribe has returned from the first Nesting Walk after their hatching, is assigned an OTsio to guide their development. The OTsio becomes a parent-analogue, though a Mutata of that age is considered independent.

otsioiue
The OTsio's student.

Raajek
Sstragh's OTsio, and a proponent of the OChiihi, or New Path—a mindset at variance with the old ways of Mutata behavior.

saorod
A species of pterosaur in Dinosaur World, with about a 3-inch wingspan.

Speaker
Translation of the Mutata title-phrase meaning "One who speaks the words of the Eldest."

tiafer
The original name of the current OColi.

werada

A death caused by a Mutata—specifically, the left-handed type of killing, not the right-handed killing that would be done to an animal.

werata

Pain.

whiaso

A "right-handed" killing, or the killing of a simple, unintelligent creature.

yeie

A modifier, indicating a negative: "I will not" or "This is not so." Also used as a quick denial: "No!"

zhiotae

The Gairk "Readers of Omens" or shaman. Functions as an advisor to the Gairk OColi in spiritual matters. The Mutata have no analogue occupation.

We want to hear from readers!

Your opinion of the *Dinosaur World* series is important to us. We welcome all feedback about this series. Write to the editors care of:

Byron Preiss Visual Publications, Inc.
Attn: Dinosaur World
24 W. 25th Street
New York, N. Y. 10010

RAY BRADBURY, one of the greatest writers of fantasy and horror fiction in the world today, has published some 500 short stories, novels, plays, and poems since his first story appeared in *Weird Tales* when he was twenty years old. Among his many famous works are *Fahrenheit 451*, *The Illustrated Man*, and *The Martian Chronicles*. He has also written the screenplays for *It Came from Outer Space*, *Something Wicked This Way Comes*, and *Moby Dick*. Mr. Bradbury was Idea Consultant for the United States Pavilion at the 1964 World's Fair, has written the basic scenario for the interior of Spaceship Earth at EPCOT, Disney World, and is doing consultant work on city engineering and rapid transit. When one of the Apollo Astronaut teams landed on the moon, they named Dandelion Crater there to honor Mr. Bradbury's novel, *Dandelion Wine*. Recently Mr. Bradbury flew in an airplane for the first time.

STEPHEN LEIGH is the author of several science fiction novels, including *Crystal Memory*, *The Bones of Gods*, and the best-selling *Alien Tongue*. He is also a contributing author to the Hugo-nominated *Wild Cards* shared-world series. Currently Mr. Leigh lives in Ohio.